Acclaim for the *Chronoptika* sequence:

'Catherine Fisher's *The Do...*  ...el fantasy, the third in her cr... *A Midsummer Night's Dream* ... ...n mirror, a son pursuing his ... ...n nightmare and a changeling child caught up in the French Revolution. Fisher's luminous prose makes you believe this cursed marriage between science, history and magic is possible.' – Amanda Craig, *New Statesman*

'An engrossing, enthralling fiction.' – *The New York Times Book Review*

'*The Obsidian Mirror* has one of the most memorable fictional openings I've read for a while. (The) book takes off into a slick, accomplished fantasy . . .' – *The Daily Telegraph*

'This is bleak, brittle and brilliant.' – *The Literary Review*

'Clever, complex and sophisticated. The book is a tangled web and Fisher jumps from scene to scene with cliff hanger moments urging the reader to unlock her puzzle.' – *The School Librarian*

'A new novel by Catherine Fisher, poet and prize-winning novelist is always worth looking out for. *The Obsidian Mirror* is both thriller and SF, and, being written in Fisher's acid-etched prose, equally satisfying to fans of many genres. Brilliantly disconcerting, scary and superbly written by the leading lady of British fantasy, this pursues Fisher's abiding interest in imprisonment and the abuse of power. Full of atmosphere, it's perfect for clever children to curl up with on a winter's night.' – Amanda

THE
SPEED
OF DARKNESS

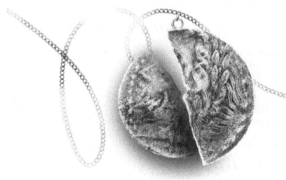

Hodder
Children's
Books

HODDER CHILDREN'S BOOKS

First published in Great Britain in 2016 by Hodder Children's Books
This edition published in 2016 by Hodder and Stoughton

2

Text copyright © Catherine Fisher, 2016

The moral right of the author has been asserted.

A CIP catalogue record for this book
is available from the British Library.

ISBN 978 1 444 92632 3

Typeset in Berkeley Book by Avon DataSet Ltd,
Bidford-on-Avon, Warwickshire
Printed and bound in Great Britain
by Clays Ltd, St Ives plc

The paper and board used in this book
are made from wood from responsible sources

33614057706714

MIX
Paper from
responsible sources
FSC
www.fsc.org
FSC® C104740

Hodder Children's Books
An imprint of
Hachette Children's Group
Part of Hodder and Stoughton
Carmelite House
50 Victoria Embankment
London EC4Y 0DZ

An Hachette UK Company
www.hachette.co.uk

www.hachettechildrens.co.uk

To Maggie

A brave vessel

Who no doubt had some noble creature in her,

Dashed all to pieces.

CHAPTER ONE

For what the Mirror truly is, or what infernal power first forg'd it in the deepest earth, who can say, nor how in lost ages it was used by barbarous men . . . ?

The Scrutiny of Secrets by Mortimer Dee

Out at sea, a glint of darkness appeared on the water.

It was very small, just a slit, as if some opening had been slashed through time and tide.

A gull flew over it, curious, then turned away with a scream of sharp fear, because out of the gap surged a storm-battered ship with torn black sails. It came prow-first with a burst of spray, flung and spun on its wild *journey*, and the single figure clinging to its mast yelled with triumph at the churning sea.

* * *

The sky clouded rapidly, with great coppery thunderclouds that piled up over the horizon. Gulls raced for cover. Seals dived deep.

All along the north Devon coast, flags began to rattle and awnings flap with sudden gusts. It was 29 October, two days before Halloween, and no one was expecting anything.

By six p.m. the first weather warnings were out, issued on TV and radio by startled broadcasters, scrawled on boards at the ends of fishing piers, passed on by urgent coastguards down the coasts of Devon and Cornwall and Wales. It was the first storm of autumn, there was a mighty Force 9 gale at the heart of it, and it had come out of nowhere.

By seven the tempest was in full fury. Defences crumbled, sea walls burst. Small fast rivers gushing down from the moors brought mud-red floods to swell the chaos. Crashing against roofs and windows, against flapping tarpaulins and smashed chimneys, heavy rain poured down all night, so that, lying curled in bed or huddled at upstairs widows with torches, people thought the end of the world might have come, and that they might not survive until morning.

A dark, slanting storm. The sedges lay flat under it. The moor became a black bog, and the Wood of

Wintercombe threshed and cracked and roared. And deep in its heart water rose from the flooding river and poured into the cellars and vaults of Wintercombe Abbey, up stairs and along corridors, under the bedroom doors, making the Monk's Walk a torrent, raging even to the foot of the obsidian mirror, chained in its harness of steel and malachite.

George Wharton didn't hear any of it.

When he opened his eyes, late on the morning of the 30th, it was to close them again immediately with a groan of agony.

'For God's sake turn that noise down,' he moaned.

His head swam. He tried to remember who he was. Where he was, even. After a few seconds of panicky concentration he dredged up the dim knowledge that his name was George Wharton, that this was a hotel bedroom, and that the giant woodpecker carefully drilling holes in the inside of his head was a hangover.

He dared not move.

Cider.

It always did this to him. He had sworn never to touch the bloody stuff again.

He lay with his eyes closed in a fuzz of pain.

The funeral.

Old Uncle Tom's funeral wake.

The White Hart, Shepton Mallet. That's where he was, and if somebody didn't turn off that rattling noise outside he would scream.

After a useless ten minutes with his head buried in the pillow he knew he couldn't stand it any longer. He dragged himself into the white-tiled bathroom, drank a whole glass of water and then went to find some headache tablets in his bag. There were none.

He groped for the phone.

'Hello? Reception? This is room . . . er, ten. Listen, do you have any painkilling stuff?'

The woman sounded distracted. 'Sorry?'

'Headache tablets.'

'Oh, we might have. I'll send something up if I can find it. But with all this . . .'

'And could you turn off whatever's rattling?'

'Rattling?'

'On the roof. Hell of a din.'

A moment's silence. He became aware of distant shouts, splashings like water, the whine of machinery. Then she said blankly, 'It's rain, sir. It's a flood.'

'Oh. OK.' He put the phone down, groaned again, and thought about getting right under the blankets and just dying there.

But the word *flood* bobbed back into his mind. Was that what she had said? It was enough to make him struggle up against the pillow.

He felt for his mobile phone. At some point last night – maybe between the speeches to old Tom's memory and the start of the singing when the second barrel of the old man's APPLE KILLER MAX got broached – he'd turned it off. Why the hell had Tom left his most potent cider for his family to drink at the wake? Was that some sort of twisted revenge?

He switched on. The screen went nuts.

YOU HAVE FOURTEEN MISSED CALLS.

'Whoa!' He rubbed his head and looked at the numbers. They were all the same. The screen said

REBECCA

REBECCA

REBECCA

REBECCA

with ferocious insistence.

He called her.

There was a buzz, and then she came on, her voice crackling and distant.

'George? Oh my God, *at last*! I've been calling you all morning! Where the hell have you been?'

He took a nauseous swallow of water. 'Asleep. The

wake was a bit heavy. Uncle Tom bequeathed his home-made and it makes dynamite look like weak tea. What time is it?'

'Gone twelve!' She sounded frantic. 'Haven't you even seen the news? I'm going mad with worry. I can't get any answer from Wintercombe – I've tried the landline, everyone's mobiles, the e-mail, and there's nothing. They must be so flooded down there, George – you know how deep in the valley they are! And it's Halloween tomorrow!'

'Wait! Wait . . . hold on.'

He fumbled for the TV remote, found it on the floor, rolled over and pressed it. Rebecca was still talking, her tinny voice drowned out by the newscaster, but even as Wharton winced and thumbed the sound down he saw the images on screen – broken bridges, floating cars, vast tracts of farmland under water, people and dogs being winched from the roofs of houses.

It looked like a real disaster.

'Where the hell did this come from?' he muttered.

Bringing the phone back to his ear he heard, '. . . pick you up in half an hour. Lots of roads are flooded but I've got an idea how we can . . .'

Fear finally pierced his self-pity. 'You can't get Jake? Or Sarah?'

'I've been telling you! I can't get anyone. Be ready, George.'

The phone went dead. He looked at it, thinking that if she was in Exeter she'd be driving like a maniac to get here in that time. He called Jake.

Straight to voice-mail. But Jake might still be on the *journey*, the last experiment.

He tried the house phone. Just a single high-pitched note. Cut off? Lines down?

On the TV apocalyptic images swam. A leisure centre with children sleeping on the floor. A seaside promenade with waves twenty feet high battering it.

Couldn't they predict these things?

A weatherman appeared; Wharton turned the sound up, cautiously.

'. . . *completely unexpected. A very sudden depression in the Atlantic, and it's as if it came out of nowhere. Certainly the Met Office have classified it as a freak storm, and we're monitoring it very closely now as it moves inland . . .*'

He turned the TV off, rolled out of bed and stood up.

The world reeled; he grabbed the wall.

'Cheers, Uncle Tom,' he muttered.

Forty minutes later the red car screeched up the drive, next to the pump churning water out of the downstairs bar. Wharton threw his bag in and squeezed after it.

'All right?' Rebecca said. She had wellies on and a heavy-duty mac.

'Stuffed with painkillers.'

'Breakfast?'

'God, no.'

'There's food in the back. Water too. I've borrowed boots and a coat that should fit you.'

She was driving with fierce concentration, her long red plait tied back tight, a knitted hat crammed on. After they had backed up a few flooded streets and on to the main road he said, 'You're worried.'

She flicked him a glance. 'I'm terrified. Everything was all ready, George! Maskelyne and David have been working so hard on the mirror they're exhausted. It was tuned to the finest of margins. They can hit anywhere in the last five years to a matter of seconds. You've seen the success they've had. And now this!'

He was silent, sharing her fear. For the last three months Wintercombe had been re-organized into a slick and efficient laboratory. David Wilde, Jake's dad, was a remarkable worker. He had taken over the lab, bossed Piers, who adored him, ordered Venn about like no one else would dare, and, in short, taken control, all with his baby son Lorenzo strapped to his belly like some dark-eyed marsupial. It had been David who had devised the strict schedule of work leading up to Halloween, the day Maskelyne had told them was the best one for Operation Leah.

If Venn was ever to get his wife back, that was the day they had to do it. The ancient end of the year, the hinge on which summer and winter turned. The night the dead return.

What's more, David even seemed to have won some grudging respect from Maskelyne, that strange, scarred ghost from the distant past, the man who knew more about the mirror than anyone, though Wharton was still not sure how far he could be trusted.

He gazed into the rain. 'I'm sure they'll be all right.'

'Yes, but it'll have been panic. They'll have had to move the mirror – that could ruin everything.'

He nodded, feeling sick.

The car took a bend at speed. Water splashed high into the hedgerow.

Sitting on a seaside bench, three years away in time, Jake said, 'Subject in clear sight. Everything in place. D minus two minutes and we're all set to move in.'

Silence.

'Dad?'

11

The modified mobile phone did not answer. He frowned. 'Dad? Can you hear me? D minus two.'

The sun was dazzling him and the ice-cream van down on the beach was playing a merry tune. His watch said 2.58 p.m.

He cursed, viciously. 'Something's wrong.'

Standing tense against the blue-painted railing, Venn had the binoculars trained on the small boy in the red shorts. 'What?'

'We've lost contact with base.'

Venn frowned. 'That wretched Piers! Can't he keep any sort of link going? That thing has worked every time until now.'

Jake looked at the watch, anxious. 2.59. 'What do we do? Go ahead?'

Venn lowered the binoculars. 'Are you mad? Of course we go ahead. If this works, we're all set.'

Jake stood up. Had he really thought that Venn would stop now? They were so close to success! One more test, to see if it was possible to save a life. It was all they had thought about for months, and today was the day.

D minus one minute.

'Go!' Venn snapped.

Jake shoved the mobile in his pocket and raced down the sunny promenade. It was a bright summer's afternoon and the beach was packed. Donkeys carried laughing kids across the tide line. Striped deckchairs were pitched everywhere.

Jake ran down the ramp into the deep sand, his feet sinking into the hot drifts. The boy in red shorts was out there on his own, near the water's edge. His name, according to their research, was James Paul Arnold. He was seven years old, and on holiday with his parents.

And this should be the day he would die.

It was a common seaside tragedy. He had wandered into the water and been swept out to sea. It happened all the time. But for Venn, for all of them, this unknown child would be the ultimate test for Operation Leah. They had worked so carefully up to it, changing all sorts of small things, checking the news reports after each intervention in the past. This was the biggest, the most ambitious. What would this do to the future? And if it worked, could they go on to save Leah, Venn's lost wife?

The sand was slippery and scorching under Jake's trainers. He kept his eyes fixed on the boy, aware that Venn was close behind, but for a moment there were so many people on the beach, throwing balls, digging, running, that he was confused.

Sun blinded his eyes. He stopped.

The kid. Where was he?

'Excuse me, would you like to make a small donation?' Some sort of charity mugger was at his elbow.

'What?' Jake stared round.

'A donation. We're collecting for . . .'

Where the hell was the kid!

Panic grabbed him. 'No! Get out of the way!'

His eyes raked the beach. Suddenly it was all so vital, so clear. Only he, Jake Wilde, could do this, at this single flashpoint in time, as if he was some sorcerer, someone from right outside the world.

He felt giddy with fear.

Then he saw him. Already in the sea.

Jake ran. He shoved bathers aside and flung himself in, splashed through a wave, fell, scrambled up. Waist-deep, he felt the undertow drag at his heels. He was too late, for a second he knew he was too late, it was all over. And then with a yell of relief he turned and the kid was there and Jake was grabbing his arm, too tight. 'Hey! Hi! Listen . . . You shouldn't be out so far! It's not safe.'

The little boy looked up, puzzled and sun-dazzled. Waves lapped high on his chest. He had floppy dark hair, pale eyes and a soaked stripy T-shirt. His skin was sun-warm in Jake's hand.

He smiled.

With an intake of relief that felt more like fear,

Jake felt the power of the obsidian mirror, a pure surge of joy and terror. He turned and led the child out of the water, and saw Venn standing close among the sun umbrellas, watching with an agony of intensity.

'Where's your mum?' Jake said.

The boy looked round and shrugged. The corners of his mouth went down.

'Don't worry,' Jake said hastily. 'She won't be far. Look, that lady waving there. Is that her?'

In the TV reports the mother had sobbed that she had only taken her eyes off him for a moment. Her photo, distraught and tear-stained, came into Jake's mind, devastated at the careless moment that would wreck her life.

But it wouldn't happen now, any of it. He had changed all that. And she would never even know.

Venn muttered, 'She's coming, Jake.'

A plump woman in shorts was running towards them. 'Oh thank you so much,' she gasped as she came up. 'He's always wandering off.'

Jake nodded. 'He was in the water.' *Be careful*, he wanted to say. *Hold him tight because you nearly lost him for ever*. But she just smiled brightly and took the child off, her hand cupped protectively round his dark head. He looked back, only once, at Jake. He didn't wave.

Jake turned away and checked his watch. 3.02.

Done.

He sat suddenly down in the sand, the strength in his legs strangely gone. Staring ahead, he felt Venn sit next to him.

'We did it.' Venn's usual arrogance was muted, as if the tiny act with its massive consequences had overwhelmed him too.

'Do you think he'll even remember this?'

'Nothing to remember.' Venn gazed out at the blue sea, his blond hair tangled in the wind. 'How many of us have brushed against death in our lives and never even realized it?'

They were silent. Then he said, harshly, 'We need to get back. Find out what's wrong.'

Jake nodded. He took out the phone again and tried it, puzzled, but there was only darkness on the screen.

Like a tiny obsidian mirror.

CHAPTER TWO

Wild storms have driven many a wrecke on the rocks of Wintercombe, and many a drowned corpse. Mermen and mermaids have been seen here, and water-selkies, and in truthe, far stranger sights, from countries that no men know. For this western coast is a strange and unfathomable land.

The Chronicle of Wintercombe

Every lane into Wintercombe was waist-deep in water, but Rebecca had a plan.

She drove across the moor by tracks and stony ways that Wharton had never seen before, and gradually bumped the car down to a small quay where a dinghy was tied, bobbing on the rough waves.

'A boat?'

'Best way. We can get round to Wintercombe Cove,

17

the nearest opening in the cliffs to the Abbey, and walk from there. It will mean going through the Wood though.'

Wharton groaned aloud. Since his captivity in the Summerland he had taken care to keep well clear of the Wood. The last thing he wanted was another encounter with the Shee, those silvery, scary creatures with no human emotions but their intense and cruel curiosity. Or with Summer, their beautiful, infuriating queen. The very thought of her smile made him shudder.

He pulled the wellies on and hauled the mac over his coat.

As they climbed down the steps a wild wind raged from the sea; the waves were choppy, and he frowned. 'Whose boat is this anyway?'

'My dad's. We keep it here. Are you OK with it?'

'Army, not navy. As long as you can drive the thing.'

She grinned, dragging the fringe from her eyes. 'Better than the car, you mean.'

But she couldn't fool him; her worry was growing and so was his. The image of the drowned Abbey, its corridors full of water, the panic over the mirror, the wreck of the carefully calculated experiments, had begun to haunt them.

They climbed down some stone steps, clutching a soaked rope that rattled through iron rings in the quayside, and Wharton clambered awkwardly into the boat. It rocked; he sat, quickly. He knew nothing about boats. This one had a tiny cabin and a few seats and some orange life-jackets in a locker. He put one on.

Rebecca started the engine. It took two goes, but then coughed into life, and as she backed the craft he felt movement against the waves, a scrape on the stone wall. Then they were running out to sea, into a swell that lifted and fell, lifted and fell.

Oh God, he wasn't going to be sick, was he?

The embarrassment.

Spray soaked him; he pulled up his hood.

The sea was a grey waste. Gulls hung low over it, and terns clouded the cliff tops. The cliffs here were high and grim, and as the boat chugged below them he saw the craggy ledges where birds nested in the summer, white-streaked and empty now, as if the tempest had come from nowhere and swept the world clean.

It took twenty minutes to beat up into Wintercombe Cove, a small inlet in the high moorland, where a stream came down to the water. It had a tiny beach, rocky and full of pools, and some dark slants in the cliff face that might be caves, probably the smuggling haunts of ancient Venns.

Rebecca said, 'Hang on. This'll be the tricky bit.' She

brought the boat in slowly, but still they crunched hard against the beach and Wharton had to scramble to get the rope out. He climbed ashore thankfully and tugged it around a huge rock.

Then he stared. 'What the hell is that?'

At first he thought it was a beached whale, black ribs spread on the rocky sand.

Then he saw it was a ship.

A wrecked ship.

Rebecca jumped down and came up beside him, hands deep in pockets. Rain spattered them. They stared in puzzled silence.

It was the strangest vessel Wharton had ever seen. Its carved prow was riddled with twining animals, the wood richly dark, ebony black, but burst open now, smashed on the rocks, its staves peeled apart. The black sails were shredded and torn into the finest filaments, as if the ship had ridden the peak of the storm for days and nights.

'Amazing.' Rebecca walked round it. 'Really old. Where on earth did it come from?'

Wharton shook his head. The dark craft filled him with dread, though he had no idea why. 'Look. Over there.'

Footprints. So someone had survived. The deep scours in the shingle showed where they had climbed out and walked – staggered? – to the steps that led up the cliff. Wharton raised his head, afraid some dark figure was looking down at him.

But the horizon was bare and windswept.

'Well, no time to worry about it.' Rebecca set off quickly. 'Come on, George. I'm petrified about what's going on at the Abbey.'

They climbed the steps, breathless, to the top, where the wind pounced, and Wharton had to struggle to keep his footing. A narrow path led between gorse that showed late patches of yellow flower, still hanging on. The path led over the open moor, boggy and soaked, so Wharton's feet sank in. 'Slow down,' he gasped but she kept going, reckless.

'Maskelyne will be fine.'

She flashed him an irritated look. 'Will he? None of us knows very much about Maskelyne.'

Well, that was true. Still he said, 'You do.'

She walked on, not looking back. Her words were quiet, snatched by the wind. 'I used to think that too. Now I'm not so sure. Once he told me such a strange story of how he made the mirror. As if he was once some sorcerer in ancient times, Egypt, somewhere like that. Maskelyne is a ghost. You can't catch hold of a ghost. You can't trust a ghost.'

He glanced at her, silent.

They came to the edge of the moor, and the path dropped into a deep valley. Trees began to rise, small shrubs at first and then, quite suddenly, the ancient oaks and willows of the Wood.

Wharton stopped. 'Here we go.'

Wintercombe Wood awaited them, green and secret. It seemed to watch them as they entered its space, as if they had crossed some border of enchantment and the very tree trunks and leaves and birds were aware of it. A starling on a branch eyed Wharton. A scatter of crows rose and circled and flew away, cackling.

'Shee?' Rebecca muttered, looking up.

'Probably.'

Their voices had become whispers. They walked cautiously. Deep as it lay, even the Wood had been shaken and threshed by the storm; great banks of fallen leaves had built up in hollows, gold and red and tawny, blotched with rime and mildew. Overhead the trees leaned, their branches dark and gnarled.

Wharton said, 'It's too quiet.'

The hush made him uneasy. He was afraid that Summer herself would step out any moment from a shiver in the air and say, 'Hello, George!' and his soul would be lost for ever and ever.

Then, as they crossed the stream through a hollow where two oaks leaned, he did see a shimmer.

A glint of green.

Rebecca stopped.

For a moment there was nothing there, but then, as if he had turned some camouflaged aspect of strangeness towards them, there was a boy. He wore patchwork clothes of russet and rain-grey, the coat studded with rubies dark as berries. His pale face was marked with whorls of green lichen; his hair threaded with a tangle of brown leaves. A bow and flint-tipped arrows lay beside him.

Wharton said, 'Gideon?'

They hadn't seen the changeling for months – not since he had re-entered the Wood at the height of summer. Now Wharton saw again that strange agelessness, that the boy had not changed or grown even by a millimetre.

Gideon stood up, tall and scornful. 'Who else would be waiting for you, mortal?'

His voice was harsh but his eyes were green with that fear Wharton recognized, the unending terror of the Shee.

'What's happened?' Rebecca said.

'Trouble.' Gideon shook his head. 'Something strange.'

'We know there must be flooding, but . . .'

He laughed his cool, unpractised laugh. 'It's not what the sea destroys you have to fear, Rebecca. It's what it washes up.'

Venn adjusted the silver bracelet and glanced round. 'Safe?'

'Safe.'

'Then let's go.'

They walked into the obsidian mirror. It was leaning at the back of the Hall of Mirrors that made up the dingy amusement arcade of the pier, and if it hadn't been for its presence here the whole experiment would have been impossible. Now, as its darkness gathered round him, Jake felt the sensation of terror and joy that was almost becoming familiar, the crackling vacuum of the black hole, the withdrawing of his entire being into its dark nothingness.

An implosion of silence, breathlessness, a flash of pain. And he was in the lab.

He stared around in horror.

In all their adjustments of time, all their delicate experiments of the last months, one fear had always haunted him. That he would come back and find they had changed the past so much that nothing in the present was the same.

And surely it had happened!

The lab was drowned. He was standing knee-deep in icy water. The benches and monitors were submerged. The green malachite web was empty. The mirror was gone.

Venn was there beside him. 'What the hell . . . ?'

'We've done something. I knew we would. We've changed the past!'

'Don't be stupid.' Venn's voice was harsh. 'A boy on a beach a few years ago couldn't have caused this. This has nothing to do with us.'

'No,' a calm voice said from the doorway behind them. 'It hasn't.'

Jake turned, fast, with relief. 'Sarah!'

Standing in the doorway, she smiled wanly at him. He had only left her an hour ago by his reckoning, but now she was dirty and her blonde hair was streaked with mud. She wore filthy overalls and wellingtons and looked as if she had been up all night and was past caring.

'Welcome back, Jake.'

Venn moved to her, fast. 'What happened?'

Sarah pushed her hair back and waded in, sending water rippling against the walls. 'A massive storm is what happened. It started last night, and there was no warning, though Piers got all restless, and seemed to sense something wrong from about six. The cats ran into hiding; Horatio just went nuts. By about seven, the sky was black. Rain, hail, the works – it fell in torrents all night. By midnight the river was rising and we knew there was no way of stopping a flood so we started evacuation.'

'Where is it?' Venn couldn't wait any more. 'Where's the mirror?'

'Safe. In the attic.'

Venn stared at her. Then he splashed out and was gone, up the corridor.

Sarah sighed. 'Yes, and we're all fine, thanks for asking.' She turned wearily. 'Can you give me a hand with this box? David needs it upstairs.'

Jake put his hands under the sodden cardboard, gratefully. 'Dad's OK then?'

She laughed her short bitter laugh. 'Jake, your dad has been the saving of this place! He worked like a madman all night and he never seems to lose his sense of humour. Believe me, without him we'd have been lost.'

He felt pride shiver through him. The box held paperwork, all of it drenched. 'I'll take it,' he said.

She let him, and waded towards the arch. 'Be careful. All the steps are drowned. It's easy to fall.'

They entered the Monk's Walk. It was a green canal;

fronds on the wall dripped into it. He had no idea how the lowest parts of the Abbey would be, the deep cellars and the lost cells of monks down the darkest stairs, where Maskelyne slept.

'Is Maskelyne . . . ?'

'Everyone's fine. We've cleaned out the kitchen – Piers has been cooking breakfast. But we were worried about you – we haven't been able to monitor anything. Did it go all right? Did you save the boy?'

He nodded, but he didn't want to talk about it yet.

Between them they manoeuvred the box round awkward corners. The Long Gallery, when they came into it, was drier, the water having drained between the warped boards, though these still groaned with damp and strain.

Sarah was quiet, preoccupied. He knew what was worrying her. If the experiment with the little boy had worked, the way was clear: Operation Leah would go ahead. And that was just what she didn't want.

Halfway down the corridor he stopped and said, 'Wait. Before we get to the others I've got to ask you. What are you planning? I know that look. It's a Venn look and I don't trust it.'

Despite herself she grinned, pushing muddy hair from her eyes. Her hair had grown quite a bit, he realized.

27

After all, she had been here nearly a year now.

Then her smile went. 'What can I do, Jake? I don't have the coin any more, if that's what you mean.'

The coin.

A Greek stater with the face of Zeus. Centuries ago it had been cut into two jagged pieces, and if those two pieces were ever to be reunited they would create the only power in the universe able to break the obsidian mirror. Sarah had brought half of it with her and lost that to Summer without even knowing what it was. She had stolen it back, but now Maskelyne had it, and where he had hidden it neither of them knew.

Or what he meant to do with it.

As if reading his thoughts she said, 'Maskelyne will never destroy the mirror. The mirror is part of him. He's obsessed with it.'

'But you would.'

She glanced at him. 'What do you care, Jake? You've got your father back. You're OK.'

He was silent. Then he said, 'That's not fair. I'm not that selfish. Well, maybe I used to be, but things have changed. If using the mirror to save Leah really causes the End Time, causes all that terrible future world you escaped from, then I promise you, I wouldn't just let Venn . . .'

'Nice to see you safe and sound, Jake.'

It was a shrewd, dry voice and it belonged to Piers, who was standing outside the kitchen. He wore his white lab coat and a pair of red and white spotted wellingtons, and his small bright eyes were watching them carefully. 'And, the sausages are ready.'

The kitchen was a warm haven. A huge wood fire blazed in the inglenook and the seven blacks cats were sleeping everywhere, sprawled and curled and content. It smelled of smoke and sizzling bacon. The first thing Jake looked for was his father, and saw him sitting at the table with Venn, talking excitedly. David Wilde leaped up at once and ran over and hugged him.

'Thank God you're back safe! O says the plan worked!'

'Seems so.'

'I knew! I knew we could do it!'

'It was such a small thing. So ordinary.'

'Not for that kid and his family it wasn't.' David grabbed a plate. 'More bacon here, Piers. Eggs too. We need to feed the troops.'

Jake looked round. His baby half-brother, Lorenzo, was on the floor, trapped in a makeshift pen and kicking tiny legs over a pile of damp toys. The marmoset, Horatio, plumped down from somewhere into his lap and nuzzled his face. 'Hi, nuisance.' Jake stroked the soft damp fur.

29

Then he realized who was missing. 'Where's Wharton? And Rebecca?'

'All lines and signals are out, so we don't know, but I'd guess they're probably racing here in a panic.'

'And Maskelyne?'

Venn said, 'The scarred man won't leave the mirror.' He poured some tea. Sarah sat in the inglenook, her hands round a mug with DEVON on it. But she wasn't drinking, and her blue eyes watched everyone.

Venn sipped the hot liquid. Then he said, 'Right. This storm.'

Piers spread his long fingers. 'Excellency, it's no ordinary weather. It's something very weird, very powerful. I felt it slide up out of the sea, a shudder of magic. In the Wood all the birds stopped singing and listened. The mirror gave the strangest spitting crackle – even Maskelyne jumped as if he had been stung.'

'How could a storm . . . ?'

'Not just a storm. A sending. A sorcery. It *journeyed* here from way out of the world.'

'Did Summer bring it?'

Piers shrugged, uneasy. 'Who can say? She can do all sorts of tricky things. But to me it was more like it came through time.'

'How's that possible?' Jake muttered.

'We have no idea what's possible and what's not.' Venn got up and paced, restless. 'I don't like it. Not at this stage, not when we're all ready to go. It's too much of a coincidence. Piers, I want every alarm up and running asap. I want the whole estate locked down tight. Maybe not only weather came through that gap in time. Maybe this is some sort of attack on us. Janus. Replicants. Time wolves. I can't take any chances.'

'Calm down, O,' David said softly.

'Easy for you to say.' Venn turned, and Jake saw the strain in him. Venn was living for this, living to rescue Leah. It was all that mattered to him any more. 'Have we checked the consequences of what we did with the boy?'

David nodded. He pulled the laptop over and found a page, then turned the screen so that they could all see it. 'OK. This is the current online page from the archive of the local newspaper for the day after you were there. Compare it with the copy I made of the original page, which now no longer exists anywhere. Here they are side by side.'

Fascinated, Jake came closer. Behind him he felt Sarah come and lean over.

The two newspaper pages, both with the same date, were completely different. On the first the headline read TODDLER DROWNS IN BEACH TRAGEDY and there was a huge photo of the crowded beach inset with the child's face. The story covered the page, its report of horror and sorrow making Jake feel uneasy.

The second was much more fragmented. The lead was LOCAL FIRM WINS BUSINESS AWARD. A man in a grey suit held a glass of champagne triumphantly to the camera. There was a lot of other stuff – a break-in at some shop, reports from a county show.

No tragedy. No death.

They were silent. Finally Sarah said, 'You know what this is like? It's like we're playing at being God.' She turned to Venn. 'It's not right.'

He shrugged, impatient. 'Saving a child's life. What possible harm?'

'Changing lots of lives. Changing time. Thinking you know what's best.' She stared at him, a fierce challenge, and their eyes were blue and identical. 'What have we done, Venn? *What do we really know about harm?*'

CHAPTER THREE

On the Eve of Hallows' Eve,
In the hollows of the Wood,
I will touch my eyes with dew,
  I will paint my nails with blood.

I have laid deep plans, my Lord,
Woven secret alchemy.
To bind your heart with golden chains
  To mine for all eternity.
      Ballad of Lord Winter and Lady Summer

'I just don't want the Shee to find me!'

'Oh stop panicking. They won't.' Gideon gave Wharton a scornful glance. 'I haven't survived here for centuries without learning how to hide from them.'

He stepped behind a tree and was at once almost lost

to sight, as if, Rebecca thought, his mortal identity had become something he could slip into and out of at will. Beyond the tree was a stream, muddy and swollen with rain. Gideon flickered lightly across its boulders to a tiny islet where willows made waterfalls and tents of leaves, already crisp and brown.

'Come on. The Shee won't cross fresh running water.'

'Useful to know.' Wharton wobbled carefully from rock to rock.

'Well, Summer might. Summer doesn't care. But the others hate it. Iron too – any metal really.'

'What about garlic?' Rebecca crouched under the willows.

Gideon stared at her. 'What's garlic?'

'A sort of bulb. Never mind.' She pushed her wet plait back. 'So tell us what came ashore.'

Gideon frowned. Instead of answering he took something from the patchwork pocket of his frock-coat and laid it carefully on the muddy ground. They both stared at it. It seemed to be some sort of wand, or baton, made of a dark bone, carved with mysterious zigzags and spirals. A strip of worn leather was wound round its handle and fastened into a loop. On the tip, tied with twine, were strange, small objects – an acorn, three pierced white stones, the tiny dried skull of what might have been a bat.

'Wow.' Rebecca touched it with chipped fingernail. 'That is seriously old. Like some sort of ritual thing. Where did you get it?'

Gideon watched the Wood. 'Last night a ship was wrecked on the beach.'

'We know. We've seen it.'

'What you don't know is that it *journeyed*.'

She stared. 'Where from?'

'Maybe very long ago. I stood on the cliff top in the storm and watched it.' Gideon crouched. He gazed at the wand with his sea-green eyes. 'The whole of the storm roared in with it, as if some sorcerer had raised it. Maybe with this.' He touched one curled thong. 'This was a knot – you see it's been undone? The ship rode before the wind. Some of the Shee were with me – others were out there over the waves, dancing in frenzy or riding their savage horses. They were screaming with delight. They loved it all, the terrible wind, the raging sea. But the ship interested me because there was a mortal on it, alone. Not steering, not rowing. Just standing. Looking at the shore. Looking at death.'

He sounded fascinated.

Wharton glanced at Rebecca, and muttered. 'The Shee wanted him dead?'

'They wouldn't care either way. The ship splintered, a great wreckage, and he dived into the sea and swam. I thought he was lost, but then he crawled ashore on all fours, sick, like an animal. Half drowned.'

Rebecca shivered. 'Where is he now?'

'Where do you think? The Shee swarmed on him like flies. As they dragged him into the Wood he saw me. Our eyes met, just for a second, but it was enough. He knew what they were and he knew I was mortal. He threw this down and I picked it up. Then he screamed and cursed at them in some lost language.' Gideon shook his head. 'I don't know what they want with him.'

'Poor sod,' Wharton said, with feeling.

Rebecca looked into the trees. 'What can we do?'

Gideon stared at her. 'Do you think you can rescue him?'

'Well, maybe we could try.'

He laughed, harshly. 'You've never faced Summer, have you? You have no idea.'

Annoyed, Rebecca started to argue, but at once Gideon turned his head, fast as a cat, then threw himself to the ground, his tawny coat blending with the heaped litter of leaves. 'Down!' He pulled her into the drift. 'Don't even breathe!'

Behind them, Wharton dived headlong into the hollow

behind the willows. His heart thudded; he felt sick. First the hangover, then the boat, now the Shee. Surely the bloody day couldn't get any worse.

He froze, waiting. The Wood across the stream seemed empty and silent, patters of rain dripping from its soaked branches. Then, as if the light had changed, or something in his brain had adjusted, he saw them. Thin and spindly and elegant, their coats and dresses red and gold as the beech leaves, they leaned and lazed and laughed, that host of silver-haired, beautiful, sly creatures that ran and whispered through his dreams. Slants of wan sunlight lit their eyes, beady as starlings', their gaudy buttons and jewels, the ribbons on their coats. Their fingers were too long, their voices the buzz of bees. Some of them still had wings for arms, one a beak instead of a mouth.

Among them was a stranger.

Careful as cats with prey, two of the Shee led him out and stood back. The whole tribe surveyed their prisoner with fascination.

Wharton stared too. The *journeyman* was young, a little over Jake's age. He wore brown, dirty clothes of some rough homespun cloth. A leather belt was wrapped twice around his waist; a pouch of skin hung from it. His face was remarkable, tattooed completely down one cheek and the side of his neck with blue whorls and

37

spirals. His hair was shaved from his temples in some savage tonsure; the rest hung down his back. He waited, alert, light on his feet, taking everything in.

From her hiding place in the leaves, Rebecca gave the tiniest gasp, and Wharton saw Summer.

Dark-haired, ivory-skinned, the Shee queen sat on a pliant branch of the birch, and it barely bent beneath her. She wore a red dress, its berried bodice all panelled with overlapping leaves in gold and ruby, its skirt a ragged mesh to her knees. Her bare feet swung in mid-air; her scarlet lips made a perfect smile.

'What brings you to my Wood, stranger?'

Wharton shuddered at that voice. So sweet. So heartless.

The stranger answered, a few words in a swift, sibilant language.

Summer wrinkled her nose. 'I see. But I don't like that sound you make. Why do mortals have those endless, foolish languages?'

She slid down and landed lightly in the leaves. The young man stepped back but Summer stepped after him. She reached up and touched his lips with a white finger, and Wharton was terrified she would enchant him into some rat or bird. But nothing seemed to happen except that his eyes widened. He said,

'Elf-woman, don't touch me.'

Summer giggled. 'That's so much better!' Then her eyes narrowed. 'Wait, though. I know you! I've seen you, in my Summerland. Once you climbed a ladder down from the sky and watched us dance. I never forget a prying mortal.'

The boy spread his hands, in a proud gesture. 'Among my people I am a shaman of some power.'

'You must be, sweetie.' She looked round. A blue wooden chair appeared and she sat on it, tipping it back thoughtfully and gazing at him. 'Because that was at least a thousand mortal years ago.'

The Shee all said, 'Oooh,' in a mocking chorus; she glared at them, and a few hastily completed the change into starlings and flew away.

The shaman stood silent. Wharton had a sudden sharp desire to sneeze; he buried his nose in his sleeve. He would rather be eaten alive by insects than let Summer know he was here; the sneeze, when it came, was a soft, muffled convulsion.

A male Shee, nearest the stream, turned its head languidly. Its cat-green eyes looked towards the willow island. Wharton willed himself to be invisible.

The Shee blinked. Then it turned away.

Wharton breathed out in a sweat of relief. When he

could listen again Summer was saying, 'So what can you want in this time? It must have taken great sorcery to get here.' Then her eyes went wide; she leaned forward. 'Ah, but you must have the magic mirror! And a bracelet!'

The young shaman looked at her. He might have been terrified but the blue tattoos made his face hard to read. He said, 'I know of no bracelet. And the black glass is lost to me now. What I seek here is its master. The great mage who rules it.'

Summer smiled. 'Why?'

'To ask for his help.'

She tinkled a laugh and all the Shee copied it slavishly. The sound was like raindrops falling down a deep well. '*Venn?* You want to ask Venn for help! You poor fool. You'd be better off asking me.'

He shook his dark head, calm. 'I think not. I know you, the elf-people, the *huldre-folk*. You're nothing but leaf and water and stone. There's no trusting you. You have no hearts. You are nothing.'

Silence.

All the Shee seemed to lean in, fascinated and intent. Wharton swore in silent dread. Was the boy totally mad? His self-possession was remarkable.

But Summer merely smiled a brittle smile and tapped a red-nailed forefinger on the arm of the chair. 'You have

40

some courage, mortal. I could do all sorts of interesting things to you, but it seems to me the very best punishment would be to send you to Venn and watch your crushing disappointment. Delicious! But first, I want to know why you need him. Sit.'

It wasn't a request. A wire park bench was there and the shaman was suddenly sitting on it. Wharton knew exactly the alarm and anger he would feel.

The stranger took a breath. He leaned forward, hand on knees. He said, 'I come from far to the north. A land of marsh and fen, of scattered lakes and deep, endless forest. My tribe is small and poor, and we are few. We are being plagued by a demon.'

Summer clapped her hands. 'A demon! I love that.'

'It came three years ago. It is a creature that crawls from a black cave in the mountains and attacks at night, or when our cattle are untended in the fields. A fell thing, a troll, not human, because our warriors have tried often to kill it; it just fades away in the night, mocking them. Perhaps one of your subjects, elf-queen.'

Summer wriggled her toes. 'I don't bother with all the grim creatures that lurk about the edges of the world. They're so ugly, and so dull. And so you came looking for help?'

He stared at her evenly. 'It took me all my skill to

bring the ship through. The ship is – was – our most precious possession. It is lost now. And probably so am I. But this was our only chance. I have left wife and children, father and mother, to do this.'

'And you end up with Venn?' She giggled, jumping up and walking round the clearing in delight. 'Venn the monster-slayer! That is so crazy!' She turned, swift. 'But I'm afraid he won't care. All he thinks of is his wretched wife.'

'His wife?'

'*Leah.*' She spat the name and at the sound the sky darkened. Wharton saw Gideon glance up in alarm. The rain fell harder, though not on the Shee.

The shaman shrugged. 'Every man can be bought, every man has a weakness. The black glass is wilful and uncontrolled, beyond my skill; its master must be powerful. Our animals are dying, we live in terror, and the blame is mine, because I am the chosen one of my tribe. I will go and see this mage, Venn. If he is mortal I will make him help me.'

Summer smiled an angry smile. 'Such haughty pride! Actually Venn is only half mortal. The rest of him is mine. Yes, I'll let you go to him. You might distract him from his stupid obsessions. But I warn you, he won't help.'

The shaman stood. He seemed undaunted, determined.

There were beads and feathers, Wharton saw, knotted in the fringes of his coat. 'I haven't come all this way for nothing,' he said quietly. 'I have powers, elf-woman. I have weapons.'

'None that worry me.' Summer came a step closer. 'I'll let you go but in return I want something. Something most precious.'

He paled then, and she laughed. 'Oh, not your greatest love! Not the first of your children to greet you when you get home. Nothing so drastic. What I want is something quite useless to you. It's a coin. Not even that. Half a coin.'

She reached out and took his hand, turned the palm up and touched it. A drop of cold water fell from her nail. It made a tiny pool and in the pool was an image, the broken face of Zeus, sliced jaggedly in half.

'That's what I want. It's hidden somewhere in the mage's house. Find it. When Venn fails you, bring it to me and I'll destroy your monster.' She touched the blue spiral on his face. 'It will be such fun for us to work together.'

He looked up. 'It must be a powerful thing, this coin.'

'Not your business. Do you agree?'

He shrugged. 'I have no choice.'

'None.' Satisfied, she clapped her hands. Two Shee

43

hurried swiftly from the trees. Turning away carelessly she snapped, 'Take this mortal to the Dwelling; give him the help he needs to get inside.' She spun on her toes. 'Now, my silver people! What shall we be? Flies on the window? Birds in the eaves? We need to be comfortable watching Venn's fury!'

The Shee emerged eagerly from the Wood. As the shaman was dragged towards the Abbey, Wharton saw how the creatures grew wings and beaks; they shivered into a bird-flock that rose in a racket of chatter and flew noisily above the bare branches. The boy looked back; his glance was sharp, considering.

Summer did not transform. Instead she smoothed down her skirt and turned, her voice suddenly as cloying as honey. 'And you, Gideon, my sweet. Did I hear your silent little sneeze?'

No answer came. Gideon was frozen into invisibility.

Summer smiled. 'Meet me at the Abbey. We'll sit on the roof and watch all the fun.'

She walked daintily down the muddy path, her shape flickering between the trees, becoming lost in the tangled branches and berried undergrowth until Wharton couldn't see her any more.

It was a very long time before any of them moved.

Finally, Gideon sat up. 'Safe now.'

Wharton eased his cramped legs out. He sat and stared at Rebecca. 'A shaman! From some ancient time? I don't like the sound of that!'

'He's pretty cocky,' she said, scrambling up.

'Maybe with reason. I only pray to God Maskelyne has that coin safe.'

Rebecca brushed leaves from her hair. She looked tense with worry. 'So do I,' she said.

CHAPTER FOUR

Venn's youth was wild and reckless. There was no expedition he would not undertake, no dangerous journey he would refuse. For months at a time he would vanish into the most remote parts of the world.

I once asked him what he was searching for.

He gave me his coldest stare. 'Somewhere no one else has found,' he said. 'Somewhere impossible.'

Jean Lamartine, *The Strange Life of Oberon Venn*

Maskelyne stood before the obsidian mirror.

The glass was black and it showed nothing of himself, as if he did not exist. As if his body and soul had been so scattered and dissipated during his long *journeys* in time that there was nothing left of him now, not even the reflection of a ghost. He had forgotten what he looked like. Now he reached up and touched the scarred skin of his face, drew forward the ends of his dark hair to see them. He was here. The mirror was here. 'You and I,' he said. 'We have come so far.'

A glimmer moved in the dark depths.

He watched it, a long moment, then turned away.

The attic stretched into dimness, the trusses and beams of the Abbey roof criss-crossing it. A shaft of dusty light slanted down at the far end.

The exhausting night had wearied him, the frantic anxiety of moving the mirror up here away from encroaching water, the worry that Jake and Venn might not succeed in their last, vital test.

And the mirror was disturbed, he could sense that. Not just from the move, but something else.

He sat at the cluttered desk and decided to find out what. He allowed his mind to loosen, exploring the dark surface of the volcanic glass, moving into its spaces. The mirror contained all of time and whatever lay beyond; too much for a man to discover in a thousand lifetimes. He had given his soul for the mirror; he had cheated death for the secrets it held. And he would never know them all.

He felt a ripple behind his eyes, a stone thrown in a still pool. As if something strange had broken through from a cold, far place. It was just a flavour, a brief touch of something ancient and and raw.

He frowned. What was it? For a moment he saw a dark, ancient ship, broken on rocks.

Then a thin voice interrupted him. 'Excuse me? Sorcerer?'

He opened his eyes, startled.

'Up here.'

It was the wooden bird with the bead eye, the one that Sarah had brought here. He hadn't seen it round the house for some time, and had wondered if it had finally gone back to the Shee. Now it flitted down from a high beam and landed on his knee, its small claws gripping him tight.

'Hi there. Sorry to disturb you . . . all that important magic stuff.'

'You're not. Don't worry.'

'Great.' The claws fidgeted. The bird tipped its head. 'Don't mind me asking, but you're the one who's got the coin, right?'

Maskelyne nodded, gravely.

'Keeping it safe?'

'Very safe.'

'Glad to hear it. I was just checking, because you know, it's probably Summer's absolute number one priority to get her hands on that bit of shiny gold. You need to be really, really careful.'

'I assure you, I am.'

'So . . .' the bird gave a nervy whistle, 'I suppose it's no use asking – just out of curiosity – exactly where it is?'

'None at all.' Maskelyne was amused; he liked the little thing, but it was Shee, and he would put no trust in it.

'Thought so.' Disappointed, the bird fixed him with its black beady eye. 'Can't blame you, really. Only – if you remember – it was me who told you where that girl Sarah had it stashed. Up on the roof, in the gutters, remember? Without me you might never have found it. So you sort of . . . owe me.'

Maskelyne knew only too well what was coming. He held out a finger, and the wood and feather creature hopped awkwardly on. Gently he said, 'I told you once before. I can't help you. I can't turn you back into your own shape. The power on you is Shee and is very strong. The only person who can change it is the one who created it.'

The bird sighed. 'Summer.'

'Summer.'

'Then I'm stuck like this for all eternity.'

Maskelyne said, 'You could try to persuade her.'

'Yes. Right.'

They were both silent, as if the impossibility of that was a shared pain. Suddenly the bird gave a brief cheery whistle. 'Ah well! It was worth a try. I'll just . . . flit around the place and try to keep busy. Anything you want, just call.' It flew, with a flash of moulting feathers, up around the beams and out through the attic door.

Maskelyne watched it go, his scarred face dark. He knew a whistle against despair when he heard it. Certainly the little thing would now start hunting, would scour the rooms and corridors of the Abbey day and night, searching for the hidden half-coin that Summer longed for.

What else could it offer her for its freedom?

He frowned.

The talisman was well hidden, wrapped in spells in a place no one would guess. But the Shee had eyes as sharp as diamonds, and were clever and quick thieves. The mortals in the house had walked past the coin a hundred times and never noticed it, but that little bird . . . A tiny spy was the last thing he needed.

He shook his head and stood up. No point in worrying. He would just have to trust in his skill.

And where was Rebecca? She must be on the way, driving too fast, panic-stricken at not being able to contact anyone.

At the thought of her he hurried out into the attic corridor, and then ran down the tight twist of the white-painted stair at the end, its newel posts carved into smooth worn spheres.

Halfway down he heard raised voices. Urgent angry voices. They were coming from the kitchen.

He frowned.

He had been expecting this.

Sarah stood alone in the middle of the floor confronting them all. She knew she had to make this work. She fixed Venn with a defiant blue stare.

'You know what I'm saying and you know what I want. Before you go after Leah, before you take that final, fatal step, I want you to see the consequences. I want you to come with me to the End World. To see what Janus will create with the mirror. You have to do that! You don't have the right to act otherwise!'

Venn was gazing into the roaring kitchen fire. He didn't look up at her. He didn't say anything. It was Piers who muttered, 'Sarah, we don't know how to travel into the future.'

She saw Jake catch his father's eye.

David glanced back, unhappy. Then he nodded, the tiniest of nods.

Jake said, 'Actually, we do.'

Sarah sighed with relief.

Piers said, 'We do?'

Even Venn turned his head. For a moment only the crackling of the fire and the slow drips of water into a bucket filled the room. Then Venn snapped, 'What do you mean?'

Jake took a breath. 'I mean that John Harcourt Symmes worked it out. Our old friend the Victorian inventor. He and Moll experimented for years on the mirror – they had a bracelet too, remember. Later Moll worked with it, setting it up for her time-travelling thefts.' He gave a wry smile at the thought of her. 'Think about it. When she *journeyed* here to kidnap me, she came into her future.'

He reached into his pocket and held up a small battered notebook with *Moll's Diary* scrawled on the cover. 'She gave me this. It's all in here, the workings, the processes.'

Venn stalked over and snatched it from him, rifling through the yellowing, badly written pages. 'Why wasn't I told about this?'

Uneasy, David undid the harness that held the sagging sleepy baby. 'Well, we didn't know at first if—'

'This is my mirror! My quest!' Venn turned on him in fury. 'Don't you trust me? Do you think Summer still has me in thrall?'

There was a guilty silence.

Piers said, 'Excellency, no one would ever—'

'Shut up!'

David laid Lorenzo carefully in the cradle. Then he straightened. 'Look, O. We know you're ready to go for Leah. It's all set. But—'

'You too?' Venn snarled.

'I'm with you, always. You know that. But we need to hear what Sarah has to say. Because she's right about consequences. We've tried small things, but changing Leah's death will be huge. We need to understand what using the mirror for that will lead to.'

Sarah glanced at the door, a dark movement catching her eye. Maskelyne had come in and was leaning there, listening intently. Outside the slow drip of the rain fell from eaves and gables and branches, the wind gusting dead leaves over the flooded lawns.

Venn stared round at them all, bitter disbelief in his cold blue eyes. He tossed the diary on the table, turned, leaned his back against it and folded his arms.

'All right.' He fixed her with a stare. 'Make your case. You've got five minutes to convince me.'

Sarah frowned. She was stupidly nervous, but this was it, this was what she had come here for and it had to work. She looked around at them all, at Maskelyne and David, and Piers with the cat in his lap, at Jake.

She pushed hair behind her ear. Then she said, 'OK. I know this is not what you want to hear. But let me start by telling you what happens next. After Leah comes back.'

'We do it? *It works?*' Venn's joy and anxiety were acute.

'I'm proof it works, aren't I? I'm your great-granddaughter. If it hadn't worked I wouldn't be here.' She faced him, suddenly angry. 'But it's not all about me, or her, or you! Do you really think that after a spectacular thing like that – bringing back the dead – that the mirror will be forgotten? That it would languish in some cupboard and no one would ever use it again? *That it would be content?*' She turned, looking at them all. 'Don't you see, every time you use the mirror, its power grows! You're feeding it, it's a caged tiger. Somewhere deep inside, it pulses with strength and desire. It won't be kept secret. It wants to grow, and grow. Ask Maskelyne.'

They looked at him.

Slowly, he nodded his head. 'That much is true,' he murmured.

Sarah took a breath. She was fighting to stay calm, to keep control. She kept her voice even and steady. 'Word gets out. The mirror is known about, first just in the scientific community. Then, after the war, by the government. Fifty years after your death it gets taken into

54

a top-secret government facility where all sorts of experiments are done with it. When Janus seizes power, possession of the mirror is his first priority. With it he can do anything, but what he creates is destruction. An empty world. A place where his enemies vanish, where people are experimented on, where cities are vaporized, where whole ecologies die. The End World.'

She had them now. They stared, fascinated.

'Janus becomes obsessed with the mirror. He lives with it, works with it. He lives lifetimes in a few seconds. His repeated use of it makes it a monstrous, demonic thing. A black hole. An *unthing* that starts to devour the world.'

She turned, staring into the obsidian glass, at her own warped eyes.

'I don't know all the details, but that's what happens. It's not some story – I've seen it. This house is a ruin in that future and the Wood a burned and hacked wilderness. My father was shot down and taken away and I haven't seen him since. I don't know what happened to him, or my mother, not even if they're still alive . . .'

Jake said, 'Sarah, look . . .'

'Let me finish!' She wouldn't let them stop her now, even though she was suddenly tired and wanted only to sit down. Instead she said, 'I'm not asking for myself. I'm asking because, if you even help to cause that, Venn, then you have a responsibility to to them, to the people of the future, to everyone who will suffer.'

She stood face to face with him; he looked at her and she knew their eyes were blue and fierce and identical.

There was silence. Then he said, 'My responsibility is to Leah.'

'What would she want you to do?'

Sarah glanced at the painting of the woman, where Venn had propped it near the mirror. Leah, warm and dark-haired and smiling, the missing character in the story. And suddenly she too wanted to find Leah, so urgently it gave her some idea of what Venn's anguish might be. 'Go to the future. Just go, and look. That's all I'm asking. See what Janus has done. Then come back and make your choice.'

Sitting on the inglenook, Piers fidgeted with anxiety. 'Responsibility's not a word the Shee know.'

'Then it's lucky he's mortal, isn't it?'

Venn's wintry stare held her. He said, 'What do the rest of you say? David?'

Jake's father was rocking his sleeping baby. He said quietly, 'I think we have to do it. I don't think we have any choice.'

'Jake?'

'Absolutely. And I'm coming with you.' He saw his father's quick turn of the head, and shrugged. 'I want to see the future!'

Venn snorted. 'If we go *I'll* decide who comes.'

Sarah held her breath. She had done it. She knew that now.

'And you,' Venn snapped. 'I suppose you have an opinion?'

Piers twisted his fingers nervously. 'Me? I'm just a genie from a bottle.'

'So you keep telling us. Speak anyway.'

The small man shrugged. 'Go. Prove it to Summer that she doesn't own you.'

'A selfish motive.'

'That's human too, Excellency.'

Venn almost smiled. Sarah wished Wharton was here. George would have had plenty to say about this, he would have backed her up, and so would Rebecca, but they were still struggling through the floods. That left only Maskelyne, a dark shadow leaning in the doorway.

As if reluctant, Venn turned to him. 'You?'

The scarred man straightened and took a few steps into the warm room. He looked round at them. '*Journeying* is dangerous. *Journeying* into the future the most dangerous of all. And have you thought of the problems

57

– how you'll return? The mirror there is huge, swollen, a raging power, well guarded.'

'I got here,' Sarah said sharply.

'I know. But remember, I've been there too. I worked with Janus for a while, in his terrible world.' He turned his face to show the jagged scar. 'I know all the power and horror of the mirror.'

'So you say no?' Venn snapped.

Maskelyne shook his head. 'Because I've seen, I say yes. You need to see it too.'

Sarah gave the faintest sigh. The fire crackled; Lorenzo squirmed in his cradle and made a small contented noise. One of the cats opened an eye.

Venn sat in brooding thought, his stare through the window to the dim rainy outline of the Wood. He was still, as if his habitual restlessness was inside his mind now, a pacing between decisions.

Sarah sank down on the bench next to Jake. Her hand was near his; she thought for a moment he meant to hold it, maybe because of what she'd said about her father. But before he could move Venn looked up. 'All right. We go into the future.'

A ripple of relief unlocked around the room. David smiled. Piers gave a small clap, then stood and hurried to stir a bubbling pot of stew as it spilled over the lid.

Sarah felt drained. She said, 'It's the right decision.'

'Let's hope so.' He turned away as if he didn't want to look at her, and picked up the diary. He threw it to Maskelyne; the scarred man caught it in surprise. 'I want the mirror ready for this in two hours. I want to know how we get there and come back, with as little time passing here as possible.'

'You're asking for miracles.'

'That's right. But you can deliver.'

The ghost of a smile touched Maskelyne's face. But he said nothing, and went out.

'Go with him,' Venn said to David.

David nodded. He came up to Venn and took his elbow. 'Leah would understand. We have to know what we're dealing with.'

'That's what I'm afraid of. That when I do know, I might not be able to go through with it. And what then, David? What then?'

David had no answer. Quickly, as if the restlessness was unleashed, Venn walked out. They heard him stride up the corridor.

'I hope he won't go to Summer,' Jake said.

'I doubt it. The last thing he wants is her opinion.' David headed for the door, then turned. 'And what's this about you *journeying* to the future?'

'Try and stop me!'

'I wouldn't dare.'

When his father was gone, Jake looked at Sarah. She had her hands round a fresh cup of coffee Piers had put there. She didn't even seem to notice.

'Well done,' he said quietly.

She said, 'You do realize, that if he doesn't rescue Leah, I or my parents won't even get born. I may have just argued myself out of my very existence, Jake. How is that even possible?'

She smiled a wan smile, seeing his fear and astonishment. Was she the only one who had thought any of this through?

Behind them, Piers clattered the pots. A waft of onion and garlic filled the kitchen.

'Mortals are so wonderfully heroic,' he muttered. 'I really admire that.'

CHAPTER FIVE

To travel to the future, Jake. Lordy, what a lark. Because you poor sods won't have a clue what's coming.

Moll's diary

Gideon said, 'I'll have to go back to her, or she'll send some of them to find me. I'll get you onto the path first.'

He led them through dripping undergrowth. Wharton glanced up – the sky was still lowering, brooding with heavy clouds. Disturbed flocks of birds broke and scattered.

Rebecca shivered. 'I hope Piers has something hot on the stove. I'm starved.'

Rather to his surprise, Wharton found he was too. He no longer felt sick, either. Grinning, he pushed through the branches on to the path, and was about to stride ahead when Gideon caught his arm so suddenly he almost fell over.

'Be careful! Don't step on that!'

Wharton froze, staring down. 'What?'

'That.'

It looked like nothing. The path crossed a grassy glade. In the centre, a ring of slightly darker, emerald grass was faintly visible, a mushroom or two sprouting from some dead wood below it.

Rebecca giggled. 'Fairy-ring. The locals say the Shee dance in them.'

Gideon gave her a sharp look. 'Maybe you should believe them. It's no dance you'd want to see. Step on it and you might pause a second. What you think is a second. Out here centuries go by. Then you step out. The Shee love them. They love watching what happens next.'

Wharton thought of the monk he had seen crumble to dust. The glee of the creatures then had chilled him to the soul. 'Death fascinates them.'

Gideon shrugged narrow shoulders. 'It's a joke to them.' He turned away and walked on. 'I wish it was a joke to me.'

Wharton raised an eyebrow at Rebecca. If only there was something they could do for the boy. His own taste of Summer's hospitality had been brief, but it still made him wake up in a cold sweat at night. How must it be to live for ever in a land of tasteless joys and unpredictable danger?

They edged round the sinister ring. Gideon walked ahead, a slim figure in his patchwork coat.

At the next turning he paused, sniffed the air and said, 'You should be right from here. Just don't step off the path, and keep going, whatever they do. Get to the Abbey.'

Wharton nodded. 'Thanks. Um, look. That wand thing he gave you. Don't you think we should take it? I mean, if Summer got hold of it . . .'

Gideon frowned. He took the bone sliver from his pocket and looked down at it. 'He gave it to me, and it might help me. I'm keeping it.'

'Whatever you say. Just a thought.'

Gideon turned, then looked back. 'Remind Venn he owes me.'

'He knows that,' Rebecca said.

'And Jake. Remind Jake.' He turned sideways, and was gone. Only a berried branch stirred. A leaf fell from a twig.

'How does he do that?' Rebecca muttered.

Wharton took her hand. 'I'm sure it's a gift he'd gladly swap for his freedom. Come on, now. This place gives me the creeps.' He was anxious to get back, but this part of the Wood was strange to him, and after only a few steps the way curved and dropped through marshy hollows and mires of mud. They pushed through a broken gate and found the path blocked by a flood.

Rebecca took a breath of dismay. 'Great. What now?'

'We don't leave the path.'

'But it's too deep.' She tugged a stick from the undergrowth and probed the water. The stick sank in up to her hand. 'We can't wade through that. We could try that way round?'

Wharton looked. A small dry path led seductively between the trees. He grimaced. 'Becky, I've learned enough about the Shee not to trust sweet little short cuts. Take my hand. It might not be quite what we think.'

They waded in. The water sloshed to the top of Rebecca's wellingtons and stayed there. Struggling in the soft mud, she took careful steps after Wharton, expecting any minute to sink deeper, even to topple and fall.

Then he laughed. 'See?'

There was no water. And when she looked back only a tiny puddle lay in the path.

Astonished, she stared. 'That is . . . nuts.'

Wharton felt smug. He strode along the path and out on to the soaked lawns, and there was Wintercombe

Abbey, its grim gables rising above him, the open mouths of its gargoyles spouting with rain.

A few starlings chattered on the roof.

The front door was shut and there was no sign of anyone, but smoke was coming from the kitchen chimney, and Wharton was sure a whiff of garlic and onions was wafting in it.

'Piers,' he said softly, 'you are a genius. And I love you.'

The Shee bird wriggled itself with great difficulty through the keyhole into the study and swooped round once, landing on the back of Venn's chair. It stared at the long-cased clock, the cluttered desk, the ceiling-high bookshelves rammed with dusty volumes.

'Neglecting the housework, Piers,' it muttered.

It flitted over, and began to tug the first book out with its beak. The book was heavy and the bird small, but finally the volume toppled and fell in a crash of pages.

The bird scanned the wreckage with its Shee-sharp sight, intact behind the black bead of its eye.

Nothing had fallen out.

Well, this was only the start, and an unlikely one. The sorcerer was far too clever to hide the coin in the pages of a book. But everything would be searched, every corner, every crack, and now was a good time, when the mortals were all in such a . . . well . . . mortal panic.

The bird whistled a happy tune, tugged another book out and let it go. Pages splattered. Dust exploded.

It tipped its head. This would take for ever.

But then the Shee have all the time in the world.

'Are you sure of those figures for the second dial?' David was consulting the diary again. He groaned. 'Oh for heaven's sake, couldn't someone have taught that girl Moll to write properly? Her handwriting is totally impossible.'

'Give it to me.' Jake took it, impatient. 'I've read all this. It's scrawl but it's not that bad.'

He stared at the page, smudged with dirty fingermarks – her own, probably, or Symmes's, made all those years ago. He read, smiling, because the words had been meant for him, straight from her crazy, bubbly brain . . .

It's not easy, Jake luv, journeying into the future. Lots of tricy stuff. But here's the list of Symmes calculations and if they don't mean nothing to you, just follow them blind. Numbers is numbers. He never got it all to work mind, but I did, *and one day I'll come and get you with it, Jake, and we'll have such larks . . .*

David, looking over his shoulder, grinned. 'She did that right enough.'

'She always does what she says she will.' Jake handed over the book, his finger on a jammed column of figures. 'That's the list.'

David took it and crossed to Maskelyne. 'Ready?'

'Yes.'

David read out the numbers; the scarred man entered them quickly on the keyboard.

Jake prowled, restless. Moll's voice was in his head now; he wished with a sudden sharp pain that she was here, mad, laughing, dangerous Moll. He missed her. With Moll, you felt you could do anything.

He turned as the whine of the Chronoptika changed. There were so many monitors and wires coming out of the mirror that it looked even more like a tethered creature, strapped down in case it broke free. Light slanted on it. It showed him a warped Jake, exaggeratedly tall, spikily arrogant, too handsome. A little cruel.

Disturbed, he turned away.

Sarah hurried in. She was wearing a knee-length grey dress, made of some smooth fabric that did not crease, and a pair of slipper-like shoes.

He said, 'Isn't that . . . ?'

'It's what I was wearing when I came. My own clothes. Piers has yours ready.'

The small man bustled in with an armful of clothing. Grey trousers. A grey shirt. Piers held them out and Jake took them from him reluctantly. The feel of the cloth was oily and unpleasant.

'Colourful.'

'Colour is one thing you won't see a lot of.' Sarah smiled, rueful. 'When I first got here I couldn't stop looking at the sky. I'd never seen anything so blue. I'm going to miss that.'

Jake looked up, caught by a bleakness in her voice, but at that moment Venn came in, carrying a backpack. The silver bracelet on his wrist glimmered, its bead of amber fiercely bright. He too wore the drab clothes, though nothing could hide his blond hair, the wintry blue of his eyes.

While Jake changed, Venn turned to Maskelyne. 'All ready?'

'Everything is as the diary says.' He was looking at the obsidian glass. 'I sense a new excitement in the mirror. A sense of turning around.'

'Turning around?'

68

'To face a new direction.' But the scarred man sounded uneasy, and sat again and checked the controls, the silver frame, the tiny fossil embedded in its unreadable words, obsessively, as if unable to be sure this would work.

Venn turned on Piers. 'I want top security while I'm gone! Not a spider gets in. Understand?'

'Always, Excellency.' Piers held out a grey knee-length coat; Venn struggled into it.

'All precautions against the Shee?'

'In place.'

'If you ever want to be free again, Piers, don't let me down.'

Piers shot him a startled glance.

But Venn had turned to David.

For a moment they were silent, looking at each other. David looked the older now, his hair greyer. Venn gave a bleak smile. He said, 'We should be back by tonight, your time. I won't stay there any longer than I need to. We'll get in, look around, come back. But these are my orders, David. *If I don't get back before midnight of Halloween you proceed with the operation.* You go and get Leah.'

'O, listen to me.'

Venn stepped close. His voice was hard as flint. 'You go ahead. The plan is all fixed; it's my life's work, it's everything. Save her for me. *Swear to me you will!*'

There was silence in the cluttered attic. For a moment David said nothing.

Then, finally, he nodded. 'I promise. We've been friends a long time O.'

'Yes.'

'Bring my son back safe.'

'That's my side of the bargain.'

Sarah came over; she watched as Venn shouldered the pack, then she held out her hand and after a second he took it, crushing her smaller fingers.

Jake hugged David hurriedly. 'Don't worry about me. I'll be fine.'

'If you're not I'll be coming after you.' His voice was raw with worry. Jake stepped back until there was a space between them.

'Makes a change, this way round.'

David managed a brief smile. 'I love you, son.'

'Me too.' He turned away.

'All set?' Piers asked.

'Do it.' Venn's voice was a growl, but it was lost in the explosion of the mirror. For Jake the power of the Chronoptika burst through his bones and nerves and teeth; it scattered him as it had never done before, a roar of nothingness that took his sight and smell and taste and destroyed them. For a timeless second he was nowhere

70

and nothing. He had never existed. He was adrift on the mysterious emptiness of the universe.

Then, with a crack that sparked pain right through him, he was there.

In the silence Piers and David stood aghast.

Papers were scattered everywhere; only one of the cats had not fled, and he was crouched absolutely flat under the desk, spitting furiously at thin air.

Maskelyne was calm but fascinated. 'So different,' he breathed. 'As if it could not wait.'

'It's never been like that before.' Piers sat down, a little numb.

David turned. 'We just have to hope that it –'

The door crashed open. 'Here you all are!' Wharton said. He was soaked, his hair plastered flat, his face dirty and unshaven. He wore a vast mac and wellingtons that looked too small for him. 'Fantastic to see the place still standing! I hope you can manage a bacon butty for the rescue party Piers, because I'm bloody starving and we've crossed wave and wood to warn you about . . .' His voice petered out.

Rebecca came in behind, took one look at the Mirror and stared at Maskelyne. 'What's happened?'

Wharton took in David's face, the devastated room.

The Mirror.

'Where's Jake?'

David shrugged. 'Hopefully, about a hundred years in the future from here.'

Far below, beneath rooms and corridors, beneath the stone walls of the Monk's Walk, deep in the flooded cellars, a trapdoor crashed open.

A hand shoved through moss and lichen; then a soaked sleeve. Water trickled from the ancient paving; it spilled and ran down the green-stained wall.

No one but spiders saw the strange, tattooed fingers grip the stone and pull, saw the boy who hauled himself through, crawled down the wall like a bat, crouched on the earth floor, hurting and breathless.

Listening.

To the vast and echoing silence of the house.

O brave new world, that hath such people in't!

CHAPTER SIX

There have been tyrants before. Men who killed for power over continents and countries. None of them dreamed of a tyranny over Time.

Janus will rule an Empire that lasts for eternity. Unless we stop him.

Illegal ZEUS transmission: Biography of Janus

Jake was lying in a dim, damp place.

He knew it was damp because his breath made a small cloud when he coughed; the air was acrid, its taste metallic.

One arm was numb, crumpled beneath him.

He pushed himself up and looked down.

'Oh hell,' he breathed.

He kept perfectly and absolutely still. He was on some sort of filthy ledge against a concrete wall, a ledge so narrow that any movement at all would tumble him off it into space. He turned cold as he thought of the odds of materializing on it and not in mid-air.

Carefully, just his eyes moving, he saw how the ledge was strewn with rubble. He straightened his elbow, and eased up, but even so his foot caught a piece of stone and sent it toppling over the edge.

There was no sound of it ever landing.

Jake took a breath, shuffled until his back was against the wall, and stared out.

He was miles above the world.

Below he saw a vast cityscape, littered with ruined buildings, most of them mere blocks of darkness, one or two pierced with frail lattices of light. Their shapes were bizarre, all shattered and corrugated. It was dark; too dark to make out streets, but from the invisible depths rose a gusty wind that wafted odd sounds – once the echoing clang of metal. And a soft, constant susurration of discreet machinery.

Nothing human.

Jake eased out from the wall.

There was so little light. He wasn't sure if he was outdoors or in; glancing up showed only dimness, but after a moment he realized that was a sky of unbroken cloud, its underside a gloomy coppery red. No moon. No stars.

Palms flat, he shuffled up the wall until he was standing. He felt sick with dizziness.

Don't look down. *Don't.*

The ledge was rough but unbroken. There were no steps down, but there were a few protruding stones, steep and far apart, leading up into the dark.

To comfort himself he called out softly, 'Venn? Sarah?' but the wind took his words and snatched them away.

Where were they? Surely not far. The mirror was unpredictable, but they had all *journeyed* together. Very carefully he manoeuvred out the mobile phone from his pocket. The screen lit, but showed only blankness.

'Dad? Can you hear me?'

Nothing.

Then Jake nearly dropped the phone. A sound rang out from somewhere far in the city, an eerie howl of incredible sorrow. It chilled every bone in him, prickled his skin with panic.

He edged hastily along the wall. There was an iron ring, rusted but still whole. He grabbed at it, eagerly.

Tiny lights moved far below. Were they torches held by people? Lights on vehicles? Their colours were peculiar – faintest purple, muted emerald.

Get a grip, he told himself. *Get off this ledge. Find Venn.*

With an effort he let go of the ring and grabbed the

nearest step. He began to climb.

It was a nightmare. The stones were thick and wet; they jutted from the wall and he had to haul himself up, sometimes with his feet kicking empty air. Even by craning his head dangerously back he couldn't see where the steps led. There must be some window. Some door.

After twenty minutes he had to stop, breathless, against the wall. A wisp of white floated against his face.

He snatched at it and his fingers went right through.

Cloud?

Was he that high?

Breathing was hard. He turned and climbed on, weary. The cloud gathered; soon he was wrapped in whiteness, even the next step invisible. He reached up, grabbed the stone and heaved; then as he wriggled over the top and lay flat, the terrible cry came again.

What could make that sound? Jake gritted his teeth, pulled himself to his knees and felt the invisible wall. It was bitterly cold, and smooth. His fingers touched a hard straight edge.

He felt along it, fast. A crack. No – too straight. *A seam.*

With a gasp for breath he scrabbled at it, desperate for a handle, for anything, but perhaps it was the simple pressure of his hands that did it, because with the softest sigh, like an airlock releasing, the panel swung inward.

Instantly Jake was through, almost falling over the sill, cloud streaming in with him and curdling in the whiteness of the warmer air.

He lay a second on the floor, gasping in relief. Then he opened his eyes, and nearly yelled aloud in fear.

He was looking at Janus.

Rebecca had decided to make herself useful clearing the mud, because she had to keep busy and try not to worry.

Wharton had gone to bed for a snooze, David and Maskelyne were taking turns to watch the Mirror. Piers, deep in the kitchens of the great house, cooked and whistled and guarded the monitors and fed the baby. He was far too busy, he said, to talk.

As she swirled a mop over the slick of mud on the wooden boards she wondered about Piers. What sort of creature was he? What hold did Venn have over him? When she had told him and David about the strange shaman from the past, and his encounter with the Shee, Piers had gone very quiet.

Not like him at all.

She squeezed the mop in the bucket. There was no

need to worry. The Abbey was locked tight as a drum. No one could get in. Venn would deal with the Shee when he got back, and then . . . She stopped, struck by a thought.

What if they never returned? Or what if they came back in twenty years' time, Venn and Sarah and Jake, and she was middle-aged, maybe with a husband and kids and a career, a completely different person, and they were unchanged even by an hour? It was too weird even to think about.

She rubbed the mop in agitated circles on the soaked boards.

She was up in the Long Gallery, where a series of buckets plipped with drips down the length of the vast room. The door to the Monk's Walk was closed; all that area below must be flooded. She had no idea how long it would be before . . .

A thump. Soft and muffled. Behind the panelled wall. She turned her head.

'Who's that?'

There was a door between two classical columns topped with Roman emperors. She knew where it led – to the east wing, a whole section of the Abbey that was never used, where the rooms were silent and shuttered, the shapes of furniture wrapped in white sheets, ghost-pale.

She dumped the mop in the bucket and dragged it noisily against the wall. Was it that Shee bird? Searching for the coin?

She turned the brass knob and opened the door. 'Is anyone in here?'

The narrow corridor was swagged in red, a dusty, stifled space. It made her think somehow of veins and a beating heart. Walking down it, her boots sank into the deep pile of an ancient carpet; she tried a door and opened it, peering in. A dim bedroom, the bed glistening with what looked like a canopy of spider web.

She backed out and hesitated. Then she saw the light switch. It was an ancient bakelite thing, but she forced it down and gasped. A whole row of elaborate candelabra, each held aloft by a silver cupid, flickered into life down the corridor, reflected in glass panels and the dusty panes of cabinets lacquered with Japanese gardens.

Rebecca walked down. Her reflection moved above her, huge on the ceiling. There was a corner ahead; around that she vaguely remembered a spiral stairway leading down to a maze of smaller rooms and store cupboards.

Then to her astonishment a voice whispered, 'Hey, girl! Up here.'

She stared at the ceiling.

A cage hung from it, a cage made of shadows. They had been spun out like threads from the cracked plaster, a crooked chandelier of dark and dust, a mesh of tangled lines. In its heart was a slanting twig and on the twig, hunched and fed up, perched the Shee bird.

'You!' Rebecca stared. 'Was it you I heard? What are you doing up there?'

'He caught me. I was having a good root around.'

'For the coin!'

'Well yes, what else. Then he came. I have to say he's pretty good. He whipped me into this thing like a shot and I can't find a way out. Yet.'

'Who did?'

'The magician.'

She smiled, a little proud, but the bird said, 'Oh not him. Not the scarred one. I mean the new one.'

Rebecca stared into the beady eye. A small point of fear quickened inside her. 'What new one?'

'He's a bit odd, even for a mortal. All stone and bone. Not a great talker, either. Look, I don't suppose you could ask Maskelyne if—'

But she had turned and was running down the red corridor, though all at once her own reflection was before her, so that she slammed into herself, palms flat. The invisible surface was sharp; she felt a sting as her hand was sliced by a sliver of glass. Stunned, she turned and met herself again, face smudged with dirt, plait coming undone.

Right, left, up, down, there was only her own face. She was in some trap of air, caged liked the bird. She stood still, breathless.

Through her image in the dusty glass, she saw the shaman. His face was tattooed. His dark eyes watched her, calm.

'Who are you?' he asked.

Rebecca thought fast. She drew herself up to her full height. 'I'm the mistress,' she snapped. 'The mistress of the mirror.'

'I don't get it.' Venn shook his head, tense with fury. 'We *journeyed* together! Why the hell should Jake end up somewhere else?'

'The mirror does what it wants.' Sarah's eyes were taking in the dimness of the place, its familiar, hated smell, its muted colours. During the months at Wintercombe she had dreamed and worried about this place. Her own world. Even though she dreaded it she knew she belonged here. She shook her head, trying to work out exactly where they were.

The street was empty, its buildings sprouting weeds. Venn stopped raging and began to see it. He turned in a complete circle. Softly he said, 'My God. Is it all like this?'

She shrugged. 'Here in London, yes. The nearer you get to the mirror the worse the effect.'

The buildings leaned. Some had collapsed under the strain, others had elongated and stretched like elastic, their bricks and stones and tiles warped to impossible lengths. Tugged by the contorted gravity of the black hole, the walls and roofs, the railings, lampposts, even the tarmac of the roads were dragged crazily eastwards. And there were holes. Empty spaces in the world, gaps of nothingness. They were small, but there were many, and Sarah knew their dangers. The whole world was being torn and sucked into the mirror, and its very fabric was ripping apart.

'Are those trees?' Venn breathed.

She nodded.

They were barely recognizable now. Stretched beyond sanity, their branches were hundreds of metres long, their trunks bloated in great burst sores, as the mirror sucked them toward itself atom by atom. They were deformities of timber, parodies of plants.

'And the colours!' He looked down at his hands, at the wall. 'Where are they?'

'The mirror devours everything. Light, colour, time, matter. Everything.'

It appalled him. She saw that and she was glad, because it was what she had brought him here for. She had begun to forget how weak colour was in this time — the drained faintness of washed-out blues, the barely perceptible reds. All the middle of the spectrum had long gone — orange and yellow and green were grey now. Her own hands were grey as she looked at them, Venn's face and hair bleached pale.

And in her nerves now, she felt the terrible tug of the mirror.

'It's a dark heart,' she said sourly. 'Everything in the world points to it.'

He turned. 'This was where you lived?'

'Near here. Come on, I'll show you.'

He hesitated. 'What about Jake?'

'Jake will find us. Everything will drag him there. He won't be able even to walk away from it. The mirror is on the point of swallowing the world, Venn, and that means us too, everything. Unless of course you let me destroy it.'

He pushed past her, but she saw his disquiet. 'Show me more.'

The street led to what had been a square of houses.

Now it was a squeezed diamond, and as they walked through it they felt themselves warp too, as if deep in their bodies cells rearranged. Venn swore. 'This is bizarre. Even in the Summerland there's nothing so—'

'This isn't the Summerland. This is real.'

He shook his head, following her down the pavement.

At the corner they passed a metal bench, so attenuated it looked like some cartoon image of arrested speed.

'How long has it . . . ?'

'Years. It started slowly. We didn't notice for a while. Then people – those left – started to get scared. Colours faded, light dimmed. We began to understand what Janus had done. Soon, there won't be anything left but darkness, and then not even that.' She shot him a glance. 'What is there when even darkness is gone? You see why I needed you to come.'

He said, 'I'm beginning to.' But he didn't look at her.

Beyond the square was a broken embankment; they clambered up on to it. It took Venn a moment just to understand what he was looking down at and when he did a small gasp escaped him.

It had been the Thames. Now the very course of the river was dragged from its bed. The opposite bank was gone; he saw flooded streets of water, alleys of mud, a swamp of sunken shipping and wrecked barges.

The bridges were contorted, torn from their foundations. And everything – office blocks, cranes, palaces, windows, pillars, every branch on every tree – pointed like compass needles to one impossible structure, rearing into the sky.

Venn stared. 'Isn't that—?'

'That's the Lab,' she said. 'Janus's HQ.'

He stared at it, baffled. It defied gravity and sanity. At its base was the ancient Tower of London, familiar, four-towered. But piled on top of that, built and propped and engineered above it, were the fragments of a multitude of structures, a patchwork pastiche of London's lost monuments.

He saw Nelson, still on his column, built into a glittering wall of office windows. He saw the façade of the British Museum and the windows of Selfridges; above that a Wren spire sprouted from the glass roof of a great railway station, and the unmistakeable chimneys and Tudor brick of Hampton Court were crowned by the dome of St Paul's. One on another, brick and stone and tile, the remnants of the city had been piled, high into the clouds, disappearing from sight.

After a moment Venn said, 'He's insane.'

'Of course he is! We – ZEUS, I mean – have known that for a long time.'

'And the mirror is in there?'

'Right at the heart, heavily guarded. Immediately below it are Janus's private apartments. Below that the laboratories and admin rooms, tech suites and galleries. The whole tower is roamed by time wolves and staffed by the Replicants of Janus. We don't know how many of those there are – hundreds, at least. There are no other people in there. You don't need staff when you can do everything yourself.'

He dragged his eyes from the building to her. Her face was drawn, her eyes almost white in the dim light. 'You know it well?'

'Well enough. We . . . the ones he called the children . . . we . . .'

She stopped.

A cry broke from the sky. A howl so terrible in its raw sorrow that for a moment all Venn wanted to do was crouch to the ground, hands over his ears, do anything to stop it.

He forced himself to stand still.

The sound rang again. When it stopped he knew he was breathing hard, his heart racing, as if after some exertion.

'What in God's name was that?'

Sarah did not look at him. Her gaze was fixed on the

top of the tower, lost in mist.

'That was the mirror,' she said softly. 'The agony of
the mirror.'

CHAPTER SEVEN

I command spirits.
I am the sun.
I am storm.
I am the web of the spider.

Be bound.
Be bound tightly.
Be held tightly.
Be held by the strength of my hand.

Shamanic spell of the Katka tribe

Rebecca walked into one of the shuttered rooms and sat on a gilded chair, very upright, watching him. She tried to look regal. Divine, even.

She said, 'I know about you. I know who you are and why you're here.'

Close up, his skin was pale, his hair glossy black. 'The lady of the mirror will know all things,' he said. Then, to her astonishment he knelt and then lay flat, his arms spread out, his forehead on the dusty carpet. For a moment there was silence. She had no idea what to do; his reverence touched and troubled her. She said, 'Get up. You may look at me.'

He drew himself up. His eyes were dark in the dim room; the strange marks on his face seemed to twist and whirl. Did he believe her? She had to show power.

'You come from a land of snow,' she said. 'Your people are troubled by a creature of darkness.'

His eyes flickered. His fear, if that's what it was, came and went like a glimmer of lightning.

'You need my help.'

He nodded. 'The lady knows all things.'

'Do you know what place this is? Do you know where you are?'

'The Otherworld,' he said. 'The home of the high people, the Ancestors. Of He-who-Climbs-the-Holy-Tree, and She-who-Stole-the-Sun. The Wolves of Ice and the Fire Woman who Punished Arran.'

Rebecca drew a breath of awe. The whole of a lost mythology was there; forgotten stories of an ancient past. She longed to ask more. But she dared not.

Instead she said, 'That's right. You came in a ship over the sea.'

She leaned back, casually. She had to make him think she was calm, that she was in control, even though her heart was thumping and all she could think of was yelling for Wharton. 'I also know you spoke to the elf-queen. And what she asked you to do.'

He said nothing. Then he took a step closer. His eyes were shrewd. 'The Ancestors are wise. You know about the creature. Perhaps you sent it, as a punishment. What have we done to offend you?'

She let the silence linger, fighting panic. Drips in the corridor plinked into buckets.

'That's secret. Don't defy us. We have powers that could crush you like an ant under a finger.'

For a moment she was proud of that; then she realized how she sounded like Summer, and hated it.

He bowed his head. 'I am less than dust.'

She said. 'Now . . . I'll take you to the other . . . er . . . Ancestors. And we will send you home safely.'

He looked up quickly. 'Without a hero to destroy the creature? I can't go back without that. My people would kill me and drink from my skull. My wife would be taken, and my children, and it would be right, because I would have failed them.'

She stared, horrified. She hadn't thought about that. It was what would happen in such a primitive society. Mesolithic, maybe?

She rose, as tall and gracefully as she could. 'Follow behind me.'

He nodded. Then, sharp as a bird's, his eyes fixed.

She looked down.

The small cut on her hand. From it seeped a red trickle.

The shaman stared in disbelief.

He muttered something, astonished, and Rebecca said hastily, 'Wait. Listen to me—' but it was too late. He snatched the flint knife from his belt, grabbed her arm, and before she could shriek or scream the blade had sliced a tiny slash in the flesh at the base of her thumb.

A bright bead of blood welled and broke.

Rebecca snatched her hand away. 'What are you doing! Are you nuts!'

The shaman's face was dark with rage. 'Gods do many things. But they do not bleed. You're as mortal as I am.' He lifted the blade to her face. 'You're just a girl. Shall I seek more proof?'

'*No!*' She tried to jerk away but he grabbed her hair, dragging her head back.

She screamed in pain.

'You mocked the Ancestors. I should kill you for that.'

She gasped. 'If you do you'll never get back to your world. We can help. OK we may not be gods but we have power. We can do things you'd never dream of.'

For a moment she thought he didn't believe her. Then he took a ragged breath, and the pain in her head released. She tried to tear away, but he held her tight. 'You'll take me to the real master of the mirror. The man Venn.'

She frowned, sucking her sore palm. 'Venn's not here. He's *journeyed*. He's in some other time. Do you understand that? And even if he was here, there's no way he'd be interested in your problems. He has too many of his own.'

The boy stared, his eyes hard. He was probably about her age. She tried to think of him like one of the students at uni, talking endlessly about assignments and techy stuff and girls, but she couldn't. He seemed ages older. Somewhere she had read the odd fact that it had probably been teenagers who had built Stonehenge, because most people died young then – looking at this stranger she understood his strange speed, his urge to act quickly, to do everything now because there was no tomorrow. For him, the darkness would come quickly.

She said, 'What's your name?'

He laughed in scorn. 'You think I'll give you that power over me? Only the woman who gave me birth knows my name. Where has Venn gone?'

'To the future.'

He looked at her sideways, like an alert animal.

'The time yet to happen.' She wondered if he had any understanding of time. No clocks or watches. Time was for him the great circling of the sun and moon.

He said, 'These others – I'll speak to them. You will be held here until they listen to me.'

She stared at him in astonishment. 'What do you mean, held?'

'Like this.' He stood, and he had the tasselled rope from the curtains in his hand.

She moved but he was faster. In minutes her hands were tied behind her back and her feet to the chair legs. Furious, she squirmed. 'Are you mad? I'll scream and they'll come running.'

'Maybe. But no one will dare to touch you.'

'What do you mean?'

He crouched close, and his eyes were bright and clear. 'There will be a spell of fading on you.'

'*Fading*?'

He smiled, reached out and took her hand, firmly in his, turned it over, took something from his belt. She saw it was a feather, small and black. With his finger he touched the blood on her palm, and anointed the feather, singing soft words she didn't catch. He walked round her three times, anticlockwise. Then he said:

'*Listen to me, red girl.*

You are a girl of cobweb now.

A girl of dry leaf now.

You are frail.

A puff of wind will unravel you.

A touch will sink through you.

You will fade and be grey.

You will fall to pieces slowly.'

He stepped back, surveyed her, made one final gesture with both hands, closing the fists tight and crossing his arms at the wrist. Then he tossed the feather to the floor, went to the door, opened it and went out, without even looking back.

She was so amazed she just stared after him.

Silent.

For a second Jake lay frozen in fear; then he realized the face was an image.

Janus gazed down at him, grave, and powerful. The same round blue spectacles, the neat dark uniform, the lank hair, the calm, superior look, but enormous now, dominating the entire wall of the corridor. Jake stared up at it, almost wanting to laugh, because Janus was a small

96

man, and yet here he looked like a giant, airbrushed into a handsome prince.

Voices.

Instantly Jake leaped up. The corridor ran in both directions, a twisting, white place with no doors.

The voices rang nearer; he ran hastily along the featureless wall. No rooms. There was a side turning; he peered round it, found another corridor and darted down. On the left a shallow alcove opened; he flattened himself into it.

Just as he did so two men passed the opening of the corridor. They were talking together; one of them laughed, a sly chuckle he recognized at once. Carefully, he leaned out enough to see.

They were both Janus.

Jake slammed back, his heart thudding. Eyes wide, he stared at the blank wall opposite, hearing the voices – the identical voices – pause and laugh and hurry on.

Even when they had died away he didn't move.

Both Janus! Replicants then. Sarah had said there were many; that Janus had experimented with the mirror too often, creating more and more copies of himself. The place must be crawling with them. Getting out of here would be almost impossible.

He eased out, and walked softly down the new

corridor. At its end was a stair leading both up and down; he leaned over the bannister and looked up, and saw a square of treads rising high into darkness. From somewhere a hum of machinery echoed.

The staircase puzzled him. It didn't fit. It was old, even worm-eaten, its rail carved with foliage and fruit, plump mahogany columns with wooden grapes hanging from them. Yet the corridor behind him was white and strip-lit, boring as a government office.

He stared to climb up. But after a few steps stopped, startled. Why up? The way out must be down. He turned, descended the steps again.

Something was wrong. His breath came hard. Each step was an effort, as if he was pushing against some invisible force. As if every bone and muscle in him protested.

He turned round and went up.

Immediately, walking was easy.

Jake leaned against the wall. Whatever this was it scared him more than anything here yet, because it was inside him. In his body. His mind.

It had to be the mirror. If the mirror was a black hole it was devouring everything. That must be the pull he felt. It would get worse, he was sure, the further away he tried to go from it. But what use was the mirror to him without the bracelet. He had to find Venn first! Venn and Sarah.

He tried to think clearly. Then a wild idea struck him. He took out the mobile phone. Piers had muttered something about internal time contact. Did he mean . . . ?

Jake touched the numbers rapidly. Surely . . .

The screen lit.

Sarah was staring at him.

Jake gasped in relief.

'Where are you?' they both said in unison.

'In some sort of high building – really high.' Jake kept his voice low, but even whispering echoed here. 'I've seen Janus Replicants – two of them.'

'You're inside the tower. We're outside.' She looked strangely pale, her skin grey. 'Listen. You *have* to get out of there, Jake. Without the bracelet you're . . .'

'How did we get separated?'

'I don't know. This is crazy! We were supposed to just come and look and go back. If he catches us . . .'

A voice said, 'Give me that.' The screen jiggled; Venn's sharp blue eyes appeared, then it pulled back to show his face 'Jake, listen to me. Get down here. Before . . .'

A bell. Softly chiming, insistent, far off in the building.

'What's that?'

Sarah said, 'They know you're there! They've picked up the signal. We—'

The phone went blank. He cursed, shoved it in his pocket and ran. Down and down, turn after turn, but even as he ran he gasped for breath, his heart slamming. Every part of him wanted to turn around, but even as he fought his way on Jake scowled in fury. There was no way this would happen. He would never be drawn into the mirror.

But he was barely walking now.

Every step was an ordeal. He forced his way through air that seemed thick, down steps that yawned like deep chasms. The walls loomed in. Shadows rose against him. He limped like an old man, like a dying man.

Finally he had to stop.

He slid down and sat, gasping for breath. Far above him the bells sent out their sinister urgent chime, then, as suddenly as if someone had turned them off, they were silent.

Jake looked up. He couldn't hear anything, but fear made him stand. There was a broad wooden landing two steps below; he forced himself down to it. In one wall was a stone arch, small, hardly higher than his waist. He ducked under it.

On the other side was a vast space of darkness.

100

He was on a balcony looking down inside the gutted keep of some ancient castle; the rooms and floors were long gone, so that now it was empty as a lift shaft, green lichens sprouting from its walls. Every stone was stretched upwards, grotesquely warped by the mirror's pull. From what Sarah had said he was inside Janus's own HQ, the place called the Lab. Would he ever be able to drag himself out?

Something rustled underfoot. He knelt and groped and his hand touched crisp, light things; he gathered a handful and stood, bringing them close to his eyes.

Dead leaves.

Where had they come from? How could there be leaves this high, without any trees? Oak and ash and thorn? He let them sift and fall between his fingers.

For a moment he thought of Summer.

Where were the Shee in this world? From the Summerlands they could travel anywhere – why not here?

He turned, and saw, set crazily in the medieval wall, a switch; he reached out and his finger hesitated over it. Then, with a sudden decision, he flicked it down.

A panel lit.

Out of it, like a ghost, a holographic image of a building materialized, walls and rooms and corridors, a tiny green spot glowing in the heart.

Was that where he was?

He studied it quickly, reached out and touched it; it turned.

Rapidly he explored the map, the sections labelled *Experimental*, *Diagnostic*, and, most chillingly, *Retribution*.

He tapped that and it grew under his fingers.

Cells.

A list of prisoners, numbers.

The word *Venn*. It leaped out at him, and he swore. *45 Owein Venn*. Had that been Sarah's father? Next to the name was one small word. *Despatched*.

As he stared at it something small and bright dripped down past him; a patch of wetness splashed at his feet.

He stared up.

The Time Wolf was grey as mist, as solid as steel. Saliva dripped from its open jaws.

It growled, a soft, satisfied terrifying sound.

Jake backed.

Until there was only the wall behind him.

CHAPTER EIGHT

There are many delicious tales of Halloween here, of a dark carriage seen on the moor, of a ghostly devil that screams down a lost mine. And of course the country people practise all the old traditions – the sliver of apple peel, the candles in mirrors. Yet I rarely look in the mirrors in this house, for fear of what I might see standing behind me.

When darkness falls, the fun ends. Everyone goes home and locks their doors. A wind rises over the Wood, and the trees stir. For at Wintercombe this is a night of terror.

Letter of Lady Mary Venn to her sister 1834

Wharton said, 'Are you sure?'

Piers was sitting at the table staring at one of the cats. 'You heard it.'

'I can't understand what the bloody animal says!

Which one is that?'

'Tertio. Always the sharpest.'

'I thought they were all Replicants . . . Identical.'

'Well, yes, they are, but—' Piers waved a hand impatiently. 'Anyway, he's sure he heard voices. In the east wing. Odd thing is, that part of the building is all shut up. Has been since the last century, when Obadiah Venn went mad and was locked up in there. Madder than your usual Venn, that is.'

'Where's Rebecca?'

'Not sure.'

'Maybe she's talking to that nutty bird.'

Piers looked relieved. 'Yes. I'd forgotten that.'

Wharton turned. He was uneasy. The attic was heaped with equipment, and papers. It looked like a tip to him, but Maskelyne was working quietly at the monitors and now David came hurrying in with a whole pile of calculations. Everything was agonizingly ready for Operation Leah.

He glanced at the clock. One p.m. Venn still had about five hours until sunset.

'Maybe I should take a look.'

'Up to you.' Piers pulled on his lab coat.

'I'm thinking of that strange boy from the ship.'

'Oh, he could never have got in here.'

'Piers, this place has more holes than a sieve.' Wharton turned.

The obsidian mirror was watching him. That was his first thought. Then he saw it was just a warped reflection of himself, a big, bleary-looking man, with thinning hair and eyes that the mirror made black and empty. It was so disturbing he turned from it at once.

'David,' he said.

Jake's father was only half listening, a great pile of calculations slipping from his hands. 'Mmm?'

'Going down to check the place out. Lock the door and stay in here, all of you. Where's the baby.?'

'Asleep. For God's sake, George, be quiet.'

'Wouldn't dream of waking him. Just don't come out, even if you hear a racket. And don't let anyone in but me. Understand?'

David looked up. 'Are you expecting trouble?'

'No. But it's best to be safe.' He headed for the door.

From a corner Piers said, 'Be careful.'

'No worries. If ten years as an NCO taught me one thing, it's to watch my back.'

Out in the corridor he pondered about going for the shotgun first, and then told himself not to overreact.

Was he getting to be worried about what *cats* said? Boy, was he losing it!

He went down to the Long Gallery.

'Rebecca? Are you here?'

Wintercombe Abbey seemed cold and silent without its owner, without Jake and Sarah.

Distant drips plopped, odd draughts whispered. The soaked boards wheezed and oozed moisture as he walked on them. Halfway down, a casement window was banging in the storm; he reached out and grabbed it.

On the roof-ridge opposite a line of starlings watched him. Their eyes were beads of black, their glossy green and purple feathers lifted and splayed.

He pulled the window shut with a bang. None of them flew.

Shee? Possible, but autumn was the time for bird flocks.

He turned. The door to the east wing was ajar. 'Becky?'

Then he saw the mop and bucket; they had been pushed to one side, and there was a clear wet footprint on the dusty threshold. 'Are you OK in there?'

He eased the door wider. He saw a corridor swagged in sumptuous red velvet, lit by candelabra.

Then, sharp as a pain, he felt something prod into his spine.

A voice whispered, 'Don't cry out, fat man. Don't even move.'

Wharton closed his fists in fury.

There was no way he was fat.

And so much for watching his bloody back.

Deep in the Summerland there was a railway tunnel.

Gideon walked into it softly, leaving behind the eternal sunlight for a green gloom. Emerald lichens dripped from the curved walls. Ahead of him parallel rails disappeared into the distance.

It was cool and mysterious and smelled of coal, and it was one of his favourite places.

He walked until the darkness was complete and then sat, his back against the filthy wall, his feet stretched out. The silks and tawny satins of his Shee clothes were stained with mud. His pale face was rubbed with patterns of lichen.

He looked round cautiously, took out the bone wand and laid it on his knees.

The small bundles of objects tied to the tip clattered softly.

Perhaps it was a rattle, or made to beat some drum. He knew there was power in it, could feel it like an itching tingle on the skin, see it like a peculiar glow in the darkness, an aura of purple and gold.

He could smell it.

It smelled of blood.

Gideon's long fingers turned the thing. But what good was it to him? He had no idea how to use it, no idea if it could get him home, back to a time before the Shee had enticed him from that cottage in the Wood.

Maskelyne might know. But the scarred man was a mystery; it was possible he might want this for himself.

And Summer . . .

As if even thinking her name had invoked it, a hum began, far, far away in the tunnel. The steel rail against his foot began to thrum.

Hastily he shoved the wand inside his coat, scrambled to his feet and began to race towards the entrance, but as fast as he ran, the circle of blue sky came no closer, and he yelled in fury because he knew this terror, knew that he could run for hours and days and that nothing would change.

'Don't torment me!' he screamed, stopping and turning. 'Do you hear!'

No one answered him.

The thrumming in the rails was a thunder now, and a great smoke was in the tunnel, making him choke and cough, and as he stood there he saw a pinpoint of light far back in the darkness.

Gideon stood still, defiant. What was the point of running?

Trembling, hands clenched, he watched the train roar out of the darkness upon him. A vast black machine, scraping the roof and wall, sparks flashing from its wheels, its whistle screeching. With a scream of brakes the train slowed; it flashed past him, all its windows lit with lamps, its tables laid, waiters carrying silver dishes expertly against the swaying motion.

As it wheezed and screeched to a halt he stared at it. He knew little about these machines. Jake could have told him more. But even he recognized the patchwork of times, the sleek Pullman carriages and the older engine, all oil and flanges and black-painted rivets.

There was no one on the footplate; this train ran itself.

A carriage door swung open in front of him, and Summer, in a russet cocktail dress of beads and lace, stood there smiling sweetly, her dark sleek hair caught in a tiara with a single feather.

'Up you get,' she said.

Gideon hauled himself up the ladder and shouldered past her, into the dining car, into a medley of steams and smells and rich velvet hangings.

He flung himself down at a table, moodily.

Summer slid in opposite. She lit a cigarette in a long silver holder, but no smoke came from it and he knew it wasn't real. 'Naughty Gideon. I told you to meet me at the Dwelling.'

'Maybe I didn't want to.'

She giggled. 'I love it when you get all tetchy. *So* like Venn.'

She signalled to a passing waiter, whose suavity and sleeked silver hair barely masked its sly Shee curiosity. 'You. Bring champagne.'

Gideon put his hands on the table and leaned over, as the train slid smoothly back to speed. 'Summer, why do you play these stupid games! Let me go! Release me. You can do it. You can take me back, back even before I was born. Back before you came peeping into my cradle.'

Even as he said it he knew it was hopeless. Her face would never lose its pretty composure, its utter certainty. The Shee did not doubt, or feel compassion.

But they did get irritated.

Summer arranged her red lips into a perfect pout. 'Don't bore me, sweetie. I have no plans to release you. Anyway, I've decided to liven things up a bit. Venn has gone *journeying*, and our new friend the cute shaman is safely in the Abbey. So what better time – if you know what I mean – for me to take out the mirror. Such fun!'

He stared at her in horror. 'And Jake? Sarah? How can they . . . ?'

'Oh, I'll get them back through the Summerland. Venn

will have to beg and plead for it, of course.'

'But this shaman – he's getting you the broken coin?'

She nodded, reaching up to take a glass from the Shee waiter. It contained a water-pale liquid that Gideon knew would have no taste at all. She sipped it. 'Delicious. So it was you eavesdropping. Yes, well, he may try, but mortals are useless. We'll find the coin. My people will find it. The midnight court. We will tear the wretched house apart.' She sat back and smiled as the train roared out into sudden sunlight. 'That little goblin Piers won't know what hit him. We'll do it right now.'

Gideon stared. 'Summer, even if you find it, that's only half. To destroy the mirror you need the other half as well, and nobody knows where that is . . .'

His voice died away. She was smiling at him with a pert smugness that filled him with utter dread.

He drew in a breath. 'You don't. You can't have.'

'I know where the other half is. I've known for ever.'

She touched her glass with one that had suddenly appeared in his hand. Bubbles burst upwards.

'Mortals, Gideon,' she said softly, 'have no secrets from the Shee.'

The Time Wolf had eyes that were small and black as berries. In their savage pupils Jake saw himself reflected, warped as in obsidian depths. His throat was dry, his heart pounding. He dared not even breathe.

The wolf raised more of its body up the stair, a stealthy, soundless movement. It was grey, like everything else here, but a grey of rain-dark cloud, so that he couldn't tell what was its pelt and what the soft fog that drifted from its mouth and ears. It crouched, belly on the top step.

Its growl made the hairs on his skin rise.

There was no way down and behind him was the wall. To his right rose a metal railing and beyond that yawned the empty space of the castle keep.

He glanced up. A low stone roof. Hanging from a staple embedded in it was a rope.

Jake blew out his cheeks. He tensed his muscles and crouched, very slightly.

The wolf rose on its haunches.

For a second they faced each other, the animal huge and grey, its muzzle drawn back to show yellow teeth, glistening with saliva, its eyes intent with intelligence.

Then Jake leaped.

He grabbed the rope; it held. The wolf gave a snarl; as he swung over it it attacked. Claws slashed at him. He swung his legs up and the rope took him out over the emptiness of the space, then back in towards the animal.

Jake swore.

He kicked out, caught the wolf on the muzzle; it made a strange skittish jerk back, yelped and shook its head. That was enough.

Jake hit the wall feet-first; with a huge effort he pushed off with all the force he could summon, right out into darkness again, the slash of the wolf's claws ripping the sleeve out of his coat. The beast howled, furious with rage. There was no going in again.

The rope swung him wider this time, almost right across the space. An opposite railing loomed. He had no choice. He let go, and jumped.

It was further than he'd thought.

Slamming against stone, his hands slithered, grabbed.

A metal rail gave way. Rust splintered in his eyes; he blinked, shook his head, slid down.

And fell.

A terrible empty fall, head-first through coldness, a scream growing and growing inside him at the thought of crashing into the stone floor that must be down there; a flashing of images – *Sarah, David, the mirror, Moll* – so fast he barely had time to feel terror.

And then there was a net, and he crumpled into it, his outspread hands thrusting through the mesh. It gave way beneath him, his weight bearing it down until he thought it would break, and then – miraculously – it elasticated him back up again, and he yelled with the delight of that.

He turned in mid-air.

The keep rose above him. Far up in its darkness a howl rang out; then another, somewhere nearer.

Jake hit the mesh again, grabbed it, held on until the bouncing settled. Then turned.

The net had been suspended above a dark pavement.

It glistened strangely, and as he lay there catching his breath he wondered if it was covered with water.

Carefully, he swung over the edge of the net and let himself down.

His boots touched the surface; it swirled away. Something crunched as he stood.

He realized with a shudder of revulsion that the pavement was deep in silvery insects; a swarming layer of them, crawling one over another, so that he stepped back hastily, crunching another dark footprint.

'Yuk.' It was a whisper, but the keep took it and murmured it round and round, as if a grave and serious crowd stood above him and watched.

The silverfish swarmed over his boots.

Jake kicked them off, looked hastily round. He was surrounded by four stone walls; each had a small door placed centrally.

He ran to the nearest, gritting his teeth against the horror of the squashed insects. Carved over the stone lintel was a single word; he reached up and brushed the dust from it and read it. The word was AUTUMN.

He glanced over at the others. Spring, Summer and Winter, presumably. What was this place?

He pulled at the door.

It was stiff, as if untouched for years, and for a moment he thought it would stick, but then he dragged it wide, the wood scraping the uneven floor, pushing a wave of silver insects before it.

Beyond it he saw a room full of pillars, each one rising and branching and intermeshing at the top, so that the ceiling of the room was hidden in a tangle of stone branches, as if this was some caricature in marble of the Wood.

Something gusted out past him. He caught it and it crumbled in his hand.

A leaf.

Dead and brown.

Jake stopped. Suddenly he felt as if the room was a trap; he wanted to get out. But even before he could turn the leaves were coming at him – a gale of curled oak and ash, the huge five-pointed lobes of horse chestnuts, shivery sepals of rowan, spikes of holly.

Jake swore. He tried to shut the door but now it was wedged tight; he put a shoulder to it but it wouldn't move.

He backed out into the keep.

Leaves flew all round him, a tempest of autumn, a storm. High over his head they swirled, and he looked up at them, and through them he saw the men.

Hundreds, maybe thousands of men. Standing all around the balconies, crowding windows and embrasures, peering down at him. And they were applauding, a soft sarcastic patter of clapping hands, and for a wild moment he thought the leaves were falling from them, generated from those small identical palms.

A thousand Januses. Most smiling, one or two laughing, a few just staring. Janus as a young man, Janus middle-aged, Janus older. Janus in a million mirrors. Janus in the lenses of blue spectacles, a giddying repetition of his face, his lank hair, his neat dark uniform.

'I've been expecting you, Jake,' one of them said. 'I've been expecting you.'

Another echoed it. And another.

'Welcome to my End Time, Jake.'

'Welcome to my Lab.'

'Welcome to my brave new world.'

Jake stood still in fury as the leaves and whispers piled around him.

He circled, staring up.

There was nothing to say.

CHAPTER NINE

My destiny lies within the mirror. It no longer shews me my selfe, because my selfe is within it. I would betray all the world for it. Betray wife of my heart. Children of my house.

The mirror knows this.

What can ever be hidden from it?

The Scrutiny of Secrets by Mortimer Dee

'So Jake's in there?' Venn looked up at the composite building.

They had crossed the river and were in streets now that he felt he should have recognized, but the nearer they came to the distorted tower, the more the contortion of the city bewildered him.

'How do we get him out?'

Sarah was sitting on the step of what had once been a

library. She looked up. 'Don't you ever stop? Thinking, planning? Don't you ever despair?'

For a moment Venn just stared at her. Then he said, 'I know all about despair. Once on Katra Simba I fell into an abyss. I hung there for three hours, turning on a fraying rope, deep in a place where there was nothing but white. Even the sunlight was fractured through ice. Nothing to see, nothing to think about, nothing below but an endless crack going deeper and deeper into the earth. So that your memory goes and in the end your mind is blank.'

She said, 'But you got out.'

'I didn't think I would. When the rope begins to jerk you up you don't even care any more. Caring is for humans, and there's nothing human left in you.'

He came a step closer.

'And then there's Leah,' she said.

Venn nodded, but she could see his reluctance. He glanced at his watch. 'I don't despair over Leah, not now. By sunset tonight Leah will be back with me. We'll have tea on the lawn – Piers will bake his best cakes. She'll laugh with Jake, charm Wharton. That's what she does.'

Sarah swallowed. 'There won't ever have been an accident.'

'No. Never.'

Was he blind? Couldn't he see the twisted, empty world? Or was he just so consumed with shame and guilt that he would sacrifice everyone else to end it?

She stood up, defiant. 'We're not going back without Jake.'

Venn laughed, harsh. 'I wouldn't dare face his father.'

'So. Come on. It's not far now.'

As she stood up and led him between the stretched buildings she thought bitterly of her own father. Where was he? Locked somewhere in the depths of this city? Or had he somehow got back to Wintercombe, that ruin in the devastated Wood?

As if he read her mind Venn said, 'When you were growing up there, at the Abbey, was the Wood there still?'

'Most of it had been destroyed. But there were remnants. Dank tangles in few valleys.'

'And the Shee? Did you ever see them?'

She shook her head.

Venn frowned. 'Time means nothing to them. They should have been there.'

'Maybe they lost interest.' Sarah stepped into an alleyway so tilted it ran with water like a stream. 'The Shee like fun and games. There are none of those in this time.'

He nodded, stepping after her, his shadow long on the

high brick walls. They rose on each side so that the sky was a slit of grey far above. She glanced up, uneasy. Fear brushed her like a shadow.

He noticed. 'What was that?'

'Not sure. Janus has flying things – black swans. Well, they used to be swans. He interbred them with snakes. And he did things to insects too.'

Venn frowned. Cautiously they paced the alleyway, wading the stream. The paved way became steeper and narrower, the walls closing in, nearer and nearer to each other, until Sarah could touch each side.

She was terrified they would be trapped here. 'We should go back.'

'I think it ends ahead.'

Beyond Venn was a sliver of grey daylight. It lit his hair like a wand.

'Yes,' she said, 'but—'

A creak of sound.

A dark shape swooped over the rooftops, its neck elegant. It plunged low, came straight down the alley at them, banking from side to side. She screamed, 'Run!' but Venn had already grabbed her arm, a fleeing shadow.

The walls closed. No wider than a crack now, the alley trapped them; Venn had to stop, his breath a magnified panic in the restricted space. He looked up, desperately; the brickwork soared, impossible to climb.

'Go!' Sarah screamed. 'Get through. Quickly!'

The crack was unbearably narrow. He turned himself sideways and shuffled, his face against the brick, and the fear of being trapped there rose up in him like panic, but then his hand was free, in empty air. With a gasp he forced himself through, arm, shoulder, his body wrenched and scraped until he fell out through the gap.

'Sarah!' He turned, both hands against the wall.

Nothing.

The dim slot of the alley was empty.

Where was she?

Then he leaped back with a hiss of terror. The swan's head came straight at him, pure black, its eyes gold. It swivelled on a neck far too long, spitting at him in fury.

Its tongue flickered out, forked.

Dripping with venom.

'Turn around,' the shaman said.

Wharton turned. He folded his arms and tried to stay calm. 'Where's Rebecca? What have you done to her?'

The tattooed boy shook his head. There was a musty smell about him, of old leather and green deep leaves. Tall as Wharton, he ran his thumb over the flint blade and said quietly, 'She is safe. If you take me to Venn.'

'Venn's not here.'

'The mirror then. The master of the mirror.'

Wharton considered. Would that be Maskelyne? If Maskelyne thought Becky was in danger he would be distraught.

'What's stopping me jumping you? A flint knife? I could take you on here and now.'

The shaman shrugged, lightly. 'I don't think so. You're not so sure as you seem, fat man. And if anything happens to me, you will never see the red girl alive again. I have hidden her behind shadows. I have made her a girl of cobweb, frail and delicate. A stray breath will destroy her.'

'Nonsense. Total tosh.' Wharton turned and strode down the corridor, flinging open every door. 'Rebecca! Where the hell are you? I know you're here'

Unconcerned, the boy shrugged, and leaned against the wall, watching.

There were umpteen rooms, all dark and shuttered. Wharton looked in them all, but there was only dust and sheeted furniture and portraits of dead Venns watching him from landscapes and horseback.

And cobwebs, yes. Certainly Piers never flicked a duster down here. Wharton opened the last door. This room was totally empty except for a dead bluebottle on the filthy sill.

And a chair.

He stared at the chair. It was massed with web, clotted with long-gathered dirt. For a moment, just a moment, it looked like . . .

He shook his head.

That was not even possible.

He backed out. 'Oh my God . . .' he breathed.

'George!' She gasped in joy as he saw her. 'I knew! I knew you'd find me. Listen.'

His eyes glanced over her, took her in. His face went white as paper.

'Don't move,' he said. 'Don't even shiver. Becky, don't even breathe!'

And he was gone, closing the door inch by inch, so delicately that it would not have dislodged a petal from a rose.

Even so, a sliver of draught gusted against her.

Rebecca stared down in disbelief.

Where the knees of her jeans had been, her knees now poked through. And even as she looked the draught took away a few flakes of skin too, barely there, grey as dust.

For a moment her breath caught in her throat with

fear. Then she screamed. 'George! Get back in here! Get me out of this mess!'

But the door didn't open.

And she heard his footsteps, running, already far down the dusty hall, and the gasping terror in his voice as he said, 'All right. I get it. What do you want? *Anything.*'

The shaman straightened from the wall. His dark coat had left a mark there, like grease.

'Take me to the mirror.'

Wharton clutched his fists. 'Look . . .'

'Take me to the mirror. Or the girl will fall apart, flake by flake of skin.'

Wharton wanted to growl; he wanted to grab this boy and punch him, but he knew already it would be no use. Instead he turned tightly on his heel and snapped, 'There's no way they'll let you use it.'

All the way along the corridor he was plotting desperately but there was no way he could see out of this, unless Maskelyne could reverse this . . . thing on Rebecca. He didn't want to call it a spell. A year ago he would have laughed at the word, before he'd come to this madhouse. Before he'd seen a grey girl, a girl of webs and shadows. His skin crawled, even thinking of it.

The cats sat in embrasures and on window seats.

They stood up as the shaman passed. Wharton expected them to spit or hiss but their behaviour astonished him; they leaped down and rubbed against the boy's legs, purring like engines. Then they followed, an eager clutch of high tails and fascinated green eyes, along the Long Gallery and up the attic stair.

Wharton marched to the door and stopped.

'Knock on it,' the shaman said softly. 'Tell them you would come in.'

Wharton scowled. He knocked. 'David. It's me.'

He heard a movement of someone scraping back a chair. 'Coming.'

'Wait.' Wharton turned so that he could see the shaman, who tipped his head, curiously. 'I'm not alone. Don't open the door.'

A brief silence. The cats watched.

David spoke again, his voice cautious. 'Who?'

'That bloody kid from the boat.' Wharton refused to be intimidated. 'He's got Rebecca under some sort of spell. Says we have to cooperate with him or she dies. Slowly.'

Nothing. But he could feel the tension through the white-painted wood of the door. Then the latch unclicked, and the door swung open.

The shaman waved a hand. Wharton entered, carefully.

As he had thought, it was Maskelyne who stood just inside. The scarred man was pale and his dark eyes cold with anger.

'Don't try anything,' Wharton muttered. 'Unless you know how to undo what he's done.'

'Where is she?'

'Room in the east wing. For God's sake, be careful. Even a draught.'

But Maskelyne was already gone, shoving past him.

The shaman came into the room, the cats at his heels. He stood before the obsidian mirror, and bowed his head before it; his tall, slim reflection warped into strange, shifting shapes, the grey slither of a seal, the shaggy bulk of a bear.

'The dark door,' he said with satisfaction. He turned. 'Are you Venn?'

David blew out his cheeks. 'No. What the hell is going on here?'

'He wants Venn. The master of the mirror. To send help to his time and destroy some monster. Or Rebecca dies.'

David met Wharton's eyes, raised an eyebrow. For a brief second Wharton was puzzled; then a flicker of hope rippled through him; he glanced round furtively. Where was Piers? Surely he had been in here?

David said carefully, 'I am not Venn. Venn has *journeyed*. Do you understand what that means?'

'My simple mind can just about cope with it.' The shaman's voice was acid. 'Well, if Venn is not here, the one who just left may come in his place. He seems a sorcerer of some power – maybe of more strength than mine. Even so, he will not release the girl.' He turned, looking curiously round the room, at the papers and wires and devices.

'*What have you done to her?*' The hoarse whisper was Maskelyne's. He stood inside the door, breathing hard. Wharton had never seen him so agitated.

The shaman moved, a rustle of fur, the strong scent of musky leaves. 'She will be released when my quest is done. You will come with me?'

Maskelyne said, 'No.'

'You have no choice. I need . . .'

'You don't need me. You have power, you can raise storm and tempest, you can control spirits. It seems that is not enough, or you would have already dealt with this … monster. Am I right?'

For a second the shaman frowned. His superb confidence flickered.

David said, 'Maskelyne . . . if you want to go . . .'

The scarred man flicked him a troubled glance.

'I won't leave the mirror.'

'But Rebecca . . .'

'She understands. I can't leave the mirror.'

His statement was flat and harsh. David shot a stare at Wharton, who stared. 'Well, don't look at me! Not with Jake away.'

But even as he blustered Wharton saw the truth, that he was the only one without a job here, that he was the only one expendable. Even as he swallowed it, Maskelyne pointed to him and said, 'This man will go with you. He is a fighter. A warrior . . .'

'A leader of men,' David said hastily.

Wharton almost choked. The shaman stared at him in frank disbelief. 'We have warriors enough. None of them dare . . .'

'None of them can handle themselves like George. Believe me. He's just what you need.'

There was a moment of silence, so intense Wharton could hear the clock down in the hall chime six. Suddenly, far off in the house there was a huge crash, as if every door and window had been thrown wide. Everyone jumped; David said, 'What the—'

Piers came hurtling in as if someone had thrown him. He slammed the door and locked it tight, the marmoset clinging round his neck and screaming wildly.

They stared at him. He was breathless and white as his lab coat. Flickering from shape to shape, he sprouted wings, shed them, his clothes shifting from white to black to red as if for a panicked instant he had no control over his shape. Briefly his face was a rat's, his hands thin and spindly, a snail's shell came and went from his back.

'They're here!' he gasped. 'Running riot! Full-scale attack.'

'Who?' David was at the window already, rubbing dirt from the pane, but Wharton knew the answer even before Piers's agitated squeak.

'Them. Her. The Shee. And it's Halloween!'

Wharton ran to the window and stared out.

His eyes widened. 'Just when you think the day couldn't get any worse.'

CHAPTER TEN

Our eyes are flame, our hands are white,
Our hair wild as the wave.
We ride the wind on autumn nights,
  Over the moor and grave.

Between mother and child, between husband and
  bride,
Between fish in the swollen streams.
Between all that is come and gone we ride.
  We ride between you and your dreams.
          Ballad of Lord Winter and Lady Summer

Jake turned in a circle, staring upwards.

Hundreds of identical faces gazed down at him. Some were smiling, others sombre. He saw Janus, again and again, a nightmare of endless reflections. Neat uniforms, blue spectacles. Young Januses of twenty, others middle-aged and thinner at thirty, others greying at forty. One Janus in a good mood, another Janus angry. Janus eating, Janus sipping from a paper cup, Janus laughing, Janus chatting to a crowd of himselves. A whole population made up of copies of one man, as if he had obliterated even the memory of everyone else, had made for himself a world where only he lived, and yet where he would never be alone.

For a moment Jake was giddy with the thought of it. They were all Replicants. In fact, thinking about it, every time he, or Venn, or Sarah had spoken to Janus that had been a Replicant too. So where was the real Janus? Was he hidden here, among all these copies of himself? After all, where better to hide. How could anyone ever know which was which?

A door slid open behind; Jake turned quickly.

The Janus that entered was young and spry. His uniform was immaculately neat, his lank hair faintly greasy. The blue lenses on his eyes reflected little in the dimness of the shaft.

'So here we are again,' he said. 'Come along, Jake.'

Jake glanced up. The others had gone, like reflections when a mirror was turned away.

'Where are you taking me?'

Janus smiled, amused. 'Where? In this time there is only one answer to where. There's only one direction, and it leads to only one place, the mirror. North, South, East and West no longer exist. Tomorrow, alas, no longer exists. There is only the now and the mirror. It certainly makes things very simple.' He glanced at Jake's wrist. 'I note you have no bracelet. That means at least one of the others is here. Sarah, I would guess. She probably persuaded Venn to come and take a look at the tyrant's terrible End Time. Am I right?'

Jake shrugged, wary. 'Maybe.'

Something went into gear, rattled. He swayed, suddenly unsteady.

The whole floor began to rise like a lift, moving slowly up through the centre of the keep.

Janus nodded. 'Yes, well I'm afraid she's wasting her time. I once offered Venn a deal and he turned me down, even though his neck was actually under the guillotine. A man like that – even I have to admire his bravado. Venn cares nothing for any of you. All he wants is his wife back, and not because he loved her either, but because he will not be defeated, even by time.'

Jake watched the walls slip down past him. There were a few doorways. Might he jump into one? But the lift – if that's what it was – was accelerating. He said,

'You don't know Venn.'

'But you do. And you agree with me.'

Jake scowled, because it was true.

Janus looked up into the darkness. 'That's the Shee in him. Venn is not mortal like you. Or me.'

'I don't know anything about you, either.'

The small man in the neat uniform turned his head. For a moment Jake saw a flicker of the eyes behind the lenses, a pale glitter that startled him. Then Janus said, 'Don't you? I'm sure Sarah has spun you stories of the horrific childhood she endured, of the torments practised on her. In actual fact she was well treated; she and her friends from ZEUS, who betrayed me. They lived in fine apartments in this tower, not in the slanting city, and they received the gifts they have from me freely. In Sarah's case, the ability to become invisible. Such power! Such ingratitude.'

Jake said nothing. Better to listen, give nothing away, and find out what he could.

'I suppose,' Janus took out a small device and consulted the screen on it, 'she will have told you her parents are held in some stinking dungeon. Am I right?'

'She doesn't know where they are.'

'And you know how that torments her. Well, why should I keep my prisoners in cells, Jake, and be at

134

the trouble of feeding them, when I have all of time to lose them in?'

The lift was roaring up now. With nothing to hold on to, Jake wished he could crouch; instead he gritted his teeth and stood with his feet apart.

'You mean you sent them through the mirror?'

'I sent them all through the mirror. All the dissidents and bores and fools. History is long, and there are so many *interesting times*.' He was watching Jake sidelong, slyly smiling. 'You know, you remind me of myself a little, Jake, when I was young. A driven and rather ruthless young man who does not let the wishes of others stand in his way. Surely you must have thought about owning the mirror. Of the power . . .'

'Forget it,' Jake snapped.

Janus laughed, a brittle amused creak.

'Are you telling me you sent everyone?'

'Only the troublemakers. Most people left the city years ago. The island is drowning, the sea levels tugged by the mirror, but they live far off, in shanties and camps and villages, in remote valleys in Wales and Scotland and wild parts of Devon, places like Venn's Wintercombe, places people think they are safe. But, of course no one and nothing can escape time. Except me.'

'Not even you,' Jake snapped.

'Wrong, Jake. I'm the master of the mirror. Your friend Maskelyne will tell you that – he helped me make myself so. I look backwards and forwards; I sit at the end of time and watch everything that happens. I control events and people move at my command like spirits. I'm a sorcerer on an island, and have all eternity to take my revenge.'

Jake was watching, curiously. Janus's fists had gripped. There was the slightest shimmer of sweat on his forehead.

Quietly he said, 'Revenge? Against who?'

'Those who set me on this course.' He stopped abruptly. Then he glanced at Jake and shook his head. 'No, Jake, you won't unpick my secrets so easily. I think we should go a little faster, don't you?'

He stabbed a control on the pad.

Jake gasped. The lift shot up so quickly he staggered and fell, splayed on the stone floor. Rolling over, he saw the tower walls fall away, doors and walls shoot past, a blur, higher and higher into the dark, without air, without sound, without colour.

He couldn't breathe.

He closed his eyes, and entered the darkness.

Wharton knew he was looking at the full splendour of the host of the air.

It terrified him.

All across the sodden lawns, out from the fringes of the Wood, a great army, thousands strong, was trooping. He saw rank on rank of restless white horses, their riders sheathed in extravagant close-fitting armour of copper and bronze and gold, helmeted with sinister masks that looked like metallic bark. The Shee were wild, their hair tangled, their eyes cold, strange bird-cries from their throats filling the air. Some wore horns like stags, others were carapaced like beetles. Their weapons were swords and lances, flint sharp. Red-eared hounds ran barking among the host, and white moths flew, and great flocks of ravens and jackdaws fluttered overhead. From somewhere deep and hollow in the Wood came a menacing drumming that made the windowpanes vibrate.

The shaman said, 'This is bad.' He made a horned sign with his left hand.

David gasped, 'What are they?'

Wharton said, 'Let me introduce you to our neighbours, the Shee. And there's Summer.'

She was standing on the grass in her bare feet, gazing up at them. She wore no armour, though Gideon, close at her shoulder, was as silver-sheathed and glimmering as the rest. The Queen of the Wood wore only a simple dress of black, and there were nightshade berries in her hair.

She smiled and waved, happily.

David muttered, 'They are so . . . beautiful.'

He was staring in utter fascination; Wharton realized he had never seen the creatures before.

'I'm afraid so.' He turned on Piers. 'Strategy. Can they get in?'

'She can. She can do anything.' Piers was sitting at the bench, biting his nails. 'We're finished. She'll lock me up in the crack of a tree for eternity. Longer than that. She's done it before. Torment me with hedgehogs. Wind me with adders. I AM JUST SO DEAD.'

'Oh, get a grip.' Wharton shot a wary look at the shaman. 'I don't suppose . . .'

The boy laughed his harsh bark. 'I have no powers against these. She is the most dangerous of enemies.'

'What do we do?' David said. 'Talk to her?'

'May as well talk to the trees,' Wharton muttered, but already David had the window open and was leaning out.

'Well, hello!' Summer said with a warm smile. 'You're Jake's dad. David.'

'Yes, hello.'

She waved a delicate hand. 'Do you like my army?'

'It's very nice.'

'I thought I'd bring them along. It's been a while since we did any serious damage. It would be such fun for

Venn to come back and find Wintercombe just a pile of ashes all blowing away on the wind. Don't you think?'

David stared, blank. Close at his back, Wharton said quietly, 'Don't trust her. Don't believe anything she says. Remember they are totally without compassion or any emotions except curiosity. Imagine you're talking to one of the cats.' He said to the shaman, 'You must know that. Even if you got her the coin, she would never help you.'

The boy tipped his head. 'How do you know about—'

'Oh I know plenty, son.'

Maskelyne paced, in an agony of anxiety. 'She must never get her hands on it.'

David licked his lips. 'Lady Summer. What exactly do you want?'

Summer shrugged. 'The coin. For starters.'

Maskelyne stopped dead. 'Never,' he breathed. 'Keep her talking.' Then, before Wharton could stop him, he'd unlocked the door and was gone, a shadow racing down the attic stairs.

'I heard that, you know.' Summer smiled coolly and a ripple of wind gusted a few more leaves from the branches. 'The scarred man thinks he has it hidden safely but don't worry, we'll find it. I intend to tear the house apart until I do. Also, I'll have the silvery bracelet that's on your wrist, Dr Wilde, dearest darling. That too.'

David said quickly, 'Surely we can come to some agreement.'

'I don't want to. I'm already bored of talking. Let's fight. We can talk afterwards.' She clapped her hands.

Banners rose among the host. Green and glittering, they shook out in the wind. They bore strange emblems: a hare, a berry on a thread, a silver apple.

'We can't fight you. You know that.' David put both hands on the windowsill, his voice urgent. 'And you must know that I need the bracelet to get Venn back. You and Venn, you're old friends, you must want him safe.'

Summer gazed up, her beautiful eyes scornful. 'Old friends. How interesting. Is that what he told you?'

'Well . . . I know he thinks so much of you.'

She snorted.

He stumbled on. 'And then, once he's back – well, obviously, we'll need both bracelets for the work we have to do.'

'Work?' The word was a drip of venom.

'Yes. His wife, Leah . . .'

'*No!*' Wharton breathed.

Piers closed his eyes in despair.

The cats put back their ears and fled.

Summer did not move. But a rumble of thunder rolled, deep and ominous, from far over the Wood. Dark clouds loomed. Wharton saw Gideon's silent, wide-eyed warning. It was way too late.

The Queen of the Wood stood there and transformed before them. Her dress shrivelled, became black armour, tight-fitting as the scales of a dragon, studded at elbow and collar with metallic devices like seashells. Wings, black as a swan's, huge as a fallen angel's, rose above her. Her eyes were weasel slits, blank with death; her voice a whisper, sweet as acid.

'I want his wife dead.'

David's hands were clenched on the sill. 'But you care for Venn. You must feel—'

'Feel?' She smiled. 'Do the leaves feel? Do the birds care? Don't you know what we are, mortal?

'We're everything you dread. We enchant you. We come between you and the sunlight, like a shadow. We are the shapes you fear in the night, under the moon. You can never be with us. You can never be without us. And I'm afraid, we don't, we really don't . . . *care*.'

She raised a slender arm.

'No,' David stammered. 'Listen . . . Please . . .'

Summer opened her mouth and her tongue flickered over her lips. She laughed, a laugh of pure scorn. 'Let's do this,' she snapped.

And the Shee attacked.

* * *

Maskelyne heard them come.

As he opened the door of the room with infinite slowness he felt the very fabric of the house shiver, the walls ripple, the doors below crash wide. The Abbey rang with sudden noise, its stones echoing with the screeching laughter of the Shee.

He stepped inside. 'Becky?'

She was seated in a chair. The spell was a grey shadow over her, the fiery hair he loved lost under it. He dared not breathe or even move, because he knew she would dissolve like a web in the slightest murmur of the air.

'I'm scared,' she whispered.

'I know. I know.'

'What's that noise?'

'The Shee are attacking the house.'

Her eyes widened with terror. He rubbed his face with a thin hand. 'Becky, I'll try stop them. I'll put every spell I know on this door, believe me. But that's all I can do. Do you understand? I can't change you back. This shaman, his work is good. He must have used your blood.'

'He did.'

Her courage made him proud, and angry. He said, 'I have to take the coin now.'

'Are you sure?'

Another crash. All over the roof the rustle of wings.

'I have to.'

Rebecca said, 'OK. But please, be careful.'

He came close to her, so close he could see the shallowness of her breathing. The steel chain glinted under the web; it lay around her neck, over the fine bones. He reached out, and took it with his fingers, and drew it out from the collar of her shirt, careful, infinitesimally slowly, but even so flakes of skin dislodged and drifted away. As he undid the clasp she said:

'Stay with the mirror. Keep it safe.'

Maskelyne hesitated. He looked down and saw the half-moon of the Zeus coin, the face hacked across, the lettering smooth from centuries of wear. 'I'll come back. I'll get you free, Becky.'

'You'd better.' She forced a tearful smile. 'Because I'd rather Summer didn't find me like this.'

He nodded.

After he'd gone Rebecca watched the door close. Small gusts of air came under the threshold and lifted the ends of her hair; the strands dissolved to grey dust.

She wanted to scream at him to come back, stay with her, get her out of this horror. But a scream would destroy her.

And he needed to be with the mirror.

She sobbed, silent and unmoving.

When had she begun to loathe the mirror?

Like Summer loathed Leah?

Everything happened at once. Wharton dragged David back from the window, slamming it shut. A hail of stones crashed against it, smashing the glass.

He turned. 'Piers. How long?'

'Minutes. The place is ringed with iron but when they're crazy like this.'

The shaman had leaped back too. 'Elf-power is strong. You are in trouble.'

David shook his head. 'Help us. Release Rebecca.'

'My duty is to my people. Not you.'

Piers was gnawing his nails. Then he stared, eyes wide. 'Wow, yes! Brilliant idea!'

Wharton whirled, felt something cold, looked down; the silver bracelet was on his wrist.

David stood back and looked at him. 'It has to be you, George. Or she'll have this.'

Suddenly he understood. 'What . . . No way! I can't.'

David dragged him across the room. 'The mirror, George! Now!'

Through the cracked window wet leaves gusted.

As they hit the floor they became tall slender people, rising up in copper and bronze, their hair silver as the moon. Doors smashed below as if the army was a madness of wind and rain, roaring through the ancient building.

The shaman gripped Wharton's arm. 'Hurry!'

He tried to tug away. 'This is crazy! They need me here. What the hell do I know about monsters?'

David's voice was almost lost in the uproar.

'Summer can't have the bracelet. The only place we can hide it is in time. Go, George! *Go!*'

Already the mirror was a vacuum, a sucking hollow in front of him. He staggered towards it, but just before he fell into its terrible, amazing brilliance Maskelyne raced in. Wharton felt something shoved into his hand, something small and icy and jagged and so full of power he cried out with the shock of it.

Then he was *journeying*, far and far and far into darkness.

And behind him the Shee were screeching with rage.

What see'st thou else
In the dark backward and abysm of Time?

CHAPTER ELEVEN

Sometimes, when sitting at my books, I look up from the pages and the mirror shows me a man I fail to recognize. A bald, pompous fellow, ridiculously swollen with his own importance. Quite inaccurate, of course.

I fear my Chronoptika has a strange, sly angle on the world.

Journal of John Harcourt Symmes

She lay on her back, flat on the floor, pressed tight against the wall. Above her the black swan beat itself in rage against the narrow crack of the alley.

'Sarah! Sarah, are you all right?' Venn's agonized yell was loud. She dared not answer. She had flicked the inner *switch* of invisibility but the creature would hear her if she made the slightest sound. Maybe it could smell her too, because it swivelled its stretched neck, hissing.

The gaze of its small black eye passed over her, then slid back.

Its venomous tongue explored in her direction.

She held her breath, squashed further in as it came closer. Its beak was yellow as an egg yolk. It made a small sound, a hiss.

Something crashed past her: a bolt of blue light, fired from beyond the alley, through the narrow crack. It hit the stones above her, and fireworked into sparks.

The swan screamed. It jerked back but the bolt came again, catching the edge of its flight feathers, blasting them to dust. Then it was gone, rising rapidly with a whistle of light bones against the copper sky. It turned towards the tower, and the rooftops hid it.

'Sarah!' Venn roared. 'Talk to me!'

'I'm fine. I'm all right.' She picked herself up, coughing with dust. 'Stay there. I'm coming through.'

She had sore palms and a scrape down one cheek. Turning sideways she wriggled through the terrifyingly narrow gap – had it got even narrower in that short time? – feeling the damp of the bricks against her cheek and backbone.

Venn shoved the glass weapon back in his belt and groped for her, finding a warm shoulder. He tugged her through fast, scared the crack would close.

Breathless, they both leaned against the wall.

'Can't see you,' he said.

All at once then he could, as if the drab grey dress she wore had always been part of the dismal half-light. She was filthy, a great smear of mud on her face. She wiped it off and looked round.

They were in a small cobbled courtyard that was heaved up on one side. Most of it was enclosed by a wall that had cracked and fallen in places; to their left was a building. Maybe it had been someone's house once. Tattered posters of Janus were plastered all over it.

She said, 'That was too close.'

'Yes.' Venn slid down and sat with his back against the wall; after a moment she sat beside him.

He looked worn; his hair greyed with dust.

She said, 'I think you've seen enough.'

He didn't answer.

'The whole city is like this. We need to find Jake and get out of here. There's nothing we can do. My parents . . .'

He glanced at her, his eyes palest blue.

'Well, they could be anywhere. And in any time.' It was hard to say it but she pushed on. 'We find Jake, we go back to Wintercombe. Then you can decide about . . .'

'I already have.' It was a small, cold sentence.

'What do you mean?'

Venn looked up. 'You were right to bring me here. To let me see this. We have to do all it takes to ensure this future never happens.'

Her heart was beating fast. 'But . . . Leah . . .'

'I'll never give up Leah.' He turned his fierce gaze on her. 'Never, Sarah. So there's a new plan. We go back and save Leah. And afterwards, when it's done, when we're sure she's safe, *then* I destroy the mirror.'

She felt a shiver of excitement go down her spine, excitement and worry. 'You mean that?'

'I'm a selfish man. But . . .'

A sound interrupted him. Terrible and eerie, far over the city, the low cry they had heard before rang in the ruins. The agony of the mirror set their teeth on edge.

Sarah grabbed his arm. 'Let's get out of the open.'

There was a door, to their left. Venn kicked it and it gave, splintering softly in a cloud of fungoid dust. Inside they found a room cluttered with chairs and tables, dark and dripping.

Venn dragged one of the shutters down to get some light. Debris fell about him in showers; he coughed and beat it away.

The building had been some sort of hotel. The bar was broken open; the few remaining bottles empty and smashed. Venn looked at it, a bleak stare. Then he pulled up a chair and sat down.

Sarah perched on a table. He was always hard to read, but the grey tortured world of the End Time had shaken even him, she knew. Avoiding her eyes he said, 'As I was saying. I'm selfish, but not a monster. If this . . . horror is what the mirror creates, if Janus is what it creates, it's a price I won't pay.'

Sarah put her fingers together. 'But we can't break it. Not without joining both halves of the Zeus coin. OK, Maskelyne has one half, but he would never never give it to us, not for this. And the other half could be anywhere in time and space.'

Venn was so still she thought he hadn't heard her. Until he said, '*I know where the other half is. The other half is here.*'

She couldn't speak. Disbelief and delight choked her. 'What?'

'There's something I've never told you; never told anyone.' He looked across the ruined room into the shadows. 'At midsummer, when we all *journeyed* to Paris, when my head was under the guillotine, and the blade fell—'

She shuddered, remembering the terror of that.

'—you said afterwards that you thought, for a second, that I vanished.'

153

'Well, I thought so.'

'You were right. Janus was there. Janus stopped time.'

She stared.

'We talked, and he made me an offer. A deal.'

She was scared now. She kept still, as if any movement would stop him.

'The deal was, my life in return for your half of the coin. He told me how you'd had the bird steal it from Summer's red box, how you had hidden it in the Abbey. I saw how desperate he was to have it. Of course I refused him. But something about his voice, his eyes behind those sinister blue wretched glasses, had given me an idea – a crazy notion. I said to him, *"Anyone would think you know where the other half is."*

He looked up. 'Sarah. I have something of the Shee-sight. I saw fear flicker right through him like a flame. It was unmistakeable, and I understood, at once. Janus has the other half of the coin. Maybe somewhere in this nightmare city. And we can't go back until we find it.'

It was a freezing cold swamp and George Wharton was knee-deep in it.

That was all he knew for a moment. Then rain hit him, a lashing, diagonal rain that came at his eyes like spears.

154

He gasped.

So this was the past! Prehistory! He tugged his boots out of the bog; they sank firmly back, and he turned, wondering. He had only ever *journeyed* once before, very briefly: that time he'd gone back to the London blitz. It had been astonishing, but there had been streets and people there, scenes he knew from old films – things about it had been familiar. But this . . . this was a vast desolation, a place of emptiness. Jagged white mountains bounded the horizon, far off a line of grey sea. A bird flapped over his head, thin and leggy as a crane.

The tattooed boy stood watching. He never smiled, but he seemed amused. 'So, big man . . .'

'My name is Wharton.' He pulled himself up straight. 'George Wharton.'

'So then, Jorjwarton. What did the scarred man push on to your hand as we *journeyed*? Or can I guess?'

Wharton opened his fingers, and then his eyes went wide. The half-coin. The Zeus stater! He stared at it, baffled.

The shaman nodded. 'I thought so. The elf-queen would give much for that. Or so she said. But I would not trust her words. They are like pale ice on a river – beautiful, but if you trust to it you die.'

'Good Lord.' Wharton shook his head. Obviously

Maskelyne had had to save the thing from Summer's clutches. But what was to stop her coming here after it?

He held it up. The stater was jaggedly sliced. It hung from a curious chain, made from tiny black metal links. He slipped it quickly over his head and tucked it inside his collar, hiding it carefully away.

The shaman turned and waded through the mud. 'It has great magic. I too had a wand of power but lost it in your time, among the elf-folk. There was a mortal there. I gave it to him. I would give much to have it back.' He pointed to the darkest corner of the sky. 'We go this way.'

'Go where?'

'Towards the lair of the monster.'

'Straight away? What about some food, a bit of warm fire?'

The boy shrugged. 'You'll have those. We're not savages. Now follow me. Or stay here in the rain.' He turned and strode away, not looking back.

Wharton sighed, and splashed after him.

It took only about an hour to convince him that this particular past was really not for him. That was when the trickle of rain running down his neck became completely unbearable, and the bog so deep that water finally poured over the top of his boots and soaked his socks. He gritted his teeth. It was cold too, a cutting icy wind from those frozen-looking hills. He walked hugging himself tight. He had had no time to bring anything, not even a coat. The shaman's sealskin, once so smelly and verminous, now looked snug and inviting. Why did this always have to happen to him? Why couldn't he get transported to some luxurious era, some palace, some tropical beach, instead of following a silent sorcerer through a prehistoric bog?

He stopped, struck by a thought.

Bog bodies. He'd read about them; seen some in a museum. Dried-out leathery fragments of men and women. Hands and torsos. Dumped aeons ago deep in the bog, maybe sacrificed. He looked at the lean urgent boy, walking purposefully towards the setting sun. He'd be just the sort to do that.

Wharton shivered and struggled on.

And how the hell was he expected to get back from here? Where was the mirror in all this northern emptiness? Did it even exist yet? But there was one good thing – he had the coin. Maskelyne for one would never leave him here for ever, not with that.

It seemed lighter now; he realized the rain had stopped. Ahead of them the sky was scarlet, streaked by long billows of frail cloud. And the ground was firmer, small bushes of whinberry and gorse sprouting here and there, and even, as he puffed his way up a rise of land, small stubby trees, growing darkly together in a dense grove.

The shaman stopped.

He waited for Wharton to reach him then said, 'This is a sacred place. The place of the Ancestors.'

Wharton looked ahead. The grove was dark and uninviting. The narrow path into it had a sort of uneasy, Shee feel. 'Do we go in there?'

'They have to see you – the warrior I have brought through time to them. They have to approve of you.'

'And if they don't?'

The boy shrugged.

Wharton didn't like that at all.

They entered the grove. The trees were so tangled, the branches meshed into a web that reminded him of the malachite protection that had been around the mirror, and he began to wonder what might be at the heart of this. The air was close; water dripped around him. Somewhere beyond the mountains the sun was setting, the shadows long, the stink of stagnant growth and weed rank in the twilight.

Wharton walked carefully. Strange green hanging beards of lichen brushed his face.

His skin prickled; he breathed loudly, as if the air was

congested. As if the dark grove had turned in on itself and swallowed him.

Sweat stung his eyes; as he wiped it away he bumped into the shaman, who said, 'Be silent now.'

To Wharton's surprise the boy fell to his knees, then lay flat, arms out, his forehead to the ground.

'I have brought a hero, old ones,' he said. 'I have brought a warrior from the master of the mirror.'

Wharton stared, chilled.

Dim in the green darkness, he saw the Ancestors.

'Get the furniture against this!' David rammed the bench against the door.

'It's useless!' Piers gnawed his nails.

'I don't care. Anything to keep them out.'

The house was being torn apart. David rammed a chair under the door handle and winced at the crashes and cold laughter of the Shee. Maskelyne had cleared the room with a whisper of cold spell that had made the air crystal; the Shee inside had shivered out in disgust. But they'd be back.

David glanced in terror at Lorenzo, grizzling in the makeshift cradle. 'Will they take him?'

'Sure to.' Piers looked round. 'If I made myself a knot in the panelling I might get away with it. If I . . .'

He stopped. A small vicious scratching was coming from the keyhole; as they stared a tiny beak squeezed through, then a bird's head.

David grabbed a metal bar.

'Wait,' Maskelyne said quietly.

'Yes! Wait!' The bird's cry was a wail. 'It's me. Not them. ME!'

David glanced at Maskelyne. The scarred man said, 'It's more scared of them than we are.'

The wooden bird scraped through, shedding feathers. It was almost bald, its eye more black than ever. 'You're finished,' it gasped. 'We're all finished. But I thought you might want this.'

It dropped something black and tattered from its beak with relief.

Maskelyne stared down at it; then he crouched and snatched it up. It was a feather, long and black, a raven's or a chough's. He turned it over, smelled it.

'Thought you'd like that.' The bird sounded smug. 'No mortal locks me up in a cage of shadows, shaman or not.' With a smug whistle it shot up into the roof and hid.

'What is it?' David said.

'It's what he used on Becky.' Maskelyne looked up. There was a dark glimmer in his eyes, his face lit and handsome, like a prince's. 'It's a start. Maybe now I can break the spell.'

Even as he said it the door shivered. There was a scatter of cold laughter outside, a skitter of footsteps. The cats dived under the furniture. David snatched up the baby. The bird hid in the clock.

As if they were liquid, as if the walls and doors were nothing to them, the Shee glimmered and flickered into the room.

They oozed and slid through cracks, walked through bricks and wallpaper. Suddenly the attic was crowded with tall silvery people, their attent eyes curious as starlings, fingers touching and tearing and exploring everything, the benches, the papers, the food; everything except the machinery, which made them shiver, and the mirror.

The mortals stood in a tight huddle, back to back. Piers was nowhere to be seen.

David was tense with fear and wonder. The Shee astonished him. As one leaped on the bench and ran along its length he saw their agile lightness, their fleet skill. Their armour was barely real; a clever replica made of bark and lichen, already shrivelling and falling away. Under it they wore clothes of brilliant patchwork, lace and denim and embroidery, russet and gold as the autumn leaves. Their hair was silver, tied and streaked in intricate ways, their whispers strange as the buzz of bees. He felt he could gaze at them for ever, even as they destroyed him, even as they tore the house to pieces around him. Their fascination was deadly. Like a beautiful flower that you know will poison you, and yet you have to pick it, and smell its sweetness.

'Out of here. All of you.' A cold voice startled him; he hugged Lorenzo tight.

Summer had not shed her armour. She stalked in, and the Shee around her melted hurriedly into fireplace and wall. Except for one.

Gideon stood inside the door, arms folded, taking everything in. He saw that David was dizzy with shock, Maskelyne a tall shadow beside the mirror, Piers a small brown moth perfectly camouflaged on a beam of the roof. Gideon smiled. It was pitiful.

Summer took one look and stabbed at the moth with a red-nailed forefinger. 'You! Goblin! Down here now.'

A flutter.

Then Piers was cringing before the Queen of the Wood.

He crawled, abject, head bowed. His white coat was dirty and torn. Every atom of confidence seemed drained from him. 'Lady Summer,' he said, hoarse.

Summer put her hands on her hips and surveyed him with weasel eyes, a long moment of silent threat. Until she said, 'If Oberon didn't value you, you insect, I'd have you carried up on a storm and hurled for centuries out at sea. I would drown you in the depths of the ocean, to be coiled by slugs and tangled in octopus limbs.'

Piers nodded, miserable. 'I suppose I would deserve it.'

'You do.' She giggled, a sudden horrible sound. 'You know, Venn's centuries away. I might just do it. Right now.' She raised her hand.

Piers cowered.

Terror froze them; David could not move, could not speak. He struggled to breathe. He had to do something!

But it was Gideon who broke the moment. Almost lazily he said, 'Summer, haven't you forgotten what we're here for? It's not tormenting that scrawny creature. It's the coin.'

Summer's eyes lit with delight. She laughed. 'Do you think I'd forgotten, sweetkin? I was just having fun.' She turned to them, ignoring Piers now, and David. Instead she faced Maskelyne.

She held out her small, delicate hand.

'The coin. Now.'

CHAPTER TWELVE

I mean, Lord luv us, Jake. What a palaver mucking round with the past is! Tricky or what??

Moll's diary

Jake opened his eyes.

He saw a large grey room. He was lying on a bed, and the bed was draped with grey hangings, frail as cobweb.

He sat up, heart racing.

The room was warped; no wall was straight, no corner a right angle. It seemed to slope in an awkward perspective to the far left corner.

He swung his legs out.

There was nothing in the room but the bed, and what seemed to be a small table, though as he touched that the top transformed to a tiled surface where cool water slid from a silver tap.

Thirsty, he cupped some in his hand and drank it.

He felt tired and confused. There was a thinness in the air that made breathing difficult, as if there was not quite enough oxygen.

And the mirror was nearer. He could feel its drag in his bones.

He went straight to the door. It was grey and solid and locked.

Jake banged a fist against it; he kicked it furiously. 'JANUS! You can't keep me here!'

'Actually, I can.'

He turned, startled. The voice was all around him, as if the walls spoke. And in a sense they did, because all of them had become an enormous screen filled with Janus's face, so close that Jake could see the very pores of the man's skin. It was hideous; he wanted to step back, away from it, but it was all around; there was nowhere to go.

'Don't worry. I'll make sure Venn and Sarah know exactly where you are, Jake. You're my bargaining tool now. A straight swap – you for the coin, and soon. Because if you stay here much longer you'll be sucked into the mirror like everything else.'

Jake's fury exploded. 'Venn will never do that. And Sarah . . .'

'Sarah is one of my children,' Janus's voice was a

whisper of venom. 'I want her back.'

'She's nothing to do with you.'

'On the contrary.' The huge face looked down at him calmly. 'She's part of my revenge. I was a small and damaged child, Jake. My parents said they loved me, but from my early years I could feel nothing for them. You see, something strange happened to me when I was small. There was a path I should have taken, but I was dragged away from it. I felt fractured, in the wrong place.' He smiled, mirthless. 'Shall I tell you about it, Jake?' The screen was suddenly a great mouth. 'In school I was always alone. As if I was living in some different element to the other children, as if I breathed water not air, was drowned deep in some green sea, so that the sounds other humans made were muffled and blurred and I couldn't quite understand them. All that talking. All that crying and laughing.' He turned, pulled back a little; Jake glimpsed the uniform collar, some blurred darkness behind him.

'I wanted to control them. If I couldn't talk to them, I could give orders. So I made myself a general, an emperor. I decided to be king of the world, but I would have failed like all the others, except that I had something no one else ever had. The mirror – a terrible device that would prolong my life if I used it carefully, that would give me time to destroy my enemies. I've had centuries to war and scheme. More time than anyone in the history of the world. By using the mirror I grew great, but I discovered that the mirror has no mercy, it's relentless. Finally it devours everything. It has eaten away all my triumphs, and left me nothing. I'm lord of an empty wasteland, Jake. King of a black hole. The mirror betrayed me, and the scarred man, Maskelyne, he knew that it would. So my last revenge is on him, and on Venn. But especially on you. On you, Jake.'

Jake stared. 'Why me?'

'Because it was you who fractured my life.'

Jake kept very still. A chill touched his spine. 'Fractured?'

Janus came back to the screen, crouching, as if he peered through some tiny door. His skin was wrinkled with tiny cracks. He looked older than Jake had ever seen him. The lenses of his spectacles were huge as the moon, blue as cloudless sky. His mouth moved, making quiet words.

'Have you never wondered about my name? Janus was the god who looked both back and forward; it was a name I adopted, it suited me. But my real name, Jake? You know it.'

'I don't. How could I?'

'It was the name of a little boy, a century ago, who got lost on a beach, who wore red shorts, who went too far out in the water. Do you remember him, Jake?'

Jake was so staggered he could barely speak. He could feel the child's hand in his, the wet cool grip.

The way he had stared calmly back, over his mother's shoulder.

'*You're James Arnold?*' he gasped.

Janus withdrew suddenly, leaving the room grey and bare. 'I am. And you should have let me die.'

David tried to think of a lie, but absolutely nothing came.

It was Maskelyne who stepped up to face Summer. 'The coin is not here.'

She stared at him, then grabbed David's arm and tugged his sleeve up. Anger flickered through her.

'Where is it? Where's the bracelet?'

Maskelyne didn't react. His dark eyes were troubled and defiant. 'I sent them through the mirror. The bracelet and the coin. Far away where you won't be able to find them.'

Summer dropped David's arm as if it was some loathsome toad.

Gideon took a step closer.

Every Shee still in the room slid discreetly into the

walls and was gone; the casement creaked open with a breeze that gusted a few dead leaves on the floor.

They expected rage. Complete fury. Instead she said, 'Who took them?'

'Wharton.'

For a second Summer just gazed at him. Then she started to laugh. A tinkle of cold delight, as wrong as if the rain laughed, or a fox smiled at its prey. 'George! Dear darling George! Lost in the wilds of the Neolithic! How delicious.'

Piers glanced up from his huddle on the floor; she noticed his movement.

'You. Up!'

He scrambled to his feet, stumbling back. 'Lady, believe me, I had nothing to do with any of this. I'm just a slave. A worm. His Excellency . . .'

'Shut up.' She gazed beyond him at David, hugging the baby tight, then at Maskelyne. 'You're a fool, sorcerer. There's nowhere in time I can't find anything I want to find. Nowhere we can't go.'

She turned to the door; Piers's breath of relief was so soft only Gideon heard it.

Summer swung back. 'That reminds me.'

She smiled at Piers and he shrank. His eyes widened in panic, his face stretched and warped, his body contorted. His skin broke out in pustules and sores; he crumpled, knees sagging, back bending horribly. Before their eyes he transformed into a nightmare creature, a child's drawing of a man, the caricature of a mortal. He opened his mouth, and could only howl.

Maskelyne moved but Summer was swifter. With a light shove of her white fingers she pushed Piers at the mirror, and he fell backwards, arms flailing, tumbling in, and the mirror opened with a sudden greediness of vacuum, devouring him with an imploding speed that made the room shiver and the marmoset hidden in the curtains shriek with terror.

Summer smiled, icily. 'Oops,' she said.

And walked out.

They had found some water that was fit to drink, but there was nothing to eat.

As she sipped the tasteless stuff Sarah thought about the strangeness of fate. If Venn was right, and Janus really did have the left half of the coin, their problems were only beginning. It could be anywhere.

'Where?' Venn said, as if he read her thoughts. He was prowling, restless. 'Where would it be?'

She considered. 'Well, he has a treasury. That's the obvious place.'

'In the tower?'

'Yes. They say it's vast; chambers and rooms of gold and paintings; a whole gallery of all the masterpieces there have ever been.' She thought of the Picassos and Raphaels and Monets, all stretched and ruined by the mirror's pull.

Venn stopped, watching her. 'You don't sound convinced.'

She shrugged. 'I don't know . . . Janus looks two ways, always. You can never predict him. There was a rumour that we heard, those of us in ZEUS, that all the things he really valued, his true treasures, were somewhere else.'

'Why?'

'I told you. He's clever.' She put the glass down and looked up at him, her blonde hair dull with dirt. 'What better way of protecting the things he values – from ZEUS, from the mirror – than to put them somewhere far from here.' She stood, walking to the unshuttered window.

Venn frowned. 'Far from him.'

'They'd be guarded.'

Watching her back, he said, 'Where, Sarah?'

She didn't answer for a moment. Then she said, 'Once, when we'd finished in the Lab, when I was lying on a

171

trolley waiting for them to take me back to the cells, I heard two Replicants talking over my head. Maybe they thought I was asleep. Maybe . . . they just didn't care.'

He stared at her, appalled. 'They. He *operated* on you?'

She shrugged. 'How else do you get to be invisible? At least I survived. Many didn't.' Seeing his face, she looked away and said, 'Anyway, they were talking about a place. A place far from London. One of them laughed. He said, "*If only this one knew what's stored up in her precious lost Abbey.*"'

'Wintercombe?'

She said, 'It was just a remark. But the way he said it – so smug . . . it made me think. I wanted to get back there, but I never could.' She looked up. 'What do you think?'

Venn pondered. It made sense. Why keep your most valuable object near the destructive power of mirror? The further away the better. But the thought of going to Wintercombe worried him.

She stood. 'You don't believe me?'

'Not that. Just . . . it's a gamble. If we're wrong—'

'We'll have wasted a day getting down there. That's all.'

'There's Jake. We can't leave him.'

'We need to find the coin. You said so yourself. We

172

can come back for Jake.' She sounded hard, even to herself. More quietly, she said, 'Jake will understand. We can never let this future happen.'

For a moment Venn was still. Then he nodded, and stood up.

'Do they have cars in this time?'

They found one a few streets away, a tiny air-fuelled thing with heavy tyres and no roof; to Venn it looked more like a golf buggy. He climbed in and looked at the controls. Sarah said, 'Don't bother. I can manage this.'

He glanced at her, then, rather to her surprise, moved over into the passenger seat. As she followed him in, fastening the safety belt and checking the controls, she realized that he would not have driven a car since the one in which Leah died.

She glanced up at the copper-grey sky. 'Ready?'

He took out the glass weapon, checked its sight. 'You mean he'll come after us?'

'He'll hear the engine. He'll know exactly where we are.'

Venn nodded. 'Not if something else is making more noise.'

She glanced at him, and grinned.

They waited. The city was silent around them, grey

dust gusting down the street. A door banged, softly, back and forth in the wind.

For five minutes they waited. And then, with a cry more terrible than any Sarah had heard, the mirror howled its anguish.

'Go,' Venn hissed.

She nodded. And fired the engine.

The Ancestors gazed at Wharton and he stared back.

They were huge and crude.

The wood they had been carved from was seamed and split with age, weathered down to a silvery grey. They leaned, as if centuries of rain and storm had battered them. Lichen grew over their mouths; their eyes, hacked from the ancient bark, watched him with an angular, incurious stare.

For a moment he couldn't move. He was seeing what archaeologists would give their eye-teeth to see – the gods of the Stone Age, the first gods of the world.

Incredible!

'Who are they?' Wharton muttered.

'Their true names are secret.' The boy stood up beside him, making a swift ritual sign with his hand as if he crossed some threshold into the precinct. 'We call them She-of-the-Flowers-and-Owls. He-of-the-Stags.

He-of-the-Thunderclouds.'

The grove was shadowy under the branches; wisps of fog drifted. Flies buzzed; somewhere there was a smell of decay and rotting flesh. Wharton shivered with the damp and a fear he could not pin down.

'Do they mind me being here?'

It was a stupid question, and yet these tall, leaning faces, these bodies barely cut from the tree trunk, had such a presence he felt in awe of them, as if they really lived.

'They welcome you. They wish you well in your quest.'

Wharton turned, caught by something in his voice. 'This . . . monster. You say you've already tried to kill it . . .'

'Of course, many times. By fire and arrows and magic. It's too quick, too clever. Our livestock are gone; our children will be next.'

'And if . . .' Wharton cleared his throat. He was feeling totally out of place. 'If, by any chance, I don't succeed either, what then?'

For answer the shaman raised a hand to the images. Wharton stepped forward. As he neared the Ancestors the smell was stronger. The nearest, the one called He-of-the-Stags, stared down with adze-cut eyes, and Wharton noticed the crude horns lopped into its head.

His foot sank into something soft. He glanced down,

and instantly scrambled back. 'Bloody hell. I mean . . .'

Bones.

White with age and green with lichen. Body parts, the flesh adhering in strips, a dried pool of blackened blood. Flies rose in a cloud about him; he beat them off in disgust, breathing hard.

The shaman watched him, dark eyes calm. 'If you should not succeed, Jorjwarton, then you will be given to the Ancestors. My people will drink from your skull, and your memories and powers will be theirs. What else is there?'

Wharton took out a handkerchief and wiped his face. He felt sick.

And far too old for all this.

CHAPTER THIRTEEN

On All Hallows' Eve the Wilde Hunt rides out and
the sea is strangely stirred.
None dare enter Wintercombe Wood.
Its long aisles are slanted with shadow.
Dark birds flutter there, like trapped souls.

Chronicle of Wintercombe

'My God!' David stared round. 'What a disaster! Piers
gone, Venn and Jake and Sarah still not back, the Shee
wrecking the house!' He glanced anxiously at the window.
'And it'll be dark in an hour.'

He had the baby tight in his arms as if he dared not
let him go. Gideon watched the small squirming thing
with fascination; Lorenzo stared back at the changeling,
eyes wide.

'You forgot Rebecca.' Maskelyne went to the door and
listened.

'Lord, yes! What are you doing?'

Maskelyne was turning the key. Alarmed, David grabbed him. 'Wait! I need you! With Piers lost I can't start Operation Leah without you. We should be preparing now.'

Maskelyne paused. 'I'll be back. But Becky comes first.'

'You don't know how to help her.' Gideon muttered.

'Still. I have to be with her.'

Gideon shook his head, curious. Maskelyne was a strange mortal – half ghost, half real. He didn't act like the others, he had no shadow and no solidity. Gideon could easily sense the glimmer of power around him, saw with the sharpness of his Shee-trained sight the man's facets and edges, the way time intersected oddly in him.

He said, 'You love her?'

Maskelyne shot a sidelong look at him with the handsome side of his face. 'I care for her. Yes.'

'Not something I'm used to.'

The scarred man shrugged. 'The Shee wouldn't understand.'

'I'm not the Shee.'

'Aren't you?' Maskelyne stepped closer. He looked curious, as if he listened to something that hadn't quite been said. David watched them both. 'I need to go to her, but it's true I don't have any real answers. If I could find something more to help me. Something the shaman used.'

Gideon went and sat on a window seat. He allowed his scaled armour to shiver away; under it he felt his green patchwork coat ripple back, his pale face swirl with lichen patterns. 'What does it feel like?' he asked quietly. 'To care?'

Maskelyne was silent; it was David who answered.

'Well, sometimes it hurts.'

'Hurts?'

'Mmm. But in a good way. Caring means a lot of pain. Being worried sick most of the time. You'll find out.'

He never would though, would he? He was doomed to exist for ever with the Shee, trapped in their timeless, brittle worlds. As he watched David lay the sleepy baby in the makeshift cradle and gently tuck the blankets round him, Gideon felt the bitter envy, the old despair wash over him. But he was mortal. He *would be* mortal. Even if Summer tormented him for it.

Maskelyne said softly, 'Gideon?'

He realized he had been staring down, hands clenched. He stood, and took the shaman's bone wand from the pocket of his coat and held it up. 'Will this help you?'

Maskelyne crossed the room in two steps, and snatched it. 'How did you get this!'

'He gave it to me. Do you?'

'It's just what I need! It's singing with power!'

Gideon nodded. He felt odd; a warm tingle inside. Was this happiness? Pride, even?

Maskelyne caressed the wand, fingered it carefully. Then he took out the black feather the bird had brought him and tied it on. The small pieces of bone flailed and rattled in their leather thongs. He turned to David. 'Twenty minutes. That's all I ask. If I can't release her in that time I'll come back, and we go for Leah. Twenty minutes.'

David blew hair from his eyes. He looked worried sick. But he said, 'OK.'

Far below some precious ceramic crashed; a wild gale of Shee laughter rose up.

Maskelyne unlocked the door, slipped through like a shadow, and with one glance at Gideon, was gone.

David locked the door behind him.

For a moment the two of them were silent, listening to the racket in the house. Outside, the autumn evening was coming down, the sky over the Wood a soft purple, the rooks descending in karking scatters to roost.

David sighed. 'Just us.'

Gideon put his long fingers together. There was more to do. He said, 'Just you. I'm going to find Jake.'

Startled, David said, 'How . . . ?'

'The Summerland. It's a maze that leads anywhere. I've done it before – found him in the past. I know ways to travel in there.'

'Yes but he's in the future.'

'It doesn't matter. It's all the same.' How could he explain the Summerland? There was no point in even trying. 'But listen, stay here, guard the mirror, because Summer isn't finished with this. And watch the baby.' He looked over at Lorenzo. The small chubby cheeks. The perfected, contented sleep. 'They started coming after me when I was that young. Touching. Looking. Singing.' He turned away. 'You never get away from them after that.'

'Gideon . . .'

He paused.

'Thank you.' David stood by the cradle. 'I'm worried about Jake. I think you are, too.'

Gideon shrugged. Then he walked through the wall and was gone.

David stood silent in the empty room. From below the rattle of the Shee's heartless destruction came up to him, and then from somewhere distant a murmur of music, so soft and enticing it made him shiver. He turned away, abruptly. And saw himself.

The obsidian mirror showed him a weary and worried

man, prematurely grey. A thin foxy face, eyes deep with doubt. It was a sight that shocked and angered him.

'I don't look like that,' he snapped.

The mirror glittered with sudden silver, like laughter. He realized the moon was rising over the Wood and shining through the high window. Darkness was coming fast. Less than thirty minutes to sunset, and then Halloween would begin.

'So it's just me. All alone.'

There was a sound like the clearing of a tiny throat. 'Um, well, no, actually, *I'm* still here. I know I'm small and useless, but still.' The wooden bird had emerged from hiding and was perched on one of the dusty rafters.

David looked up at it. 'Is there anything you can suggest I can do?'

Another enormous crash echoed through the house.

The bird shook its head, irritatingly cheerful. 'Nope. Sorry.'

Jake sat on the bed with his head in his hands.

The screen was blank now, the room silent. Not a murmur of sound came in to him, nothing but the fast pulse of his own heart.

The boy in red shorts!

The small boy on the beach!

182

The boy they had chosen at random from a dozen similar news reports, chosen because that was the one Dad and Venn had thought easiest, the simplest death to change.

And by doing that, by taking his hand and leading him out of the water they – he Jake – had created Janus?

He shook his head, stubborn. No way! He refused to believe it. And yet Sarah's words rose up inside him; he remembered her anger, her fierce accusation.

'It's like we're playing at being God. It's not right.'

Had their changing time sown the seeds of the End World?

He jumped up and prowled, unable to keep still.

How could evil come from an act so good in its intentions? Saving a life! That was always right, wasn't it? He felt bewildered and devastated. All at once nothing he had always held true seemed solid or safe. Everything he had taken for granted might be wrong. As if the ground had shifted under his feet.

And then it did.

The floor rippled.

Jake was flung against the wall; he grabbed at it but it slid away from him. Something crazy was happening to the room – it was dropping, stretching out like elastic.

The bed crashed past him.

He hung on and wriggled back furiously, towards the door. It was above him now, the floor up to it a slope, a smooth hill. He rolled over and tried to climb, but started to slide instead, and though he grabbed with his fingers and the toes of his boots, he couldn't stop, he was slithering down, and he knew this was the mirror, dragging at him, and he would fall into its black hole for ever and ever.

He panicked, yelled, screamed in terror.

The room spasmed; there was a crack, a tang of burning.

And he was spread-eagled on a flat floor, one nail bleeding, all his muscles taut.

Breathing hard, Jake picked himself up and stared round. Whatever had happened it had transformed the room; now it was distorted into a diamond shape, and there were holes in it, small black empty patches, as if the very fabric had been sucked away, as if reality had been stretched too far, and split.

He stepped back, looking at the wall.

It had faded. He could see stonework through the plaster. He could see the corridor outside through the stones.

The End World was wearing thin. He moved quickly to the door; the grey metal seemed the same, but when he thrust his shoulder against it hard it crashed apart so suddenly he staggered and was almost thrown out.

He stood in the corridor and relief flooded him, because for a moment he had dreaded that he too would be somehow thinned, as if the black hole would weaken his very bones and skin.

Now he'd get out of here!

He set off, found some stairs, ran down them. It seemed easier than before. He ran through dim halls and dismal lobbies, along passageways that twisted and broke into stacked sections so that he had to clamber up or down. He knew Janus would be watching on some camera system, but he didn't care any more. He would escape the tower, get out, find Venn, try and—

He stopped dead.

In the centre of the tiled floor in front of him was a great chasm, gaping like a crater. He approached it carefully, and crouched.

The edges were not jagged; this was no collapse of tiles and cement. Instead the pattern of the tiles just faded out, its colours gone. He put his hand into it, cautiously; his fingers vanished and he snatched them back with a gasp, and then raised his head.

On the other side of the chasm a Janus was watching him. A dim, small figure standing in the dark hall, two of the grey Time Wolves lying at his side; their eyes charcoal black now, eyeing Jake hungrily.

Jake stood slowly, scornful. 'Another Replicant.'

Janus shook his head. 'No,' he said. 'Not this time.'

And he came forward into the light.

The Abbey was being torn to pieces.

Rebecca could hear the distant smashes of china, the ripping of curtains. How long before they got to her? She wanted to jump up and run, to move, but forced herself to keep still, because any movement, even the slightest, would be death now. So when she heard soft footsteps rustle down the corridor her heart leaped with a mix of panic and joy.

Maskelyne! At last!

She watched the door, so intent it hurt.

It opened. Summer strolled in.

Rebecca took in a sharp breath that sent minute flakes of her skin spinning through the dark air.

Summer put her hands to her red lips in delight. 'Oh how fantastic! I *love* that!' She took a step forward, stretched her fingers out.

'Don't!' Rebecca's gasp was a whisper. 'Please!'

'It's so . . . delicious! I've never thought of anything so tormenting.' Summer's dark armour dissolved as if she

186

had immediately lost all interest in war; she wore a short gold shimmery dress now and as usual her feet were bare. 'Our shaman friend did this? And there was I thinking him rather crude! It only goes to show, mortals have some good points. They have ideas. New ideas.' She sat on a stool crossing her legs and dangling one foot. 'The Shee are not very original. We've done everything already, really, over and over. But this! Oh I can't resist. All I have to is open a window. Or even—' she pouted her red lips together, '—just blow you away.'

Rebecca said, 'Don't you understand? I would die.'

'That's what makes it so interesting.'

She wanted to say, *I've had time to think about it, sitting here. About leaving everyone behind, going out of their lives for ever. What they'd say about me. Who'd come to my funeral.* But there was no point in talking about the terror. Instead she said, 'Would you like to die, Lady Summer? That's one experience the Shee never have. Or do they? Will you die, one day?'

She was talking for her life, whispering for time, but it was dangerous.

Summer's beautiful eyes were fixed on her, fascinated. 'Die? Me?'

'In the End Time, Janus said, there are no Shee. Why not? Where have they all gone?'

187

The door creaked as it opened, softly.

Summer shrugged. 'Why should we go there? It's grey and cold and empty. No parties, no hunting.'

'Not because you fear Janus then?'

Summer stood up, swift as light. 'No.'

'Then we really can do something you can't. We can die.'

'It's a dubious privilege, if you ask me.'

There was a change in the room, a shiver of draught. Summer stood elegantly and crossed to the window seat. She raised her fine white fingers to the catch of the casement. 'There's quite a wind rising out there, you know. Tonight is Hallows' Eve, and my hunt will ride across the skies. I like it all dark and wild and stormy. Just look how the leaves are flying!'

One plastered itself to the glass and was instantly whipped away.

Summer turned her head and smiled. 'So sorry about this. But I just *have to* see it!'

With a quick, spiteful twist, she undid the window.

It banged wide.

A cold wind whirled through the room.

Rebecca gasped, but a darkness burst in from the door; and she realized Maskelyne was inside. Even as she dissolved he touched her face and fingers with the shaman's wand, and in that instant she felt herself shiver and gather together; her whole body was firm and strong, and with a scream of delight she jumped up and flung her arms about his neck.

'Are you all right?' he gasped.

She nodded. For a moment all her words were gone.

The window banged in the gale. A starling sat on the sill, glossy green, its beak thin and sharp. It looked at them in distaste. 'There'll be other times,' it said.

And launched itself into the storm.

CHAPTER FOURTEEN

After Katra Simba, Venn travelled obsessively. Cities, rainforests, the Greenland interior – he spent years on the road.

Once in Rome, I came across him on the Janiculum, gazing down at the domes and houses.

'The Eternal City,' I said, foolishly.

He looked at me as if I was a stranger. 'If there only was such a thing,' he said.

Jean Lamartine, *The Strange Life of Oberon Venn*

The city was a nightmare to drive through.

Every street was angled, every corner warped. The roads buckled and ran over dangerous, filmy places that Sarah was terrified the car would fall right through. The noise of the engine seemed hideously loud in the silence, and as they sped under walls and the empty houses she imagined hundreds of Januses hurrying to windows to watch them pass.

She shook her head. Already her arms ached from gripping the wheel too tightly.

Relax.

Concentrate!

Venn had the glass gun in his hand; he watched the streets intently.

'He must know,' she muttered.

'Maybe he doesn't care.'

She flung him a glance. 'He will when he realizes where we're going. And why.'

Grim, Venn nodded. 'Left here. Left!'

They passed deserted crossroads. Vast office blocks and shops, underpasses and road bridges confused her. She had never known London well; it was Venn who navigated, from memory and guesswork, and she was amazed at how the ancient ways of the city still existed, the roads and thoroughfares that might have been here for centuries.

She spared him a glance. 'You must find this strange.'

'The silence is. In my time over six million people are crammed into this city. A swarming ant heap. All those lives, all those plans and dreams. Just gone.'

She slowed at a junction. They were back near the

river. 'Where now?'

'Westminster Bridge. Straight ahead. If it's still there.'

She saw him searching for landmarks. 'Where's Big Ben?'

'Built into the tower. Sometimes you hear it strike in there, at odd hours.'

They came to the bridge. It had been stretched to over a mile long and was barely wider now than the car. The lampposts were black, elongated slices of metal; each took half a minute to pass.

'This part has been pulled a long way.' Sarah bumped the car over debris. 'The warping is different in different places. Have you noticed?'

He nodded. 'Maybe if we can get far enough things will be more normal. Out of London.' He looked back. High and unsteady on the horizon, the tower rose like a nightmare silhouette, a child's interrupted game of stacked pieces. Rain blurred its outline. Cloud streamed from its top. 'I hate leaving Jake in there.'

'No choice.'

'If anything happens, David will.'

'It won't. Janus will hold him as a hostage, and he'll be kept alive, I'm sure.' But she wasn't sure, and both of them knew it.

Suddenly the world convulsed. Sarah swore, slammed

the wheel sideways, the car skewing along the pavement, shearing the parapet, and then along the façade of a building, sparks scorching up.

The road buckled under them. She jammed on the brakes but the car didn't stop; for a second the world was contracting, withdrawing and taking them with it, like elastic snapping back on itself.

Her breath went; she felt a terrible dragging agony.

Then everything was still.

Venn breathed, ragged. For a moment neither of them dared move or speak.

Finally he cracked the car door open and climbed out.

Sarah had her arms wrapped tight around her body. She was shaking, icy with shock.

'That was the mirror. It even felt like the mirror.' He looked back. Everything seemed the same, but to both of them it felt all wrong.

Sarah said, 'Look.' She pointed to the small navigation screen. 'We've been dragged back, three miles back.'

Venn frowned. 'But we're still here.'

'Yes, only here isn't where it was. The mirror is collapsing the city. We'll never get out! However fast we drive it will just pull us back and back. There's no escape.'

She knew her voice was panicky but she didn't expect

his laugh. It was bleak but really amused. He swung himself back into the car.

'What?' she said.

'The Shee do this. All the time. They make some poor mortal walk and walk for hours and really they're never getting anywhere. The Shee love it.' He looked round, his eyes blue and sharp. 'Maybe they're even here, hiding and giggling.' He shook his head. 'Let's go, Sarah. Nowhere is going to hold me. I'm not giving up. And think of it this way. Wintercombe is being dragged towards us. Everything in the whole world is.'

She glanced at him sideways, and shook her head. He had that Shee look about him, that indefinable arrogance that Summer had, that carelessness. It infected her; she felt stubborn and defiant. She started the car. 'Must run in the family,' she muttered.

The village was like places Wharton had seen in archaeological reconstructions; a collection of small buildings made of wattle and thatch, surrounded by a stockade. The people surprised him though; they were all so young, and yet their face were worn, their bodies bent with subtle diseases.

They fed him with some sort of meat stew, and a harsh beer that tasted of hops, and watched him eat and drink as if he was some other species. Even the few children, crouching beyond the firelight, stared fascinated, their eyes bright with curiosity and dread.

At first it rather embarrassed him, and then he realized it felt like being with the boys at school all over again. To these people he was old. More than that, a freak of nature, because no one else here was anywhere near his age. It annoyed him. OK, a few wrinkles. The odd grey hair. But he wasn't past it. Not by his standards.

When the brief meal was over the tribe sang, long soft choruses of chanting, the song moving round the attentive circle, the children sleepy now, the women gazing at Wharton as they crooned the slow words, a story of infinite sadness that made him feel uneasy, troubled with strange longing.

The shaman came and sat next to him; Wharton had noticed how the others treated the boy with the utmost respect.

'Is there anything you need, Jorjwarton? A woman?'

'Er . . . no. That won't be necessary.' Hurriedly he said, 'What are they singing?'

'The old songs of our people. They remember all those who went out into the dark and never came back.'

'The dead?'

The shaman nodded. 'Darkness comes quickly here.

In your world, each man has more time.'

'I suppose so.'

'I saw that. When I was there. The buildings, the speech, the objects in the rooms. Everything had needed much time to be made.' He folded his fingers together and leaned his chin on them, thoughtfully. 'It's different for us. We have few years in the light. Our things are frail, our knowledge shallow. This is a new thought for me. I will not forget it.'

Wharton nodded. 'Except for the mirror. That lasts.'

The shaman met his gaze evenly. 'Yes. Except for the black glass.'

So he did have it! Wharton smiled. There was a musky smell now, of some narcotic, maybe. Perhaps that was why he felt so sleepy.

'This creature,' he mumbled. 'It's only killed your livestock. No people?'

'The people keep away. They leave offerings of food and these are taken.'

'So maybe it's just some wild animal. Doing what animals do. I mean.'

The boy's tattooed fingers unfolded. 'It thinks. It plans. Don't deceive yourself. Soon it will come after us. Are you afraid?'

He thought about it. 'A bit. But I've been more afraid.'

'The reply of a warrior.' The shaman looked a little surprised. 'And your spirit weapons, you have them safe?'

Hardly weapons. He heartily wished he'd brought the twelve-bore shotgun. He said, 'Safe.' The coin was in his inside pocket; the bracelet clamped tight on his wrist. But the mirror seemed well hidden, so how could he find it to get back?

And what on earth would he find at Wintercombe if he did?

As if he guessed the thought the shaman said, 'Don't worry. Your friends will defeat the elf-people. Those spirits have no purpose; they flutter like leaves in the wind, here and there, this way and that. They are soon bored.'

Wharton blinked. 'They come here?'

'Sometimes I have seen them.'

Great. That was all he needed.

He said, 'You left my friend – Rebecca – in great danger. How could you do that?'

The boy looked at him. His eyes were dark and steady; they had an intelligence Wharton knew was deep. 'I left the wand. The scarred man will release her with that. As I said, we are not savages. We too have our mercy, our rules. I was in a dangerous place, and she insulted the Ancestors.'

Wharton raised an eyebrow. 'Then I just hope they get to her in time.'

Finally the songs ended. Wharton was led out politely, and given a hut to himself; he ducked under the doorway and found a deep pile of bedding, so inviting that he just wanted to collapse into it at once. But he made himself sit in the darkness and think.

Should he make a run for it, now, while they were all asleep?

A rustle of sound came from outside; a careful footstep.

Well, maybe not all asleep. Wharton frowned. It made sense. Someone would be keeping a sharp eye that he didn't run off in the night. These people needed their hero.

He took his shoes and jacket off and lay back, staring up into the musty dark rafters of the thatch.

Well, they'd get one.

He hadn't wanted to come, but he was here now, and his duty was clear.

If this bloody monster wanted a fight, he, George Wharton, would be happy to provide it.

He smiled a grim smile, and closed his eyes.

Moments later, he was asleep.

* * *

Gideon walked swiftly through the Wood. It was a landscape of autumn; crammed with the red fruits of hip and haw, plump blackberries, shiny conkers. Fungi sprouted from fallen wood; he saw death cap and toadstools and fly agaric in the cloven stumps of decaying trees.

The air smelled chill, of twilight mist.

This was the most dangerous time, the coming of darkness on Halloween. He knew the Wood was alive with Shee, all of them were here, even the weird solitary beings, the distorted half-animal creatures and deadly hollow women that usually haunted pools and swamps on the moor, far from people.

He slowed, more careful now.

The path ran downhill. From the overgrown valley rose the grey tower of an ancient church, its stones yellowed with lichen. As he came down to it Gideon paused. Then he opened the lychgate to the churchyard and went in.

The graves were ancient. On some of them stones and granite crosses leaned, worn down by centuries of rain, cherub faces and grey angels. Others were bare, lost under tangles of bramble, but he could feel them, the long rows of the dead, could see with his Shee-sight the pale glimmer of their bones under the wet grass.

There were names on the stones; he couldn't read them, but he had often come here and wondered which of these names was his. His family were here somewhere, his father, his mother, the people he could barely remember. This was one of his secret refuges from the Shee. They disliked the place, complaining of its dullness.

He traced a lichened letter with a long fingernail. Death fascinated him. Sleep was strange enough, the sudden dreamless state he sometimes knew, but to sleep for ever, to merge slowly into the soil, to go back to the earth, how must that feel? Or was there no feeling?

Wharton had told him about the soul, a secret magic mortals believed they possessed, that left the body at death and lived on, elsewhere. He had once asked Summer about it, but she had been furious and he had never mentioned it again.

He had a soul.

Did the Shee have souls?

As the thought came he heard them, a sliver of laughter. Glancing up, he raked the trees with an angry glare.

'Gideon!' they called, soft as honey. 'Find us, Gideon!'

He snatched his fingers from the stone and left the churchyard, hearing the gate clang behind him. He walked under the trees and said, 'What?'

A male Shee, tall and spindly, slid round a silver birch and leaned against its peeling white trunk. 'Summer wants you. Night's coming, the host is all ready to ride. You have to come now.'

Wary, he said, 'Who are we hunting?'

'Not you! Not this time.' Another one, up in the branches, her silver hair piled up, her dress like lizard skin. 'It will be such fun! All the hounds are here, and we'll ride out, far over the land, over the sea. Come on, Gideon. Be quick!'

He managed a smile, and a lie. 'I will. But I'm going to fetch Summer a gift first.'

Their eyes went wide.

'What?' the male said greedily. Its fingers, thin and spidery, gripped his sleeve. Its arm was the webbed wing of a bat.

Gideon shook his head. 'A secret. She knows. She'd be furious if I told you, or came without it.'

'Is it the silver bracelet?'

Gideon shrugged. 'Secret.' He pulled away. 'See you there.'

He walked away from them, forcing himself not to look back. There was a creak of sound, the whisper of a branch. He sensed them go, flicker into the western sky.

He nodded, grim.

Now for the Summerland.

The entrance he chose was one he had used once or twice before; as the track through the Wood came through a certain gate to the moor there was a tiny muddy pond almost lost in bracken.

He waded into it and at once was in the car park of a huge supermarket, its neon letters enormous.

Ignoring the drivers' stares, he ran round the back of the building, past the bins where a plank crossed a grimy stream.

Behind him, some mortal shouted.

He crossed the bridge, arms wide.

Beyond it the slanted worlds of the Summerland lay crashed and fractured. He passed from a confined hut in an arctic wilderness of snow to the corner of a street in Venice, where a gaudy procession passed him, the sumptuous gold and red and black of the people's clothes delighting him. He changed his own to match, then flickered back to green as he found himself running down an endless avenue of lofty oaks under a brilliant starry sky, towards a fountain that rose in one solitary column of splashing water.

Laughing, he ducked under its rainbow of drops, the sun flashing on them, and out into a dark hillside under a blood-red sunset, where a solitary body hung on a gibbet, swinging, the rope around the man's neck creaking in the breeze.

Breath held, Gideon stopped.

He wanted to climb up, and stare into the mortal's lost eyes. He wanted to talk to the dead, as he had often tried to before, and for a second he almost turned aside. But he had to find Jake. He had to find the future.

If there was no map for the Summerland there was also no time, and though he passed through a hundred worlds and eras he was untired when he crawled through a hedge into a strange grey world where the sky was coppery red and the air tasted of salt.

Standing, he found himself on a cliff top, looking out to sea.

It was all wrong. The very shape of the waves, the sluggish silver, was unbalanced, as if more than the moon tugged at these tides. He felt a strange, shivery pull at his heart; he had to turn, to face east, and even then it was all he could do not to stumble forward a step. The sky was lit with an eerie glow, but there was no sunset and no moon. No stars. Nothing but clouds of copper.

He wrapped his long arms around himself.

He knew where he was. This was Wintercombe Bay,

where the shaman's ship had been wrecked on the sand. There was no sign of it now.

This was the future.

All around him, the world felt empty and torn.

CHAPTER FIFTEEN

We only want to warn you. We've seen the evil Janus
has done. He's done it to you and to us. But there is
nowhere to hide now and nowhere any of us can go
where he won't be.

Unless we destroy the mirror.

We dedicate our lives to this. We won't give up
until we succeed, until there are none of us left.

Illegal ZEUS transmission: Biography of Janus

Jake walked around the edge of the great chasm and
faced the tyrant.

Janus wore the familiar uniform, the usual blue-lensed
glasses. But now a sash of black silk was tied diagonally
across his chest, and a small row of silver and gold medals
hung there, all stars and ribbons.

The man himself was subtly older, his skin waxy and

lined. He leaned easily on a thin black cane.

Jake said. 'How do I know you're the real Janus? How can I ever know?'

'Ah, the difficulties of the world!' Janus smiled, and one of the wolves raised its head and looked attentively at him. 'How they try us! Perhaps you remember your hand in mine, Jake, as you led me out of the water.' He turned towards a small door in the wall. 'Shall we go?'

'Go? Where?'

Janus looked at him sideways, and Jake saw the man was not as calm as he appeared. 'Venn and Sarah have made a very irritating move. They've gone after my gold coin. And that's your fault, you know, all your fault. I won't forget that.'

'Your coin? We have the coin.'

'You have half.'

Jake felt a shiver prickle his nerves. 'And you have the other half?' Suddenly everything was changed. If those two fragments were joined . . . Quietly he said, 'Let them find it. You said yourself . . .'

'Not before I *journey* one last time, Jake.' He turned. 'If Venn is going to Wintercombe, so are we, and I certainly intend to get there first.'

'Are you crazy!'

Janus stopped and tapped the cane thoughtfully,

as if he was seriously considering the question. 'Some have said so. The ZEUS children put that about. They are all dead now, of course. For my part, I always felt I was bringing a certain order and excitement to the world, that it was everyone else who was mad. I still think that.'

'You can't go through the mirror! It's . . . so unstable. It's become a monster. If you do you might—'

'Trigger the black hole? Devour the universe?' Janus's eyes glittered. 'What a way to go out! Don't you think?'

He had to be insane. Jake turned, took two steps towards the chasm and leaped, but even as he moved a huge heaviness flung itself out of the dark and hit him hard; he crashed down on to the tiled floor with a thump that knocked all the breath right out of his body.

The wolf lay on top of him; he stared up into its charcoal eyes, and they smouldered with the tiniest of red flames. Jake couldn't breathe; the weight of the beast was crushing him. Its pelt stank, saliva from its jaws dripped on his face. As he struggled for air he felt the rough tongue of the thing rasp against his throat.

'All right!' he gasped. 'All right! Call it off!'

Janus stood looking down at him. 'If I gave the word it would tear your throat out with one bite.'

'Get it off me!'

'It's not often I've seen you scared, Jake. I mean really shaking with fear.'

He gritted his teeth. The tongue was hot and scorched him, the long teeth yellow. He knew it was true.

'I'll take pity on you.' Janus was amused. '*Up!*'

The wolf gave a low growl of disappointment and dragged itself off; the relief was so great Jake gasped in a huge breath and felt his ribs expand.

He rolled, groaned, and picked himself up.

Janus already had the door open. 'Come on. We have to hurry. I'm sure you want to be there.'

He rubbed his face. What option did he have?

And at least he would find the mirror.

Maskelyne thumped on the door; David had it open in seconds; as soon as he saw Rebecca he gave a whoop of delight and relief. 'Oh my God. The wand worked. Are you OK?'

'I'm fine.' Wanting to forget it all, she glanced rapidly round, taking in the cradled baby and the wooden bird on the curtain rails. 'Where's Wharton? And Gideon?'

'Gideon's gone for Jake. Are there still Shee out there?'

They listened. Suddenly the house was very quiet. No more crashes and bangs, no more laughter.

'Have they gone?' David whispered.

The bird chortled. 'You should be so lucky.'

In the growing evening dusk the attic was silent, studded with the tiny red lights of the monitors.

A tiny scratch made Rebecca turn. 'What was that?'

It came again, soft and delicate, at the base of the door.

For a moment none of them dared move. Then Rebecca gave a murmur of recognition and went and turned the key and tugged the door open.

The seven cats strolled in in a line, tails high.

'Are they gone?' Maskelyne asked at once.

One of the cats made a soft mew. It sat and began washing its tail with rapid concentration.

'Was that yes or no?'

'No idea,' the scarred man muttered.

'Maybe we should we go down there and see the damage.'

'Later.' Maskelyne turned to the window and stared out at the thin scarlet streak fading over the Wood. 'The sun has set. Halloween is here.' He looked at David. 'If you want to do this – if you want to go ahead with Operation Leah – then we have to start it now. Timing is crucial.'

David blew out an anxious breath. 'Yes, but without Venn . . .'

'You heard what he said. If he wasn't back he told you to go ahead.'

'I know, but it's the responsibility. If we mess up . . .'

Quietly, Maskelyne walked to the controls. 'The risk would be the same if he was here.'

David groaned. 'If only Piers was!'

'Forget Piers. Piers is gone – Summer could have sent him anywhere. He'll never find his way back.' Maskelyne's voice was harsh; he sat at the controls and touched them with his fingers. Red shimmers flickered on the unscarred side of his face. 'We have to do this without him. Becky, give me readings every two minutes. We need to be accurate – more accurate than we've ever been before.'

She looked at David.

He shrugged, and glanced in the mirror as if for help, but all it showed him was his own uncertainty. 'Right,' he said, seeing how his dim reflection squirmed. 'OK. Let's do it.'

He would have to do this alone; he would have to kill the monster, or be killed by it.

Which would certainly be a bit of a strange end for George Wharton, who'd got through three tours in the army without a scratch and two years in Compton's

College, aka the hell-hole, which had been tougher by far.

Now, escorted by a small group of young men splashing their way through the swampy ground, he wondered if it was too late, too late for everything. He thought about his life. It wasn't as if he'd achieved much. No house, no wife, no kids either. No one to mourn him. Probably better that way.

Of course he'd never see Jake or Sarah again. Compton's owed him back pay too – he'd never see that either.

He laughed, a bitter amusement; the shaman, walking behind, glanced up at him curiously.

The swamp was masked with drifts of mist. Gnats swarmed in circling clouds; it was warm, even muggy. Wharton loosed his tie and tugged it off, then undid his shirt collar.

On the horizon the mountains were white peaks. He stretched, still feeling stiff from the night.

Around his neck were corded pendants, festooned on him this morning by the women of the tribe. They had been sombre, even silent. He had the definite feeling they thought they would never see him again.

He slapped a gnat.

As if that was some invisible signal, the escort party stopped.

The shaman touched his arm. 'These men won't go any further. Come now, Jorjwarton.'

The swamp ended. The rocky ground rose up into low hills, outcropping oddly, topped with strangely shaped crags and mounds of earth. One hill, the nearest, was crested with four wind-bent trees.

Wharton toiled upwards. Great clouds sailed over his head; birds rose in flocks, wheeling high and giving eerie cries that echoed in the bare rocks. When he glanced back down, the group of men were tiny, lost in the emerald green of the saturated land.

They came to the four trees, and crested the ridge. Wharton whistled. Beyond lay a vast moor, its earth blasted and bare, the vegetation shorn to nothing; a tortured landscape, as if some legendary beast had laid it waste and burned every bush and brake.

The boy stopped on the hilltop, and pointed with his tattooed finger. 'There.'

Breathless, Wharton shielded his eyes from the sun.

'You see those broken rocks, the smashed teeth of the hills? In their heart is the lair of the creature, deep in a secret cave. There it sleeps, and there it drags its food. The birds and beasts keep clear of that place. Even the insects fear it. That is the place you must go.'

Wharton straightened his shoulders. 'Whatever you

say, son.' He held out his hands, and the shaman put a flint knife into the right and a flint-tipped spear in the left.

He looked at the weapons, trying to blink away the infuriating longing for the twelve-bore. These would be sharp, but he had no skill with them.

He said, 'Will your Ancestors go with me?'

The boy shook his head. 'Who knows? The dead have their own dreams. They will wish you well, but this is not a place where they have power.'

Wharton nodded. 'Right. Well, I'll have to do it without them then.'

He started to climb.

The shaman's voice came calmly after him. 'Don't hesitate. Strike once and strike to kill. It is deadly and has no mercy – nor should you.'

Wharton nodded. He had climbed almost out of earshot when the shaman spoke again.

'Don't believe anything it tells you.'

'Eh?' He turned, almost slipping. *Tells me?*

But the rocks were empty.

He was alone.

Sarah drove for an hour, then Venn took a turn. They tore through the empty land. The motorways were bare and the countryside grey as dust. No livestock cropped the fields. No smoke rose from farms and chimneys; they saw only a few other vehicles, and those too were all speeding west. The convulsions of the mirror came again, and then once more, sending them skidding, so that the very land seemed to be rolling up under them, even as they passed villages and cities and came at last to the great moorlands of the west country.

Venn, his face dirty from the grey dust, muttered, 'Not so far now.'

Sarah was aching with tiredness and thirst. She drained the water-bottle of its last drops and dumped it, stretching her arms, wriggling warmth into her cramped muscles. 'What then?'

'Find the coin. Get it back to our time.'

'Jake . . .'

'*I know!*' Venn's reply came through gritted teeth. 'I know, Sarah. You don't have to keep reminding me about Jake.'

It was clear he did know, and piling on more guilt wasn't helping. She pushed hair from her eyes and stared out at the bare spaces of the moor, and saw, beyond, like a faint green streak of lichen, the glimmer of the poisonous sea.

They were coming towards Wintercombe and they would find the other half of the coin. It was what she had dreamed of for months. So why was she so scared?

The ground quivered.

Venn swore. 'Hell! What now!'

Sarah squirmed round in the seat. She looked back. She saw the horizon shimmer, then completely disappear. Before her eyes, a slit began to open in the fabric of the world.

'*The black hole*,' she breathed.

The lift shot up, until Jake felt giddy. When the doors snapped open he stood a moment, not even realizing what he saw.

Then he said, 'Is that . . . ?'

Janus nodded. 'I'm afraid so. Our old friend the Chronoptika. Looking a little . . . bloated, I'll admit.'

It was a huge laboratory, but the obsidian mirror filled it to the ceiling. The dark glass was swollen, unrecognizable, the frame burst wide, all the silver letters shattered. The blackness at its heart seemed to have spilled out, as if it had melted and reformed, become molten in some vast lava flow that clogged the room, its surface not smooth now but pitted and faceted, so that he saw not one Jake reflected in it but hundreds, all slightly different, a hundred variations on that tall, dirty, astonished boy. It was solid and yet he could look right into it, and there was a terrible emptiness at its heart, a great vacuum, and it was a threat, unstable, as if at any second it would expand uncontrollably, eat up the tower and him and everything in the world.

He stepped back, but Janus grabbed his hand, and he saw on the small man's arm the glint of the silver bracelet, its amber eye.

'No!'

'We'll be safe.' Janus walked forward, perfectly calm.

'No! Can't you see? It's—' But it was too late, he was already dragged in, and he knew with a sharp terror that the emptiness was at the heart of him, that it had always been there, and it erupted around him like a volcano, and devoured him.

Gideon faced east. He felt the shock wave coming before he saw it, a shudder in his nerves, in his teeth, and bones. The world rippled, the sky sang. He flung himself to the ground, arms over head. In that moment he was mortal, only mortal, and he laughed, because now he knew he would die. He would escape the Shee for ever. He was going where they couldn't follow.

His hands clutched the thin grass.

He closed his eyes.

Wharton stared at the cave. It was a black, empty maw in the hillside.

It shimmered in a miasma of gas – or maybe that was him. His terror.

He took a breath, and crouched. 'All right,' he yelled, in his best parade-ground bellow. 'Whatever you are in there, come out! NOW!'

Behind the car the world cracked. A black stain spread from horizon to horizon; it rose over the grey land like some satanic aurora, bloomed upwards like a dark and decadent flower. It blotted out everything, even the dull coppery evening light.

'Hold on!' Venn yelled. He put his foot down and the car screamed down the twisting road, while Sarah stared back in terror, sure that this was it, the ending of the world, the black hole opening.

'He's done it,' she breathed so quietly Venn barely heard the words. 'He's killed us. He's killed us all.'

This thing of darkness
I acknowledge mine

CHAPTER SIXTEEN

When the Wood is no more
> There will be woe in the World.
> There will be no more laughter on the wind.
>> Traditional proverb

The mouth of the cave was black.

No sound came from it; nothing had answered his challenge.

Wharton moved cautiously on. Small objects crunched and slithered under his feet; looking down he saw bones, piles of them, cracked and gnawed, and skulls too, of wolf and bear and fox.

The smell was almost unbearable; he wanted to retch but he fought it down and crept carefully from rock to rock until there was nothing between him and the opening.

It was a great slanting gash in the hillside.

Nothing, not even flies, disturbed its stillness.

'*Childe Roland*,' he muttered, '*to the bloody Dark Tower came.*'

He took a tighter grip of the flint knife, hefted the spear up to his shoulder, and slid in.

The rock face loomed over him; he stepped into its shadow. Dimness surrounded him; he crouched, all too aware of how starkly visible he would be against the sky. But the creature made no sound.

He knew it was watching. There was a soft shuffle, a rattle of pebbles somewhere back in the darkness. For a moment he thought he saw a grotesque shadow flicker on the cave wall; he turned, but there was nothing, except a stink of fish.

Tactics?

A bold front.

And as the man said, strike first.

A rock flew out of the darkness and past him, so close he felt its draught. He flung himself down, just as another sizeable stone whacked into the cave wall.

Wharton rolled, picked himself up, and ducked behind a boulder. He was shaken and exhilarated all at once.

If the thing wanted a fight, it would get it!

He risked a glance round the boulder.

Immediately missiles came at him like arrows; high and wide. He jerked back, taking a breath. Then he ran.

It was a crazy, zigzag process, into the dark, from crevice to salt stack. The cave was deep; it divided into a myriad of openings, stalagmites, grottos of glistening crystal. And always the creature flitted somewhere ahead, a dark shadow.

No animal, though. As he paused, heart thudding, Wharton realized that this thing thought. It was drawing him in.

And it had a very poor aim. Suspiciously poor.

He frowned. Gripping the spear and knife, he stepped boldly, unprotected, into the darkness.

Stones spattered past him. Ignoring them, he walked steadily on, eyes alert. Now, in the shadows ahead, he could make it out, a grotesque, huddled shape squatting deep in the cave.

There was a fire burning somewhere back here; smoke caught in his throat, the stink of singed wood making him stifle a cough. As he closed in the light flickered, flame-red. The monster's shadow rose up behind it like dark wings; he glimpsed a misshapen eye, a hunched back, a small white human-like hand. Fascinated, he took another step, and saw it.

Scaly, shadowed and swollen, it crouched in the darkness and watched him. Wharton took a breath. What was this? Half man, half monster? It appalled and terrified him. The single eye watched him. He couldn't tell if the thing was ferocious or as terrified as he was.

He swallowed, and raised the flint spear quickly to his shoulder.

Strike fast, strike once, the shaman had said. He should do that.

But his hand held the spear still.

Was he getting soft? Old? He clenched his fingers round the ash pole and drew it back.

The creature didn't move. It just watched him, a dim grotesque huddle.

And then, before he could let fly, before he could save himself, it spoke.

The darkness was a great arc of raw emptiness across the horizon. It had already swallowed half the sky. Sarah stood by the car and stared back at it. It hung like the dawning of a terrible new sun, a black sun without light or heat. The sheer vacancy of it chilled her.

The city must have been destroyed, with everyone and everything in it.

With Jake.

She had tried the phone over and over, but only static came through.

Venn slammed the door of the vehicle in fury. 'It's over. This thing's useless. Useless.'

The final contortion had distorted the car out of all shape. The front wheels were crumpled, the bonnet steaming. The entire chassis was stretched into a parallelogram of warped metal.

Venn wasted no more time on it. He stormed off, walking quickly.

Sarah ran after him.

'We're not far now. Six, seven miles maybe. We'll take a short cut over the moor.'

She hadn't needed him to tell her that. As they ran down the road, as it dwindled to a dusty lane, the gorse growing high and dark and furzy at each side, she smelled again the old smells of her childhood, and knew she had come home.

The lane became a track, and there was the gate to the moor. Venn stepped up on to a tussock of grass and stared round.

'This hasn't changed, anyway.'

But he was wrong. Both of them sensed the emptiness here; the silence. Few birds made any sound, and in the rooted hollows of the ground she knew there were no rabbits, no badgers, no shrews. Janus's world was an empty one, even here.

Venn leaped down and walked fast. He said, 'We'll go in through the Wood.'

'There is no Wood.'

He spared her a sideways glance. 'Sarah, don't . . .'

'There is no Wood. You'll see.'

They hurried over the low, boggy moor, the uneven ground tripping them and the acrid salty smell of the poisoned sea growing stronger, its livid green line visible now.

She watched how Venn saw it all, but he said nothing, and she wondered if all this was fuelling his decision to destroy the mirror, or whether in the end he would endure it, even all this – for Leah. Because it would come down to a choice. She was sure of that. Pushing back her wind-scattered hair, she decided that if Venn could not act, in the end she would do it for him, even if it meant she had never been born.

He said, '*Unbelievable.*'

She knew what he was looking at. Slowly, she climbed to the edge of the valley and looked down with him.

The Wood was gone.

The trees had been cut down and hacked; in places the bare trunks still stood, grey and brittle, all life drained from them. Down the slope of the combe the earth was brown and desolate, its secret places open to the sky.

Venn stared, appalled. 'It looks so small.'

She nodded. In his time the Wood was so vast, so tangled, so full of mystery that you thought there would never be an end to it.

'How did they . . . Summer . . . how did she ever allow it?'

'I told you. The Shee don't come here. I lived here till I was ten and I never saw one of them.'

He shook his head. Stealing a glance at him, she was struck by the paleness of his face, the cold blue of his eyes. The city had shaken him, but it was this – the disenchantment of one small, secret wood – that had really struck home. She nodded to herself.

'Come on,' she said.

Taking the lead, she led him through the devastated trees.

'Anything?' David hovered anxiously behind Maskelyne.

Softly, Rebecca said, 'D minus one hour now.'

'Something. A ripple.' The scarred man gave a glance up at the mirror. 'Did you feel it? It came from far away, but it was immensely powerful.'

'Will it affect us?'

'Slightly.' He frowned. 'I need just a few changes.' His fingers worked the controls, hurriedly.

David stalked to the door, opened it and listened. The Abbey was silent. He turned. 'I'm going down to check things out.'

'The Shee,' Rebecca whispered, but the tiny bird hopped down on to the window seat and interrupted her.

'It's OK. Really. They've gone. It's Halloween. They won't hang around.' It nodded wistfully at the window. 'Take a look.'

David came over; Rebecca crowded behind.

They saw the moon, a silver crescent over the Wood. Dark, flitting shapes were moving over it, as if geese were flying, or other unearthly, impossible birds.

'Oh it's such fun.' The bird flapped its weak wings, sending a feather spiralling. 'You find some stupid human, out on their own. I mean, they're asking for it, right? And then you spook them, just a bit. And they run. And then ... bang, the whole hunt looms up, the hounds and the horses, and we snatch them up and they get dragged and dumped and they run a bit more . . . and then maybe they collapse, and beg, and scream . . .' It sighed. 'Wish I was there.'

David glanced at Rebecca.

They moved back to the mirror. He said, 'Can you spare us? Ten minutes. I've got to secure the place.'

Absently, Maskelyne nodded. 'While you're there get the uniforms. Don't be long.'

David gave a mirthless laugh. 'Believe me, we won't.' He went to the door, unlocked it and peered cautiously out. The attic corridor stretched into gloom. Dead leaves drifted in a draught.

'All clear.'

He slipped out, and Rebecca followed him.

They waited until they heard the door softly locked behind them. Then he whispered, 'Quiet as mice.'

She followed him down the small winding servants' stair to the Long Gallery. David flicked the light switch on. Nothing happened. But the moon came out from behind a cloud and briefly lit the windows of the lengthy room with slanting silver rectangles.

They were both silent.

Then David said softly, 'I hope O's got insurance.'

There was not a curtain unshredded, not a marble bust left whole. Every cabinet had been torn from its place, every book ripped to pieces. The floor was a sea of pages and sherds, of gleefully scattered ceramics, of tipped and broken cabinets.

'His collection,' Rebecca muttered.

'Priceless. All gone.'

Appalled, they picked their way through the wreckage. Smashed china crunched underfoot. There were berries and leaves everywhere, and as they came to the top of the stairs they saw that mushrooms and toadstools had sprouted all down the carved wooden bannisters.

'Crazy.'

David nodded. He leaned over and looked down. The front door was wide, banging wildly in the rising gale. There was no sign of the Shee.

They hurried down. 'Give me a hand.' he said. It took both of them to drag the door shut; it had been half hauled off its hinges, and they had to slam it in the frame and force as many of the heavy bolts across as they could. Even so, once it was done Rebecca felt much safer.

'Cameras.' David set off for the kitchen.

If anything, this was worse than upstairs, and she put a hand over her mouth, imagining Piers' dismay and fury. David pushed the table back, kicked saucepans aside and waded through to the small control room.

One look told them the cameras would never work again.

'Right. Forget that. Cloister door.'

They worked their way round securing every door and window they could find whole. The Shee had ripped the place to pieces looking for the coin, but the metal fastenings were all untouched, and odd things like copper pans and steel wires stood safe in the sea of wreckage. David looked up at the grandfather clock in Venn's study, its face askew and coils of clockwork springing out of it. 'Thank God we sent Wharton off with the coin. If they'd found it . . . it doesn't bear thinking about.'

In the storeroom, David dug out a few cardboard boxes, still soaked from the flood, and stacked them in her arms.

'What are these?'

'Stuff for Operation Leah. Piers had it all ready. Just as well.' He paused, shaking his head. 'What a disaster, Rebecca! How can I face Venn when he gets back?'

'Let's just hope he does,' she muttered.

Halfway back up the stairs, a small brown shape swung itself down from the ceiling and leaped on to the boxes, then hurriedly on to David's back, hugging his neck tight.

'For God's sake, he's choking me! Get him off, Becky!'

She reached up and took the small furry body. Horatio was shaking; his small brown eyes were wide; he started at shadows, and the moonlight caught his panic. His fur was electric with fear. He snuggled rapidly under her arm.

231

'Well, that's one worry off my mind,' David muttered. 'I thought they might have snatched him.'

Once back in the attic, the marmoset clung to Rebecca anxiously. She gave him a grape, but he turned away from it.

Maskelyne said, 'They're gone?'

'Looks like it. Left the place totally zeroed.'

Rebecca hurried to the screen. 'D minus fifty.'

'Right. We need to hurry.' David tore the boxes open. Inside she saw the dark material of uniforms, POLIZIA on their backs. There were tabards too, striped with yellow high visibility tape.

'The power's getting low,' Maskelyne murmured.

'Thank your stars for the generator, because the rest of the house is dark.'

The gale rattled the window, like fingers trying the catch. David looked up. Clouds were streaming over the moon. The night was wild, the storm rising like a low moan of wind off the sea. Even as he looked he caught the first glimmer of lightning, and then, immediately after, a rumble of thunder.

Horatio dived into the makeshift cradle and hid under the blankets.

Lorenzo grizzled, hungry.

The cats looked at each other.

David laid the uniforms out to dry. He felt sick with anxiety. Where was Jake? If Jake was here, it would all be fine. '*Come back*,' he found himself murmuring. 'Come on. Come back. Now.'

But the mirror leaned in its darkness, and showed him nothing.

Rebecca said, 'Don't worry. Venn knows he has to get here.'

'How do we know what's happening there, Becky? In that terrible future.'

'Venn can deal with it. And he'll look after Jake.'

He looked at her. There was doubt in him, and he opened his mouth as if to say something, but in that second, like a spiteful word, the lightning struck. It scorched a white shiver, a bolt that crashed into the house, burst tiles apart, shook the walls. For a second they were all blinded with it, the cables crackling and curling. Rebecca screamed. Fire ran round the room in a white glee.

Then it was gone.

David lay on the floor, on his face, and the hairs on his neck were stinging. There was a jagged crack inside his eyes.

And the world was in darkness.

CHAPTER SEVENTEEN

I lie awake at night listening to the wind. It has voices in it, and they whisper. The latch of my window rattles as if fingers pull at it.

Outside, for miles, the storm rages through the Wood.

This is such a house of secrets, my dear.

Letter of Lady Mary Venn to her sister 1834

When the world had finished moving, Gideon picked himself up.

He felt cold, and the night wind whipped his hair. Half the sky seemed to be missing; far to the east an arc of darkness had eaten it. He shivered. There was something else he felt, and for a moment he struggled to put a name to it, because it was both familiar and alien. Then he realized.

234

He felt alone.

He was used to that. Being a mortal among the Shee meant always being alone. But here – he turned, facing the wind, smelling – here there was no one at all. *No Shee.*

Had he really escaped them, at last?

It was so overwhelming it made him want to crouch down on the muddy cliff top, and rest his head in his hands, and just wonder at it.

But he had to find Jake.

He ran, with the swift speed the Shee had taught him, because far back in the past the Host was hunting, and Halloween was here, and the black hole had opened in the east. He ran over the cliff moor and into the combe, past the graves, past the shell of the church, down the track and into the Wood.

Though there was no Wood.

He stared in astonishment as he leaped between the skeletons of trees, at the absence of green life. Lost, strange sounds came to him, whispers and sighs, dreams of sad music. He frowned, and hurried on. In the dark he made himself a shadow, his coat black, his face masked by its swirls of lichen.

He came out on to the soaked lawns almost before he knew it, and looked up at the façade.

Wintercombe Abbey was a ruin. Its walls were smothered with ivy; its windows bare holes. The roof and gables reared to the sky, but no smoke rose from the chimneys and nothing stirred here, not a bird, not a bat, not a moth. It was a dead place.

He ran hastily up the steps.

There was no door. But as he entered the tiled hall he felt, just like a warning finger on his spine, a shiver of power. He stopped, waited, getting the sound of it clear in his head. A faint, high ringing, as if someone had run a finger round the rim of a glass, centuries ago, and the ghost of that echo still sang in the stillness.

No one but he could have heard it, his senses taut with the Shee-brightness.

He crossed the hall softly, and ran up the stairs.

The Long Gallery was an empty shell, the night wind whipping the rags of its curtain. There was no roof; he looked up and saw the coppery clouds that never seemed to break.

He walked down. Floorboards creaked – old, familiar sounds.

The door that led to the Monk's Walk was the only one left; he opened it, and immediately smelled the damp of the subterranean cloisters, heard the roaring deluge of the river below.

The faint sound rang, beyond hearing. It prickled his skin.

Curious, he walked down the stone passageway. At its end, in the cellar where the mirror had once been kept, all that was left were the remnants of the green malachite web. Ducking under its sticky strands, he made his way to its heart, noticing how the web had been carefully reconstructed at some time, how it was thicker now, rewoven and so tightly meshed he had to scramble over and through it, and how it trembled with the invisible vibration of the thing at its heart.

He stopped, listening.

There had been a scuttle of a leaf. A draught over the stones.

He glanced back.

Nothing.

He slid under a strand of web and it stuck to him; he tugged his coat tails from it, but then it snagged his hair and arm. When he brushed it away his fingers stuck.

Gideon breathed a hiss of annoyance. He struggled on, but the further he went the more tangled he became. Finally he couldn't move at all.

This was crazy.

The Shee had many things like it, traps and webs to snare mired mortals, but this was no Shee spell. The web had been animated somehow; it held him softly but firmly at hand and elbow and hair, and as he pulled and ripped himself free he suddenly wondered if it would hold him here for ever, because he would not die like the other humans it had snared. Their remains lay about him. Bones. Ragged strips of clothing.

They had hung and rotted here. All of them struggling to reach that thing that sang at the labyrinth's heart. He wondered if any of them were Sarah's friends, if any had been from ZEUS, desperate to end Janus's tyranny. Because he had begun to understand what that silent, ringing power was.

He took a breath, and fought his way on. Lithe, slippery, he transformed into the thinnest of Shee-beings, ducked and wriggled, slid lizard-like through the trap.

The nearer he came to the centre the more he struggled to breathe, as if even the air here was meshed and strung tight, but then, quite suddenly, the pressure was gone, and he tore himself free and stepped out into empty space.

There was a table, and on the table a casket made of gold. His eyes widened at the sight of it; the Shee would have had it torn open in seconds, greedy for its beauty.

It was plain in design, with no markings, no lock.

He walked round it, listening.

The ringing was like a voice.

Or rather, *half a voice.*

It was too faint to hear the words or know what language they were. As if the sense of them had faded to mere vibration.

Gideon paused. He knew all about the dangers of magic. He reached out delicately for the lid of the casket, putting one long finger under the clasp.

Then he lifted the lid.

The note of the ringing rose in the depths of his being.

Inside, on a bed of white satin, lay a broken coin. It was ancient, worn with use. It had been jaggedly cut down the middle, and this half showed the edge of the face, one eye, part of the nose.

Zeus, king of the gods, stared up at him.

Gideon breathed in. *This was the other half* – not the one Sarah had brought, that Summer had stolen, that Maskelyne had now.

This was the left half, never seen by anyone before. With this he could buy his freedom from Summer for ever.

Eagerly he reached in; his fingers closed around the thick rim.

Until a voice from the dark said, 'Don't touch that. That is not for you, changeling.'

'You would not believe,' the monster said acidly, 'just how really stupid you look.'

Wharton stopped breathing.

'I mean. A flint spear! And all that stuff around your neck. Going native, teacher? How on earth did it take you this long to find me? I know they can't do a thing without me but I would have thought Maskelyne at least could have made more of an effort.'

'*Piers?*' The word was a hoarse gasp. He stood there frozen with the spear whipped back; then he lowered it abruptly. 'Is that you?'

The shadowy grotesque laughed bitterly. 'Who else?'

'How can it be you? You were at Wintercombe when I left! How can you be a monster who's been here over a year when . . .'

'Oh get a grip!' Piers sounded more than angry. 'This is time travel. I may have left after you but I got here a long time before you.'

The intricacies of it made Wharton's mind whirl. 'But how?'

'Summer,' Piers snapped. 'That's how.'

It was enough. Feeling oddly deflated, Wharton propped the spear against a rock and thrust the knife into his belt. 'She did this?'

The monster's voice was raw. 'I stood up to her. I mean, it's clear she sees me as a threat. I can understand that.'

Wharton couldn't, but just shrugged. 'Well, I'm here now. How can I help?'

Piers seemed not to hear. He shuffled a little forward into the flamelight. 'But she's gone too far this time. Look at me! I've lived like this for months, waiting. Eating anything they tossed in here – raw fish mostly. I am so hungry!'

'They – the people here. They're terrified of you.'

'Of course they are!' The monster made a strange snuffling sound, oddly smug. 'I made absolutely sure of that, and the reason is that otherwise they would have come in mob-handed and fought it out. And of course, I had no desire to hurt them.'

Wharton shook his head in admiration. Whatever else had happened to him, the little man still had his complacent self-possession. 'You mean you were terrified of them.'

A bark of scorn. Then Piers, his voice smaller, said, 'George. I need you to get me out of this.'

Wharton was baffled. Stepping forward, he moved into the flamelight and saw a bizarre hunched creature perched on a rock before him. Summer had done her usual excellent job. Piers was unrecognizable; this was a scaly, tailed, huddled thing, one eye huge and red, the other tiny, the only thing left of Piers his small hands, the fingers crooked and too long now, absurdly clutched together.

'What can I do? Summer is the only one.'

'Don't say that. You've got stuff on you. The coin ...'

Wharton shrugged. He unslung the purse from his neck and tipped out what it contained, the right half of the coin. 'What can this do?'

'I don't know. All I know is it has power ringing from it like rays. Try touching my skin with it.'

Awkward, Wharton scrambled closer. The stink of fish and worse things was pretty unbearable, but he tried not to let Piers see that. The creature's huge eye watched anxiously as the gold coin met its scaly hide.

Nothing happened.

'Well, what did you expect?' Wharton grunted.

Piers sniffed. 'OK. Well, you've got the bracelet . . . ?'

'On my wrist.'

'So we go back through the mirror, and—'

'Whoa, whoa. Wait a minute!' Feeling suddenly weary, Wharton sat on a slab of quartz. 'First, I haven't a clue where the mirror is. Second, how can you go back to Wintercombe looking like that?'

'Oh so you think that matters?' Piers was furious. 'Look, I have been here *months*.'

'I know but—'

'You know? You have NO idea! You swan in here, and have the nerve to refuse . . .'

'Swan in!' Wharton leaped up. 'I thought I was facing some ferocious beast. Imagine how *I* felt!'

'That is so selfish. JUST like a mortal.'

Wharton gasped. 'Do you know I could just walk out of here right now? Maybe I will! And what the hell are you going to do then?'

The monster spat. 'Go ahead. Leave. Run away! Let the tribe out there slaughter you and drink from your skull, and your friend the shaman's too, because your failure is his, you know that, don't you?'

Wharton stopped.

He felt ridiculous. He turned, slowly, and blew out his cheeks. There was a moment of silence in the cave, the echoes of their anger ringing slowly back into silence. It occurred to Wharton that the tribesmen must be hearing a great roaring and howling down there. Well, maybe that would impress them.

'OK. OK. Sorry. We need to sort this.'

A small hesitation. Then the monster muttered. 'Too right.'

243

Wharton looked down at the Zeus coin, then held it to the flamelight. 'This has to be of some help to us. I don't know what but . . .'

His voice went.

In the middle of the sentence it just stopped.

He tried to close his mouth but it wouldn't. He tried to drop his arm but nothing would move. He was frozen in his pose, and even before the dreadful understanding washed into his mind her small white hand had come from behind him and taken the coin very carefully from his fingers, and her voice said, 'So *sweet*, George, of you to keep it safe for me.'

Piers gave a small howl of dismay.

From the corner of his eye, Wharton watched Summer walk round and stand in front of him. She tipped her head.

Suddenly he could move. He gasped, jumped back. 'Summer, please—'

'And you were so ready to fight each other! That would have been really entertaining.'

'Look. That coin . . .'

She dropped it carefully into the neckline of her berry-red lacy dress. 'Too late. But look at the hobgoblin, George. Our poor lost monster. Shall I turn him to something even more hideous?'

244

'No,' he said.

'Shall I turn him back to Piers?'

'Summer, don't torment us. We . . .'

She smiled, kindly. Then to his utter astonishment she just nodded at Piers and the hideous shadow shrank and there he was, small and irritable and normal in his white lab coat.

Piers leaped up and stretched; he gave a whoop of joy.

Summer turned daintily away. 'But I don't want to disappoint you. You so wanted to fight something terrible. I see it in you, George. You wanted to be the hero for those mortals out there to admire, so they could sing about you in their ghastly songs. And I wouldn't want you to be sad. So, if you want a monster, George, if you really really want one, then do, please, have it on me.'

He stared. The cave wall cracked and fell apart, with a roaring of stones.

Beyond he saw a vast cavern huger than a cathedral, all pillars and chasms. Curled in its heart, asleep, smoke rising from its nostrils, was what he could only describe as a dragon.

Summer giggled. 'You never know,' she said, as she faded softly out of sight, 'you might even start some sort of legend.'

* * *

Gideon turned his head.

Jake was standing there, looking worn. Next to him, neat and small and deadly, was Janus. The tyrant leaned on a black cane, now he lifted it, threatening. 'Move away from that casket, changeling. Or I'm afraid our friend Jake will pay.'

Gideon didn't move.

'What's in there?' Jake snapped.

'The left half of the coin.'

'Then get it, for God's sake! Don't worry about me. *Get it!*' He seemed simmering with anger and frustration.

For a second Gideon hesitated. Then a voice from behind Janus ordered him like a whiplash of scorn.

'Do as he says, Gideon. Get the coin now.' Venn had the glass gun thrust into the tyrant's back. Janus's smile had frozen on his lips. He turned round and faced Venn. Sarah was there too, standing a way off, looked filthy and tired; she flashed a surprised glance at Gideon.

'Sorry, Venn. No one else has this – this is mine.' Ignoring the weapon, Janus walked to the casket; he swept past Gideon and took the coin and backed away, his hand in his pocket.

'Be careful,' Jake muttered. 'I think he's armed.'

'So am I.' Furious, Venn raised the glass gun.

'Why not use it?' Janus smiled. 'It's your only chance, *Oberon!*'

'No,' Sarah breathed. She went to grab at him; Venn held up a hand to keep her away.

'I will use it,' he said. 'Time's run out for you at last, Janus.'

'No,' Jake snapped. 'Don't shoot. It's not . . .'

Venn smiled, said, 'Too late. I've been wanting to do this for some time.'

He took careful aim. And he shot Janus straight through the heart.

CHAPTER EIGHTEEN

One time, Jake, I was in a gondoler in Venice and it
was Carnival, which is this party thing they have. I
wore a black and silver mask and as we come under
this stonking great crib of a palazzo we was breaking
into I thought of you.

'What do you think Jake's doing now?' I asked
Long Tom.

'Lords knows,' he says, dipping in the paddle. 'But
it's probably something just as daft as this.'

Moll's diary

The attic was dark and there was a white echo behind
David's eyes. His ears rang. He dragged himself painfully
to hands and knees and saw that Maskelyne was
already moving.

'Becky?' The scarred man's voice was sharp. 'Becky?'

'I'm OK.' She was sitting on the floor, looking quite sick.

Maskelyne crouched by her. 'Are you hurt?'

'No. Sort of shaken.' She looked out at the window. 'We were struck by lightning?'

As if in answer the storm rumbled, far over the moor. He helped her to her feet.

The wiring and screens around the mirror were smoking; small blue flames ran down the sockets in the wall. David grabbed the fire extinguisher and sprayed them, fast.

Then they stood and surveyed the wreckage.

The mirror seemed enhanced in its blackness, Rebecca thought, startled. Almost it seemed a little bigger. She glanced at Maskelyne. 'Is it . . . ?'

'It's absorbed the power.' He was already hurrying back to it; she felt, like a prickle of cold, the familiar sting of jealousy. 'I can feel the difference.' His fine hands touched the silver frame, caressed the secret letters. '*I hear you,*' he whispered, and she knew it was the mirror he was speaking to, as if, in some secret communion with it, he had forgotten her.

She looked at David who said, 'Maskelyne. For God's sake. What's the damage?'

He turned. In the fleeting moonlight they saw the

scarred side of his face, the ugly dragging of the flesh. He blinked at them, and then said, 'The mirror is the mirror. Nothing can change it or destroy it but the reunited coin. It's fiercer now, engorged. It shivers with new strength. But as for all this—' he waved at the wrecked machinery, '—this is gone. Fused to uselessness.'

Appalled, David said, 'Surely we can salvage . . .'

'It will never work again.'

'It has to! We have,' he glanced at the clock, 'less than forty minutes.'

As if the baby understood him it gave a great cry of misery; hearing it Rebecca realized she was hungry too. The wooden bird, high on the rafters, cheeped and flew down to the cradle; it stared at Lorenzo curiously. 'The mortal child wants feeding.'

David didn't move; he seemed struck still by disbelief. He touched a wire; it smouldered and he had to snatch his fingers away. 'But . . . Leah! We have to go ahead. We can't fail Venn.'

Maskelyne sat. His long lean shape was a ghost in the dim room. Not a light flickered on the panels. The only sound was the soft tick of the clock, and outside, the moan and rustle and roar of the wind in the branches of the Wood, and the dead leaves, flying in hosts.

'All we can do now is ask. The decision is the

machine's. My Chronoptika must decide if it will help us or not.'

The cats mewed. One by one they gathered in a tight, uneasy group.

Horatio scrambled on to Rebecca's shoulder, gripping her hair tight with his tiny hands. She stood by the table.

'So it's all over then?' she whispered.

As if he agreed, Lorenzo screamed, a crescendo of need.

'Leave this to me.' Piers rolled up his sleeves. 'I'm handling this.'

Wharton stared. 'Piers, that's a huge creature. That's a . . .'

He faltered to a stop. Was it a dragon? He had thought so, but now he wasn't sure. It was certainly a great dark slumbering mass, it rose and fell and breathed and snuffled. Hastily he took out the flint knife and looked frantically round for the spear.

'This is all your fault, of course.' Piers advanced steadily, his white lab coat ludicrous in the dimness. 'Mortal pride. She could see that. *Man-stands-alone-against-impossible-odds*. You people! You have absolutely no idea how stupid you are. Even your thoughts are stupid. Well, I've had enough of it.'

'Keep your voice down!' Wharton whispered. There was a smell too, a scorched, sulphurous stink. It reminded him of volcanoes. The vast sleeping creature rumbled like a distant storm.

'No way!' Piers turned and walked backwards, tiny on the immensity of the cavern floor. His anger seemed to boil up inside him; his voice was loud and hard and steely with it. 'I've *had it* with you. All of you! Mortal and Shee. Her and Venn! Had it up to here.'

His face was fierce with passion; the earring in his ear glinted like fire. 'Never mind Summer – *I* am a spirit of no common rate, and it's about time people around here realized it. So let's have a bit of respect. The worm is turning, and it's no more Mr Nice Guy. Step well back out of the way.'

Wharton stared. The lab coat had become a silver suit, elegantly fitted. Piers seemed taller, younger, slimmer. Strange glimmers like wings of light rustled behind him.

He stood directly under the sleeping beast.

Wharton held his breath.

The thing woke. It uncurled, and they saw how immense it was. Its hide was dark purple, leathery, stiff with plated scales, its tail scraped the floor like a coil of steel. It unclicked claws thick as Wharton's arm and opened a green eye embedded as deep in wrinkled flesh as a jewel far below the sea.

It breathed out a satisfied scorch of steam.

But Piers was too furious to care. He spread his hands. Tiny before it he stood on the stone floor.

And he began to sing.

It was a song that made Wharton feel very strange. Dizzy, even. A song of cloying, sweet music, clear and high. The words he could not distinguish, but the very sound of them was somehow familiar; they made him think of things he had forgotten for years; of sitting on the rug playing while his mother did the ironing; the flap of clothes on a washing line, the taste of honey on his fingers; distant happy, painful things.

And the dragon – if it was one – began to rearrange.

Its hide peeled back like water from rocks. Its bones became coral, white as lace work. The deep green eye filmed over, grew white and fell, rolling like a great pearl to Wharton's feet. And he realized that his imagination had created the entire thing, that Summer had reached into his mind and concocted it out of all the debris in there, and he laughed, because for a moment he felt as if everything in the world could be changed, everything could be new and rich and strange.

Soft and delicate as the secret words of the song, a drum began to beat.

Piers stopped singing. The cave was silent, except for a fading echo, a sound like the wash of the sea.

Wharton stared at the rubble and scattered boulders. Finally he said, 'How the hell did that fool us? It doesn't even look like a monster.'

'Not now it doesn't.' Satisfied, Piers turned, dusting his hands. 'Whoopee. I haven't done that for quite a while.' He set off for the cave mouth. 'I am so *wasted* in that kitchen. It's time His Excellency Mr Oberon Venn was reminded of that.'

Wharton followed. He was deeply impressed, but there was something that niggled him. Then he realized. The soft beat of the drum was coming from the entrance to the cave.

'What's that?'

'One way to find out.' Piers marched towards the sound.

Wharton hurried after him. This newly bold Piers was slightly hard to get used to. Across the cave floor they ran, to a wide entrance, and as they came out into the darkness he saw night had fallen on the neolithic world, and over his head the stars were more breathtaking and brilliant than he had ever seen them before.

Dark landscape stretched, with not a light, not a glimmer. He saw the world when men were tiny in it, when they were insignificant and lost in it, invisible and silent.

Except for the soft beat of the drum.

'There.' Piers pointed.

For a moment Wharton saw nothing. Then, like a red spark, a pinpoint of fire flamed up, in the shelter of the rocks just below.

As they scrambled down they saw a figure standing waiting for them, and as Wharton came nearer he realized that this was no random assemblage of stones; that they had been selected, and shaped, and placed here, that this was a circle of monoliths.

He stepped into it, Piers behind him.

'So you came back, Jorjwarton.' The boy put down the small drum he had been beating, and stood. Even his superb calm seemed shaken with relief. 'I have to say, I did not expect it. I was making your death-song.'

Wharton shrugged, awkward. 'Well, it had nothing to do with me. It was him.'

The shaman peered behind him. 'Who? I see only your shadow.'

Wharton whirled; Piers was gone; there was only a darkness stretching out from his own heels, and then a tiny moth that came out of the dusk and settled on his lapel like a gilt brooch.

He said, 'Er . . . yes. Well, look here. The monster . . . well, there is no monster now. I've destroyed it. You're all safe.' He stood more upright, raising his head. 'Your people, your children. All safe.'

The boy nodded, his long dark hair swinging. He took off his sealskin coat and put it around Wharton's shoulders. He took off all the amulets around his neck and added them to Wharton's. Then, with a small flint knife he began to cut the ornaments of bone and shale from his hair.

Wharton stared, baffled. 'What are you doing?'

'These things are yours now.'

'Mine?'

The young man stepped back. His face was pale; the tattoos dark against his skin. He said 'There can only be one shaman in any tribe. You have done what I could not, so my life is yours now. My wife, my children. My power.'

With both hands he held out the flint knife.

Numb, Wharton took it.

The shaman knelt and bowed his head. 'Strike,' he said. 'Quickly. Drink from my dreams.'

Wharton stared down at him. For a moment his mind was a blank; then the overwhelming horror of what was being asked of him flooded in. He threw the knife down,

256

grabbed the boy's arm roughly and yanked him to his feet. He was furious.

'What do you think I am! There is no way I would ever . . . Good grief!' He took a breath, trying to get calm. 'We're not bloody savages, I thought you said?'

The shaman watched him. 'You have different ways.'

'Yes I bloody do.' Wharton thrust the knife back. 'Keep your wife and children. Keep your power. All I want is to get home. Where's the mirror?'

The boy allowed himself a small smile, looking down at the knife in his hands. 'You do know, Jorjwarton, that I should now kill you? It is my right and my duty. But it is not my desire.'

Wharton went cold.

'I will show the way home. Because you are a strange man. You are strong and yet foolishly trusting, like a child. I'm younger than you, but I am older too.' His eyes flickered to the gilt moth 'And yes, I sense your familiar. A powerful spirit.' He turned. 'Follow me.'

He led Wharton out of the circle, to a place where three stones made a doorway. There, propped between them, was another, a black slab, smooth and familiar, though without its silver frame. It leaned like a door of darkness; as Wharton approached it he saw his distorted reflection, and in it he was tall and strong and handsome like a hero, and he frowned, because he knew it was mocking him.

He turned, and held out his hand.

The shaman took it, uncertain. 'May the Ancestors watch over you.'

'And you. Good luck.'

'Tell the changeling who has my wand,' the boy said softly, 'to keep it. It may be of benefit to all of you.'

'Thanks.' Wharton faced the mirror. He put his hands in his pocket and checked – the half-coin was there, safe. For a moment he frowned – after all, he was taking it back, and he had no way of knowing where Summer might be. But he had no choice.

He adjusted the bracelet.

Then without looking back, he strode into the mirror.

It opened to receive him. It was younger here, and raw, and eager, but its power was already huge, and he felt it open and devour him hungrily until the vacuum imploded and tore him into its heart.

The shaman waited.

When the mirror was quiet he touched its solid surface gently with the flat of his hand.

'Goodbye, Jorjwarton,' he said softly. 'I have learned much from you.'

Then he turned and walked down to his tribe.

The blast of the glass gun was a white fire but Janus did not disappear or shatter, or even fall.

Instead he stood unhurt and smiling at Venn.

Jake said gloomily, 'I tried to tell you. It won't work. He's not a Replicant. *This is the real Janus.*'

For a moment Venn seemed not to understand. It was Sarah who said, 'What? After all this time?'

Janus turned to her. 'Yes, Sarah. After all this time here we are again, truly face to face. I have missed you.' He glanced at Venn, then at Gideon, who stood by the empty casket.

'If you're mortal,' Venn growled, 'you can still die.'

'Not now,' Janus smiled. 'And not here.'

With one swift whipping motion he raised the black cane, but Jake was quicker; he kicked it aside and hurtled into the tyrant. Janus fell; as he did the weapon fired, missing Jake by inches, blasting a scorched arc through the ruined malachite mesh so that the whole web fell, crashing down on Sarah and Venn, snaring Gideon with sticky green threads.

Only Jake was outside. Before Janus could fire again Jake grabbed his arm; for a moment they wrestled furiously, face to face, while Venn's shouts of wrath rang in their ears.

Then Janus slipped. Jake yelled; the cane rattled to the floor.

Janus grabbed at it, *and dropped the Zeus coin.*

Sarah screamed, flung herself flat and scrabbled. Inside the web her fingers stretched but couldn't reach. Janus was on it instantly, but Venn whipped a tangle of web round his feet, and before he could kick himself clear Jake had the golden sherd in his hands and was running out of the room, down the stone corridor, racing down the stairs so fast he stumbled and fell and picked himself up and ran again. A bolt of flame scorched the doorway as he flung himself through it, out into the night.

He looked round, then raced into where the Wood should have been, dodging round splintered trees and the wreckage of bushes; diving into a hollow where the ground sank.

'Jake!' Janus stood on the top step of the Abbey, his voice hoarse with fury. 'Jake, listen to me. Bring it back. NOW. Bring it back or I kill all of them. All of them, starting with Sarah.'

Gasping for breath, Jake crouched over the pain in his side.

His hand clutched the gold coin; he felt its hidden

hum tingle his palm.

What should he do? He couldn't leave them there! And yet, with this half of the coin, joined to the other all this nightmare of the End World could never have been.

He took a breath, raised his head.

Janus was a small shadow in the darkness. 'You must know you have no choice. You won't leave them to die. You couldn't leave James Arnold, and you didn't even know him.'

There must be some way out of here. If he could just find some cover.

Jake edged sideways.

The hollow gave way.

And he fell straight into the Summerland.

CHAPTER NINETEEN

He took the purple berries,
The webs of spiderkind.
He made a drink of darkest dye
  And held it in his hand.

'I will not let you bind me.
Nor I your lover be.
Through death's strange silver doorway
  You will not follow me.'
        Ballad of Lord Winter and Lady Summer

Maskelyne stood before the mirror and spoke quietly to it.

As she listened, in the dark of the attic, Rebecca's skin prickled. Behind her, David made soft crooning noises to the baby, letting Lorenzo suck at his fingers.

They had twenty-six minutes to start Operation Leah.

Maskelyne said, 'I know you can hear me.'

The black glass faced him, empty of reflections.

'You've always heard me, since I found you, millennia ago. Do you remember that? I found you and I awoke you, and all through the centuries I guarded you and lost you and finally I flung myself into you. I *journeyed* for untold years through your heart. You and I were the same then. We are the same now. We are one.'

He talked to it like a lover.

Rebecca set her teeth and tried not to be so stupid. They were desperate and he needed to do this. She flicked a glance at David, an anxious shadow in the moon-striped room. Outside, the storm howled; thunder rattled the casement.

Maskelyne moved his hands to the silver frame. Carefully he touched the secret letters. Then he spoke in a language she didn't even recognize, and as if in reply the surface of the glass gave the slightest, softest ripple.

The wooden bird flew down on to Rebecca's shoulder and murmured in her ear. 'Oh my. Is this even safe?'

She wondered that herself, because the cats were fleeing, diving under benches and furniture.

Lightning flickered, and she flinched.

Danger.

She felt it like a sweat on her spine.

Suddenly she couldn't stand this; she reached out and caught Maskelyne's arm, and immediately snatched her fingers away again with a gasp, because the dark energies of the mirror were coursing through him, and for a moment she had thought he was only the outline of a man, a silhouette of space, scattered with galaxies and stars.

'Stop this,' she breathed.

As if she had not spoken, Maskelyne went on. 'We need you to help us. We need you. You must know I will never let them destroy you. I promise you that. We will be together, you and I. For ever. I promise you that.'

Tears blinded her. Through them she saw the mirror tremble, felt the build-up, the crackle in the air.

Maskelyne turned. 'Get back!' he hissed, but even before he'd got the words out the Chronoptika opened; it imploded with the terrible sucking vacuum of the *journey*.

A figure strode through.

'Jake!' David cried, but already Rebecca could see it wasn't Jake, because the mirror was cold and hard and still, and Wharton was standing there.

He was incredibly dirty, his clothes muddy, his hair tousled. Bones and carved stones hung from grimy strings round his neck. He carried a flint-tipped stick, and as soon as he saw where he was he flung it on to the floor, gave a great whoop of joy and went and sank into the nearest armchair.

'I can't tell you,' he said, 'how good it is to see you all!'

David said, 'You've been gone less than an hour . . .' Then he stopped, staring.

A small gilt moth had fluttered from Wharton's lapel to the bench. It transformed into a small, slim being in a silvery suit, his hair shining, his earring a long diamond.

It said, 'I turn my back for five minutes and this is what happens. Complete and utter chaos.'

Maskelyne smiled.

David stared.

The baby howled.

Piers folded his arms. 'Let's get this show on the road.' He shook his head, and winked at Rebecca. 'You mortals. Thick, or what?'

Jake had been in the Summerland before, but the chaos and confusion of it shocked him every time. Already he had passed through an icy river ravine and a ruined fairground, its Ghost Train stark and empty against a rainy sky. He had walked down a long canal towpath into a 1960s schoolroom where the children chanted their times tables with robotic monotony, arms folded on graffitied desks, and only a small fair-haired girl in the back row had noticed him walk in through one wall, and out through another.

Now he stood in the corridor of a French Riviera hotel, where guests followed a porter carrying a pile of suitcases. Out of the window he glimpsed a sunny seafront – it made him think of Janus and the small boy he once had been. He frowned. The tyrant was right. There was no way he could go back and let the child drown, see him choke and scrabble under the waves. Even knowing what he knew. He could never go through with it.

He took out the half-coin.

It was cold on his palm.

So this was the other half, the missing half, and he was holding it! The thought made him dizzy. Now they had both, because Maskelyne had the right side safe and hidden. They finally had the means to break the power of the Chronoptika, if they chose.

He tucked the fragment safely into his inside pocket, ran quickly to the end of the corridor, opened a door and found himself in a dark street.

Trees clustered overhead; he stood on the pavement outside a row of substantial Victorian villas, and, with a shock of recognition, knew at once where he was.

Fascinated, he walked along the street until he found Symmes's house. Then he went up and gripped the black railings of the area and paused, looking in.

The study window was lit. Inside, standing by the fireplace and obviously talking importantly and at length, he saw the bald, portly figure of John Harcourt Symmes, the man who had once stolen the mirror; whose diary had given them the knowledge of how to use it.

Symmes was lecturing someone. He gestured extravagantly, his red velvet waistcoat bright in the firelight.

And there – Jake could just see it, sticking out from the edge of the sofa – was a small leg, and a foot. A girl's foot, in a dark stocking with an old slipper on it, slightly too big and falling off.

Moll.

Moll as he had first known her.

For a moment all he wanted was to see her, to edge forward and make that cheeky pert face turn to him, to wave, to shout, 'Moll! It's me! It's Jake!'

But Symmes, as if he caught some prying shadow through the firelit reflections, gave a frown of annoyance and came and drew the curtains, and Jake stood alone on the pavement.

He stood, considering. The mirror was in that house.

He could just knock, and Moll would come running; she'd scream in delight. But she would have told him, if he'd ever done that, so he couldn't have, could he?

Confused, he stepped back.

Against a great grey standing stone.

With that simple step everything changed. He was on a grassy hilltop, the stone high beside him. Fires were burning and all around him a wild, eerie party was going on.

The wind from the sea made him shiver; the moon flickered through fleeting clouds showing bare downland, a domed hill of dark grass.

He took one look at the people and ducked behind the stone with a gasp of dismay.

The Shee were dancing. Elegant and strange their music rang out, manic fiddles, whispering pipes. They were dressed as if for some ancient hunt: the females with top hats and veiled faces, the males wearing tail-coats of russet and tissue of gold, the ripe richness of autumn. He glimpsed their feet, light and free, their long fingers, the bright mischief of their eyes, felt their mounting desire of the chase like an electric charge in the air. Tethered all round the hill, horses waited; impatient and proud, shaking their tangled manes and pawing the air. There were hounds too, white lithe beasts with red eyes like points of fire, prowling and baying, eager for blood.

Jake crouched lower.

Summer was in the middle of the host. She was swinging round and round on the arms of a dozen male Shee, laughing with delight.

And she was wearing the other half of the coin.

It was displayed for all to see on a ribbon round her neck; as she danced and laughed the gold of it flashed and swung – jagged, unmistakeable.

Jake let out a breath, almost a moan, of disbelief.

How had she got that! Surely Maskelyne had had it safe! Suddenly he felt a flicker of panic. How long had he been lost in the future? *What had been going on since he left?*

One thing was clear: he had to get that half of the coin too. Though if he even stepped out of hiding they would be on him like flies and he would never stand a chance of getting away.

Unless . . . He glanced round.

The horses.

It was dangerous. But he had no choice at all.

He nodded to himself, braced himself, stood up. Then he flung himself into the dance.

* * *

Janus had forced them to their feet and outside, all three still bound with malachite threads, down the steps and out to the ruin of the Wood.

The night was totally still.

'Well,' Venn said into the silence. 'Are you actually going to do it? Kill all of us, starting with Sarah?'

He was the one who had recovered first from the shock of Jake's vanishing, his whiplash scorn almost admiring.

Sarah glanced at Gideon. The changeling shrugged. 'Jake's in the Summerland,' he whispered.

Janus seemed the most surprised of all. He stood with the weapon pointed at them, and even through the tangled mesh that held her arms and feet Sarah could see his astonishment, his devastation.

But he recovered fast. He said, 'You think too much of yourself, Venn. None of you matter now. Only Jake does.'

'You can't find him.' Venn struggled, hands working restlessly at the mesh. 'You're in trouble. You haven't time to go back to the city and anyway you know the mirror is far too unstable to use.'

'I have all the time in the world.'

'Not any more,' Sarah said quietly. She stood still, not attempting to escape. 'You're just as trapped as we are. You're stuck here at the end of time and Jake has the coin. That means we have both of them now. All he needs to do is reunite them and what you've done to the world never even happened.'

Janus flicked a venomous look at her. 'He won't, Sarah. Because that would mean losing Leah. And Venn would never forgive him.'

She looked at Venn. He was silent, and grim.

'So you see, I'm not too worried.' Janus stepped back, the coppery darkness glinting on the edge of the lenses that hid his eyes. 'And I have a plan. I could use the mirror again. I could just enter it and go back to some earlier time and trigger the black hole. Why should I care? I would be safe.'

They stared at him in cold dread. Sarah swallowed; her mouth was dry with terror. Carefully she said, 'You could. But I think you have a better idea.'

He laughed. 'How you know me! All those years you lived in my Lab, Sarah! You were always one of the brightest of my children.'

'*I'm not one of your children.* My parents . . .'

'Are lost,' he said. 'Lost like all those who opposed me.'

It was a stab so painful she could not even think about it. She had to push it away and not let him see her flinch, not let Venn or Gideon see.

271

But maybe Gideon, with his Shee-sharp eyes, noticed something after all, because his voice was cool with curiosity. 'How will you find Jake? He's in the Summerland. You'd never dare.'

He stopped.

Janus was smiling at Venn. 'No? You see, there is one person left who can help me. She can help me and herself, at the same time. We have always circled each other warily. Now, at last, we should join forces.'

Venn snorted a laugh. 'You mean—'

'I *mean* to make alliance with Lady Summer. Together, who could stop us?' Janus turned, and looked at the hollow where Jake had fallen.

'You can't.' Gideon moved, nervous. 'She doesn't have allies.'

'Neither do I.' Janus probed the ground cautiously with his cane, until the end of it seemed to shimmer and warp. 'Well, not until now. So, this is one of those places where the slanted worlds meet ours. It will be so interesting to travel there.'

He glanced back at them.

'Goodbye, Sarah. I doubt we'll meet again. And you, Venn. I am so sorry you'll never get to ease your guilt over Leah's death. But you do know, don't you, that you don't really want her back. Your need is purely selfish; all you want is your peace of mind. And I'm afraid that's gone for ever.'

He turned, and walked into the hollow.

They saw how he vanished, quite abruptly, as if through some invisible door.

CHAPTER TWENTY

The horses and dark beings are shadows on the moon. Flee, pray, guard your soul.

Chronicle of Wintercombe

'D minus fifteen,' Maskelyne muttered.

'Presence of mirror?'

'Confirmed.'

'Local conditions?'

'Within parameters.'

'Power?'

'Ninety-five per cent.'

Piers and Maskelyne's voices murmured in a strange harmony, Rebecca thought. Like a song. She watched Piers curiously, because he had been so decisive, had made the cables curl and reconnect through his hands, had repaired the terrible damage with an impatient, scornful magic.

He was changed, she thought.

All the cats knew it. They rubbed and purred against his legs, a furry crowd of joy.

The Shee bird sang bright whistling songs to itself on the rafters, its bright eye watching everything.

David said, 'Get changed.' He handed Rebecca a uniform; she stared at it.

'Me? But . . .'

'I can't ask George to go, not again. The others need to be here.'

She looked at Wharton, sitting with the baby in one arm and a bottle in the other. He shrugged, or tried to. 'Sorry, Becky.'

'A bit of a comedown for a hero,' she said.

'Believe me, I'll get over it.' He wiped a white drip from Lorenzo's chin with a tissue. 'I'm not cut out for bloody knighthood.'

She changed quickly into the neat dark uniform, with POLIZIA on the back in white letters, then tied her hair back firmly, wondering how many Italian policewomen were redheads. And she didn't know a word of the language. Jake did, of course. She remembered how he had spoken it in Florence, in that terrible plague-ridden city. Was Jake in a place as bad as that, in that unknown future?

She wished he was back, and Sarah too.

She slipped on the cap.

David's uniform had three stripes on the sleeve; his cap was peaked.

They looked at each other.

'Flattering,' he murmured.

She glanced at Maskelyne, but he didn't look up. He was engrossed in the mirror, in the cables Piers had rigged.

'Right.' David turned to Wharton. 'George, this is it. Culmination of all our work. Operation Leah. I just wish Venn was here to see it.'

Outside, the night flickered, thunder rolled, the window flying open with a crash that startled them all.

Rebecca went and grabbed the handle; cold rain slashed her face, and for a moment it felt like sharp-nailed, thin fingers; she ducked back quickly, slamming the casement.

The wind screamed round the house.

'OK.' Piers straightened. 'We're ready.'

David held out his hand; Rebecca took it, and the silver bracelet gleamed, its amber stone shimmering.

'We're putting you in place as near as we can; hopefully within two kilometres from the Mirror, in that warehouse in Amalfi. If the timing's right it will give you one hour exactly to get the diversion in place.'

David frowned. 'Cutting it fine, Piers.'

'Best we can do.' The small man ushered them towards the mirror, where it leaned, shadow-dark, against the wall. 'I suppose I don't have to remind you that you have the last bracelet. If anything goes wrong no one can come after you.'

'No. You don't.'

Wharton laid the baby down, and came over. 'You'll both be fine. Couldn't have finer operators.'

'Thanks, George.'

Maskelyne stood. He reached out and took Rebecca's hand. 'Good luck.'

She nodded. 'See you soon.'

She wanted to say more, so much more, but it was awkward with the others here. He let her fingers go, and she dropped her hand to her side, and saw in the mirror's sly reflection how she stood alone, how he wasn't even there by her side. Annoyed, despising herself, she turned away.

David said, 'Let's go.'

He pulled her forward. She took a breath and walked boldly into the darkness, and it filled her stomach and her lips and her eyes, and it was a roaring, sucking emptiness like some unending unhappiness at the heart of the world.

It was eternity, and it would never be filled.

Jake was flung from hand to hand. The dance was ferocious, he had no idea of the steps, but that didn't seem to matter. Breathless, aching, he was whirled and bumped; thin hands grabbed him and spun him. The music was everywhere, a pounding of drums, the eerie wail of pipes, and already it had got into his blood like an itch and he realized his heart was thudding too fast and his pulse racing; he was crushed under the arms of the Shee and their faces – pale and bright and cold – were all around him.

He snatched a look through the crowd.

Summer was close; then she whirled away with a giggle of laughter.

He tried to work his way towards her, ducking under arms, circling thin bodies. Beautiful faces and grotesque masks stared at him; the swish of taffeta and tail-coat, flounces and fingers. He felt velvet and lace, smelled the sharp notes of lavender and lemon and rose. The shimmer of lizard skin touched him, the gloss of starling feathers.

He twisted, took a few decorous steps in and out of a small group, turned on his heel, and there she was.

Within reach.

He had to be fast. His hand shot out; he grabbed the coin, tugged it hard. The thin ribbon snapped, and he ran.

Summer put both hands to her neck and gave a scream of absolute wrath that sheared through the music and froze every dancer in mid-step. Heads turned. Eyes slid.

'There's a mortal here!' Her voice was acrid with hatred. 'Find him! NOW!'

The dance split apart like a burst of panicking sparrows when a hawk falls, like angry bees from a hive. They swarmed over the smooth darkness of the hilltop until a shrill whinny made every head turn.

Jake had leaped on to the nearest horse. It went wild, rearing and kicking; even as he hung on and grabbed for the jewelled reins it was galloping, fleet and furious as the wind over the stormy down.

Head down, breathless, he glanced back.

The Shee were a dark whirlwind. He heard cries and strange calls, saw birds rise from the host, hounds streak after him like arrows.

Gasping, he turned, just as the Shee horse jumped a hedge and clattered down into a lane, chalky white in the fleeting moonlight. Jake grabbed in panic. Under him the horse felt alien; its skin cool, its mane white and flowing. One red eye flicked malice back at him.

He fought to control it but it ran faster. He risked working his hand free and was about to plunge the stolen coin into his pocket when the realization of the appalling risk he was taking turned him cold.

He had both halves of the coin!

It was so terrifying that he shouted aloud, snatched his hand back out. Which pocket was the right side in? Because if he put them together, if they joined, the mirror would be destroyed right now, and he would never see his father or Venn or Sarah or Wharton ever again.

He had to think!

Crouching low, he felt with his fingers until he found the right-hand side, the coin Janus had dropped – yes, there it was deep inside the grey jacket.

He shoved the other half deep in his trouser pocket.

As he rode, the terror of it came home to him. Both halves of the coin! And between them, like a barrier, his own body. He was all that separated them from rejoining, from fitting perfectly together, becoming the single piece of gold they once had been.

He felt as if pain was shooting through him. As if each broken fragment of the ancient god, its single eye, its wide, jagged mouth, was screaming out to the other through his blood and bones and veins.

The horse plunged downhill. He yelled, holding

desperately on. Silver hooves slid through rubble.

Behind, like a shadow flowing over the land, dark and intent, came the host of the air.

The downland fell away into a deep combe of smooth turf. There was no cover and nowhere to hide; Jake urged the horse on; it made a laughing whinny that terrified him, and then he was crashing through a thin copse of gorse and out again on to the white grass, aching with fear.

The hounds bayed with deep chesty hunger; the Shee were close now. Risking a glance back he saw other things too, flying shapes, and things that ran and even slithered, deep in the mass of bodies.

Then the horse came to a stop so suddenly Jake crashed right off.

He picked himself up, breathless.

A fast stream of water ran in front of them, a raging torrent in the moonlit night.

Jake grabbed the rein, dragged the creature forward. 'What's the matter with you. It's nothing. Come on, stupid!'

The horse flickered its silver ears, tossed its mane. It gave him a wild defiant look from its scarlet eye.

And he remembered what Gideon had told him once, that the Shee would not cross running water.

He swore, abandoned the horse and plunged into the stream, scrambling through, splashing deep, slithering on submerged stones; he climbed up the bank on the other side, dived behind a tree and crouched, aching.

The Shee came to the riverbank. There was a moment of milling horses, confusion, shouting, fury. Then Summer forced her way to the front. She was wearing a red riding habit, a jacket, a veiled top hat. Her pure white horse swished its tail restlessly. She stared at the stream in fury, then snapped, 'Upstream. Quickly!'

She turned the horse's head, but a voice said, 'Maybe we should talk first, Queen of the Wood.'

Jake's heart almost stopped.

Summer's eyes glittered under the fine black veil. 'Well, well.' She drew rein and sat calmly, looking into the darkness. 'So the tyrant of the End World is back.'

Janus came out of the shadows. He gazed at the hunt with intense curiosity. 'So this is the famous and terrifying wild hunt. Impressive. But stopped in its tracks by a trickle of water?'

Summer paled. She shook her head, a curt, suppressed gesture, her lips pressed tight. 'Don't anger me, mortal. I assure you I could turn you into an ant and stamp on you with the greatest of pleasure.'

Janus didn't move. He looked up at her through his

blue lenses. 'I think not, Lady. Because you and I, we have the same aim now, and it's time we worked together. Against Venn, against all of them.'

'Why should I . . . ?'

He interrupted her, calmly. 'Because they have robbed both of us. And the boy has both halves of the coin.'

Jake took a breath of dismay.

Summer stared at the small man in the blue spectacles for a long moment. Then she swung down from the horse and stood, slim in her flowing dress.

She smiled with her perfect red lips. 'Let's talk,' she said.

The mirror was silent.

'That's it,' Piers said. 'They're through. We've done all we can. It's up to them now.'

As if in answer the wind howled round the house. Wharton said, 'Are we safe here?'

Piers shrugged. 'It's Halloween. The hunt will be dragging some poor half-dead mortal through bush and briar. They'll have other things on their minds. But still …' He turned to the cats. 'Primo, Secundus – the cloister. Tertio, Quintus – on the roof, and make sure you keep flat. The rest of you patrol the lower floors. I want to know the state of the flooding in the cellars and how the defences are looking. Move yourselves.'

The cats gave him an identical glance of adoration and paraded out. Restless, the wind unnerving him, Wharton prowled. 'What can I do?'

'Keep everything crossed.' Piers folded his arms, but in that instant the mirror crackled, a great snap of energy.

Wharton swore; even Maskelyne stepped back.

Because within the silver frame there was no longer black glass, but a blue sky, a hot, shimmering empty road, spiky trees of some unknown species.

'Where the hell is that?' Wharton breathed.

Piers' eyes were wide. 'That's it! The road in Italy. The road where Leah dies.'

At that instant, deep in the Summerland Venn stopped dead, as if something had touched him.

Sarah, glad of the rest, doubled over, hands on hips, taking deep breaths.

As soon as they had struggled out of the mesh they had followed Janus, running through at least ten of the slanted, colliding worlds, each different; now she realized they were on a run-down seaside pier in a slot arcade full of gambling machines that slid heaps of coins back and forth inside grubby glass cases.

Venn said, 'It's now!'

'What?'

'Sarah, it's begun. *I have to get to Leah.*'

She had never seen him so agitated. 'Have they?'

'I can feel it! The hot road, the car. The way she screamed. Maskelyne and David must have the plan under way. I have to get there!'

He slammed one of the machines in fury. The pier shuddered, as if a great wave had hit it.

'How can you know?' Sarah said.

Venn glanced down at the bracelet on his wrist; the amber stone was shimmering strangely. 'Maybe it's the Shee-blood of the Venns.' He turned. 'Gideon, listen to me. Find Jake before Summer does. I have to get to Leah.'

Gideon said, 'Yes, but in all these worlds, there's no logic here, no way of knowing where you'll end up.'

Venn shrugged. 'Remember what Maskelyne told David once? That love is the only thing stronger than time? Well, now we'll see.' He faced Sarah, and she saw his agitation.

'Are you coming?' he said. 'If I save her, then you can have the mirror. It will all be over.'

She looked at him a long moment, his blue eyes cold and fierce, and wondered how long she could keep what she knew from him. 'How do I know you'll let me?'

'Trust me, Sarah. I've seen the future. It was enough.'

He turned away.

With one dark glance at Gideon, she followed him, out of the door, along the pier, into a drifting sea-mist.

When they were gone, and he knew he was alone, Gideon walked over to the nearest slot machine, where a tottering pile of coins balanced on the metal edge inside the glass.

Curious, he put out a thin finger and touched it, very gently.

The pile collapsed, a great slither and rattle of brass pennies and halfpennies falling through the slot, cascading and rolling on the wooden floor.

'So who wins?' he murmured. 'And who loses everything, for ever?'

In the glass his face was reflected. His own eyes were Shee-bright. They scared him.

We are such stuff
As dreams are made on; and our little life
is rounded with a sleep

CHAPTER TWENTY-ONE

I had never thought Venn the sort of man who would marry. He would only have chosen an extraordinary woman, and Leah was certainly that. I only met her once, and briefly, but I saw at once that she was a match for him.

Mostly I remember how she laughed at him, and how he let her.

Jean Lamartine, *The Strange Life of Oberon Venn*

'Someone's coming.' David ducked back into a doorway.

Rebecca slid into the shade of the building.

It was hot here; the sky was pure blue. The park smelled sweetly; there were neat beds of scented roses, all gold and red, and purple bougainvillea climbing to the terracotta roofs.

When the man with the dog had ambled by, giving

them no more than an idle glance, the street was empty. David stepped out. 'That lock-up. Walk slowly.'

Behind her sunglasses, Rebecca watched the Italian street. It sloped downwards towards the sea, a glint on the horizon, and the buildings shimmered in the heat-haze of early afternoon. The lock-up was small and whitewashed, insignificant among the houses and shuttered shops. David had a key; he pulled it out and unlocked the padlock, and they slipped quickly inside.

The darkness smelled of petrol; there was no window, so he snapped on the light.

She saw a car, small, white, ordinary, slightly dusty. It wasn't a police car. David went over and lifted the lid of the boot; coming behind him she saw the space was crammed with stuff – high-vis tape, cones, plastic barriers, road signs reading DEVIAZIONE.

'What does that mean?'

'Diversion.' David checked the equipment carefully. 'The plan is very simple, like all the best plans. We drive out there, park up in a lay-by and wait. Exactly five minutes before Venn and Leah's car is due we get out and set all this stuff up, closing the coast road to all traffic. They arrive, see it, back up, go another way.' He looked at her. 'No accident. No death. Time goes on, but Leah is alive and they never know what might have happened.'

Rebecca shook her head. 'That's all?'

'Why not?'

'It just seems . . . too easy.'

David laughed, a little bitterly. 'That's how life is, Becky. Everything is balanced on a knife-edge. We think we're so secure, don't we, that everything will always go on just like this, but all it takes is a second's indecision, a mistake, a swerve on the wrong road, to wipe a lifetime away. There are mere seconds and inches between normality and disaster. If all my *journeying* has taught me anything it's that safety doesn't really exist.'

'But—' Rebecca put her hands down and leaned on the cold metal of the car bonnet. 'Think about this. You say nothing will change except her survival, but surely the truth is nothing will be the same. If Leah lives, Venn will never need the mirror – so he'll never own it. I won't know him, or you, or Jake. Or maybe even Maskelyne.' Her heart chilled at the thought. 'None of this stuff with the mirror will have happened. So then how can . . . well, how can we have saved Leah then?'

The unending paradox bewildered her.

David shrugged. 'Don't ask me. Jake told me Summer once laughed at a question like that. Gideon says that for the Shee time is just now, there is nothing else. Even in nature the seasons are circles, things are born and live and die. Maskelyne thinks there are infinite universes, each subtly different, like reflections in the mirror, and we might cross from one to another. Maybe it's just us humans that have this weird idea of time as a single line stretching into the future. Maybe it's all wrong.'

'Yes, but Sarah's argument was that the mirror becomes world-famous after Venn uses it to save his wife. That's why Janus gets hold of it, and starts his reign of terror. But . . . if . . . I mean . . . if Leah never dies, that can't be true. Can it?'

He stared at her, startled. 'No. I suppose.'

For a moment they were silent, looking at each other. Then David shrugged, stubborn. 'God . . . Look, I don't even pretend to understand any of this. Logic is useless. All I know is Leah can be saved, and we're the only ones who can do it. And I promised Venn that I would.'

Rebecca nodded. 'So we go ahead?'

'We go ahead.'

He opened the car and they slid in, David in the driving seat. He handed her a map. 'Pre sat-nav, I'm afraid. How are we doing for time?'

She looked at her watch, changed to local time from the clock outside the town hall.

'One forty-five.'

He nodded. 'Venn thinks the accident was about

three thirty. The witness statements agreed.'

'Is it far, this coast road?'

He started the car, and began backing out. 'Not if we don't get lost,' he said.

Summer stood gracefully at ease on the grass. Behind the veil her face was scornful. 'Do you know, tyrant,' she said, considering, 'for a mortal of such power, you are really very small and . . . dull.'

Janus smiled, cold. He said, 'I'm afraid I can't do anything about that. But what I told you was true.'

'That Jake has both halves of the coin? Impossible.'

'I assure you. He has mine. And now he has yours.'

She turned her head and gazed over the stream, straight at the cluster of trees where Jake had flung himself. 'So you're telling me he could destroy the obsidian mirror at any moment. How wonderful.'

'He could. But he won't. You know that. It's the last thing he wants to happen. But you, Lady, you could. You could do what you've wanted to do since Venn made his crazy plan in the first place.'

Her beautiful, sceptical eyes slid to him. 'And you wouldn't care if I did?'

Janus shrugged. Jake saw how he stepped forward, leaning on the dark cane. 'My time is over. Even as a *journeyman*, there is only so much time a mortal can steal, only so long one lifetime can last. In our long contest it seems time will defeat even me. To be blunt, I am dying. Like everything in all my world I am coming to an end.'

Summer stared in instant fascination. 'Really! How do you know?'

Some of the Shee had dismounted. They clustered around Janus, tall and silver-haired and interested. One reached out and touched his lank hair.

Jake edged his elbows into the soft soil and wriggled forward, feeling the jagged edge of the coin in his pocket stab him.

Janus seemed amused. 'How death draws you! Like bees to honey. Almost as if you had the same greed for it.'

Summer made a soft snort of derision. She reached out with her red fingertips and carelessly tinkled the medals pinned to his chest. 'Does it hurt, mortal?'

'Not yet. But it will.'

'How wonderful.'

He smiled, sourly. 'Forgive me if I don't quite see it that way.'

'And so you want to join our Wild Hunt?' Summer laughed, softly. 'It's an interesting last request. No mortal has ever asked that of me before. What can you offer, for the bother of taking you along? After all, we can tear the boy to tiny shreds quite easily on our own, and after what you've told me I certainly intend to.'

Janus shrugged. He seemed remarkably at ease, Jake thought, in all that whispering crowd of silvery beings. 'What can I offer you? What indeed is there that the Shee don't already have? Only knowledge, and I've already made you a gift of that.' He swept his cane irritably and the prying crowd of Shee leaped back. 'Bring me a horse and let me ride.' He raised his head and gazed across the stream, and Jake caught his breath, because Janus was looking straight at him, the blue lenses tilted in the moonlight, as if the words he spoke were not for the Shee now, but for Jake. 'My life has been longer than any man's but it's over. Once I imagined a great realm, a brave new world, where time would have no power, where I would rule free from its tyranny, because time is the tyrant, not me. But all I see now is my failure. Destruction and ruin, and yes, I made it like this; my obsession with the mirror caused this to be. You wouldn't understand, Lady, if I talked now about regret. Or shame, even. Those are just words to you. Jake understands though. Jake knows it was his own trespass through time that created me.'

Summer was listening avidly. 'You mortals,' she said, fascinated, 'are so . . . *intense*.'

Janus smiled at Jake, as if he could see him under the

brambles. 'Perhaps we are.' He turned. 'My question stands. Will you let me see the destruction of the mirror before I die?'

Summer hummed. Then she clicked her fingers. The Shee remounted, hurriedly.

'I'm not sure if I believe a word you say.' Summer stepped on a male Shee's back and swung herself lightly up into the saddle. 'But I can't resist seeing your face when I join those two gold fragments. If only Venn could be there too.' She pointed at a Shee in a starling-green satin coat. 'You there! Get the mortal a horse. We'll go upstream and cross at the spring. And then, tyrant from the World's End, you'll see something no mortal has seen and lived to tell of it. You'll see the host of the air in all its terrifying power.'

Jake swore silently.

He began to wriggle furiously back, panic flooding him. He shouldn't be here, he should be running for his life, before they found him and . . .

Then he thought, *No. Wait! Think!*

Janus had climbed on to the horse with surprising suppleness and turned its graceful head. As the host streamed after Summer he paused, looking over to where Jake was.

'Guard my coin, Jake,' he whispered. 'It's all I want

from you now.'

Then a Shee hand dragged at his bridle, and they forced him to gallop away.

Jake waited till they were over the brow of the hill then leaped up and ran. His plan was cunning and he was proud of it. Back across the stream again for one thing, that would slow them even more.

He splashed over and ran easily into the tangle of wood, then climbed over a field gate and jogged across a sloping meadow into a small tight lane between high hedges. It ran steeply down, its pebbles loose and slippery, and they rattled noisily under his feet, setting off an avalanche of dirt.

The moon came out, showing him an expanse of dark and woldy countryside. He slowed and took a breath of delight, because far off in the darkness there were tiny points of electric lights in isolated cottages, and to the west the orange glow of a hidden village with its streetlamps.

So he wasn't in some remote past. That was good! With luck he might even be back in his own time.

He loped down the track until it turned a corner towards a scatter of farm buildings. They were just barns, bulky and unlit, and he was about to pass them when he heard a noise in the darkness of the lane behind that made him stop and turn.

A strange, almost crisp, rustle.

The sky was dark; a high wind gusted. One edge of the moon appeared like a brilliant sliver and then was gone again, the clouds around it pale and torn. Puddles near his feet reflected silver light.

Jake waited, leaning one hand on the wall. His breathing was short, uneasy.

Something small and dark flashed past him. He jerked back.

Bats?

And yet – that noise—

It was a soft deep murmur, a tremor in the wet ground. Like the pounding of hooves.

He raised his head, and saw, out of the canopy of the Wood, dark as a tempest of leaves, the Shee host were riding, closer than a nightmare. And yet something was wrong – they were oddly above him, and like a thousand tiny stars in the night their eyes were all turned on him. As Jake backed in despair he knew no running water would stop them this time, because the horses and hounds galloped in the sky, as if on some invisible road metres above the dark hill, a wild, oncoming mass.

He turned, and ran furiously for the nearest barn, but

never even got near it; a few steps were all he managed, and then something snatched at his coat, and he yelled and was dragged up by his collar, lifted into the dark, up and up, kicking and struggling, higher and higher until the ground was gone far below and he was sick and dizzy and from somewhere very close Summer's laughter was a cold delight, like a blade in his heart.

Venn said, 'This way.'

He walked to the end of the foggy pier, opened a door and stepped through. Sarah followed him. What she saw terrified her.

A wide blue bay of the sea, its waters glittering to the horizon. White yachts moved leisurely across its waves; a ferry churned towards a distant misty island. Far across, on the mainland, a dormant volcano rose like a shimmering mirage, so faint in the heat it might almost be a watercolour painted on the sky.

She stepped out.

They were on the verandah of some grand hotel. Two sunloungers faced each other; one had a purple jacket draped across the back of it. On the table was a half-empty wineglass.

'Sarah.' Venn stared round. 'This is it! This is the hotel room we had on that trip!' He caught up the jacket and held it to his face, breathing in the perfume. *'This is Leah's, Sarah!'*

Sarah's heart missed a beat. She had to stop this.

'Wait a minute. We need to be sure.' She stepped back into the room.

An Italian newspaper lay on the dressing-table; she turned it quickly. 'What was the date? The date of the accident.'

'28th October.' He was behind her; he snatched the paper up. She didn't have to ask; she could see by the sudden flash of triumph in his face that the date on the newspaper was the same.

'This might not be today's,' she said, hating herself.

With a hiss of impatience he threw it down, went to the TV and switched it on. A flood of voices came out; he flicked to a news channel and they saw the calendar behind the news desk.

28th October.

Venn shook his head in awe. 'It seems the scarred man was right after all. Maybe there is something stronger than time.' He glanced at the clock on the TV. 'We're early. Two hours early . . . I think . . . yes, I remember. I'm at the bank down the street. Leah, think of it, Sarah! Leah is outside in a café in the piazza! I remember she complained about waiting for me for so long. I could go out there now . . . *Right now, and—*'

He took two paces, but Sarah was quicker. She dived in front of him and stood with her back to the door. Groping behind her with one hand she snicked the lock across.

'No,' she said, breathless. 'No. You can't.'

'Don't you understand? I could see her. Talk to her.'

'That wouldn't be wise.'

Venn's eyes were ice-cold. 'Sarah, get out of my way.'

'I'm not moving.' She licked dry lips. This was her own fault, she should have done this before, but the time had come and there was no way she could put it off any more.

'There's something I haven't told you,' she said, quietly. 'And I'm afraid it's something bad.'

CHAPTER TWENTY-TWO

It is not wise for a mortal man to gaze too long into the darkness. He comes to see strange shapes and cold imaginings.

He comes to doubt all that he once held true.

Alas, I have gazed too long. Even mine owne face is lost to me now.

The Scrutiny of Secrets by Mortimer Dee

The mirror showed them an empty road and the blue sea below it. Every now and again a car or lorry drove by, but traffic was light.

Finally Wharton said, 'They're all having a siesta.'

Piers nodded. 'Do we know the local time?'

They both looked at Maskelyne who muttered 'One fifty p.m.'

'No sign of David and Rebecca.'

'They'll be there.' Piers turned as the final cat came back. 'Well?'

The animal made a few careless mews. As he listened Wharton felt something small swoop down and land on his shoulder; he flicked at it but the Shee bird said, 'Hey. Don't dent my feathers.'

Wharton frowned. 'Are you still here?'

'Nowhere to go. Not with that lot kicking off out there.'

It tipped its head at the window. The night was a raging storm, the clouds ragged over the moon. Crashes of hail beat at the windows. Wharton grunted. He certainly would not have wanted to be out in it.

'Well, the house isn't at all secure,' Piers said, 'but there's nothing we can do about it. Too many broken windows and all the doors torn off.' He began to pace, a scurrying worry. 'Something's wrong, though – something more than that. I can feel it.'

Wharton looked at the animals. The marmoset had gone to ground under the blankets of the cradle; only its small nose peeped out. It was oddly silent and still. The cats, who had all come back and were sitting around the room, were stiff and uneasy. Their ears flicked at every wail of the wind.

'What about you?' he said to the bird.

The tiny bead eye was very close to his. 'Scared stiff,' it whispered. 'The Shee are out there and they're hunting. The thunder is their hooves and the lightning the flashes of their spears. It happens every year and it's wonderful. But only if you're with them.'

Wharton looked at Maskelyne. The dark man was face to face with the mirror, staring into its arid landscape. 'Where are you, Becky?' he was whispering.

Wharton went to the window; after a moment Piers joined him.

'What happens on the hunt, Piers?' he muttered.

Piers looked out at the moon. Small wild flecks sped across it. He laughed, a short mirthless bark. 'I told you. They hunt a mortal, and then they catch him, and he dies. If he's lucky.'

Jake wanted to scream.

He was high above the ground; below him shadows of hedges loomed up, trees rushed under him against the night. He dared not struggle, or the Shee horse might drop him; he felt its teeth tearing his coat, its hot stinking breath at his neck.

Then fine threads were flung and looped about him, a tangle of cobweb. The horse let him go, and now he did scream, plunging down head-first till the threads caught and held him, snagged in some dark tangle of power.

He wriggled over, looking up.

The Shee were above him. Their speed was terrible, the roar of the horses' hooves a storm on the wind. They cried out and sang in strange voices, and though it terrified him, the rush of it exhilarated him too, and he felt madness and fury spasm in his heart.

'Faster,' Summer cried, her voice clear above. 'Faster!'

Jake gasped. He saw a great landscape below him, a forest that spread for miles, and then suddenly the net dropped and he hit the canopy of branches with a crash that sent moths and bats up in a cloud about him.

'No!' he yelled. '*Wait!*'

But he was already among the treetops, dragged and torn through thin twigs, snagged and stabbed and scratched, tipped up, tumbled. He tried to protect his eyes, then thought of the coin fragments, but it was too much, there was no way of even breathing. A tree of huge size was before him, and seconds before he smashed into its trunk the Shee yanked him up and away, wild with laughter at his terror.

Jake fought to breathe. Head down, hands through the web, splayed, he saw the landscape far below. Beyond the forest was a town; the roofs of its houses loomed; a church spire stabbed up at him, a wind vane was torn away. Rain crashed down; in the streets people fled the storm. He saw the glint of a river, and as the Shee whooped and plunged towards it he knew what was coming, and gasped in air, barely filling his lungs before *splash!* he was deep underwater, in a streaming chamber of bubbles and foam, the moonlight blinding him in facets and broken slivers. He wanted to breathe, but couldn't; he wanted to open his mouth and scream, but only a great bubble of air came out, and the pressure on his lungs was a knife and an agony, until, just as he knew he would die, he was out, streaming with water, whipped up over a bridge and a factory, where machines churned and a great wheel turned, and a railway line where a train roared, all its windows ablaze.

Jake howled with rage. 'Summer! Let me go! Let me go!'

If she answered he could not hear it. All he could hear now was the rush of the host, the scream of the gale, and then the town was gone, and there were hillsides, and a whirling wind turbine that the Shee streamed round and round in delight, so that its great blades slashed past his face and he ducked and tried to drag in his limbs and head.

When they tired of that they rode on. Though he was exhausted and chilled to the bone he managed to slick the hair from his eyes and see they were over a high country, bare moorland, cragged here and there with rocky tors, the grass and gorse flattened with the mad rush of the host.

A narrow road flashed under him, the red tail-lights of cars. A tower, with one light at the top. Farms, snug in the folds of the moor. A skein of wild geese were suddenly all about him; their eyes wide, their wings huge. And then with a shiver of dread he saw what he had dreaded all this time.

The coast.

He squirmed round, upside-down.

'Summer!' he screamed. 'Listen to me! If you drown me Venn will make you pay! Venn will never forgive you!'

It was useless. The glittering mass of the sea convulsed in the storm, he saw waves raging on the cliffs, the tide lashing high. He groaned and struggled, wriggling his hands deep into the pockets of his coat.

Already they were over water; the Shee horses were swooping low, their hooves splashing on the waves, light as frost.

He flung out both arms wide.

'Summer! LOOK! I'll drop the coins! I'll fling them into the sea and they'll sink and you'll never find them.

Watch me, Summer! Watch me do it!'

He raised both closed fists. Again that terror coursed through him. For a moment he held the fate of eternity in his hands; the gold fragments seemed to burn his skin, to whisper to him in their broken voice, to beg him to reunite them.

He kept his arms wide, far apart, but the effort cost him something like agony.

Her high scream answered him. It seemed to come like the lightning; it pierced through him. Her voice was a cold whisper in his ear. 'You wouldn't dare!'

'I've got nothing to lose. Let me go. Put me down. Now!' He was frozen and blazing with fury. He drew back his arm.

'Wait!' Summer's cry was sharp.

The host skidded to a halt. Like a great storm cloud they hung over the sea. He realized he was being dragged away from the water, swung and lifted and tossed and dumped on to the hard ground that came up like a wall and knocked all the breath out of him.

The web shrivelled.

He rolled into nettles and sand. Without waiting, without even looking round, he was up and running, still clutching the coins, leaping and racing through the rough terrain, instinct taking him over the thin tracks of the moor.

As he ran he caught the smells of the place; rain lashed horizontally into his face, water dripped from his fingers, but he knew this place. With a yell of pure joy he leaped a wire sheep fence and plunged into the gorse, because somewhere ahead of him in the storm lay Wintercombe, deep in its valley below the Wood.

He spared one glance back.

Where were they?

Had they gone?

He caught his foot in a rabbit hole; his ankle turned and he crashed down.

Flat in rain and mud he lay winded.

The night was silent. Only the wind screamed, only the rain spattered.

He lay there a few moments, breathing hard, aching in every joint and muscle, all energy gone, all thought gone, as if he could lie there for ever.

Then a wiry hand grasped his coat, hauled him up. Cold fingers touched his neck. 'Are you alive?'

Jake tried to answer but he had no strength.

Gideon pulled him to his feet. 'Arm round my shoulder. Quick.'

'Can't. Can't walk.'

'I'm not surprised. They've hunted you hard. But they won't have finished yet.'

He was half dragged into the dark. Bushes swished against him. Trees loomed. He recognized the Wood. Craning upwards he gasped, 'Where are they?'

'Don't know. And that scares me.' Gideon hurried, bent under his weight. 'Listen, Jake. Operation Leah is under way.'

Jake swore, silently. 'Can't be . . . Have to speak to Venn. Have to warn him. About Janus.'

'Venn's not back. They've lost him. Sarah too.'

Jake took it in. Branches whipped him; he stumbled, was dragged up. 'Janus . . .' he muttered. '*Janus is with Summer.*'

Gideon's shock was almost a shiver. 'What? Are you sure?'

'I saw them. And I've got the coin. All of it. Both parts.'

Gideon stumbled. 'Then we're dead.'

The Wood had fallen silent around them. Outside rain fell, the wind gusted, but in here water dripped from the bare twigs, dark branches moved uneasily against the sky.

'Where are they?'

'Close.' Gideon didn't slow. 'I can feel them.'

They hurried down a track, through a grove of oaks. Then, abruptly, they were on the lawns, knee-deep in soaking, flattened grass, and Wintercombe was rising before them, dark and ominous with one single light high in an attic window.

'Piers!' Gideon yelled. 'Maskelyne!'

He tried to run but stumbled. Jake fell forward; his right fist opened and the coin fragment fell like a spark into the grass. 'Wait!' He searched for it, panicky. 'God, where is it! Find it! Find it!'

Jake groped feverishly; his fingers touched warm metal; he snatched it up, and turned.

Gideon was already on his feet. In an instant, without thinking, Jake flipped it to him; Gideon caught it with one hand.

They stood together, and he looked up.

On her white horse, Summer sat calmly looking down at them. Next to her Janus fought to control his restless beast. Behind, rank on rank, staring, shuffling, fidgeting, silent, their beautiful eyes fixed on Jake with terrible desire, the host of the Shee regarded their prey.

'I'm sure I heard a shout.' Squeezed into the attic window, Wharton put his hands to the panes to block out the light, and peered down. Shadows shuffled on the lawn. For a moment he could not quite make out what they were. Then he swallowed hard.

'Bloody hell, Piers. Have we got major trouble.'

Venn stared at her a long moment. Then he said, 'What could be so bad it makes you look like that?'

Sarah felt weak; she had to sit down. There was a striped armchair in the hotel room; she sank into it, and poured herself some water from the carafe.

It was cool and fresh and she gulped it gratefully.

Then she put the glass down; a soft click on the glass table.

She said, 'You can't save Leah.'

'Sarah . . .'

'Hear me out.' This was so hard, she thought. She said, 'I told you, long ago, that your saving of Leah made the mirror famous. In my time – in my universe – that's what happened.'

'Yes.' His eyes were icy. 'I succeeded.'

'You did. Leah never died. But it wasn't as if her death had never happened. It had – and *you brought her back to life*. Do you think something like that could ever stay secret?'

'Sarah, I swear . . .'

'It doesn't matter!' She shook her head in despair. 'I know what happened! To me, it's already over! It got out. David's notes, your own secretly written account.'

'I won't write a word.'

'But you already did!' She leaped up and started pacing round the room, then paused at the balcony, looking out at the haze of Vesuvius. 'This idea that you can save her and then destroy the mirror, it's impossible! We don't have the complete coin. You can't do it. Once you've brought her back it will all start, and nothing you will do will stop it. The End World will happen.'

Venn shook his head. He was pale with anger and despair. 'Listen to me, Sarah. The operation is already under way. David is probably driving out here already.'

'We could find him.'

'No! And do you know what I'm going to do? To make sure this works? I'm going out of this room and down the street now, and I'm going to find myself. Myself, Oberon Venn, the Venn that was here four years ago! I'm going to stare into my own eyes and I'm going to tell him – me – not to take that road. Not even get in that car. I don't care if that turns me into some Replicant. I'm doing it. Now.' He made for the door.

Sarah jumped up, but he was already turning the lock; desperately she tugged his hand away and he flung her off, so hard she fell crashing on the tiled floor.

Breathless, she looked up.

Venn wasn't moving. He stood rigid, the door half open.

For a moment she thought that time had stopped; then he turned and held a hand out.

Wordless, she let him help her up.

After a moment he said, 'I'm sorry.'

She gripped his frost-bitten fingers tight. 'Please. You've seen what Janus does. If we had the coin, yes, OK, but we don't. Leah has to die. Leah, and me, and all that terrible future. And you have to accept that.'

He looked at her and she saw that behind his cold blue eyes there was more pain than she could ever understand.

All he said was, 'Sarah, I'm sorry.'

He turned, opened the door and went out. It snicked shut behind him.

She stood there a moment, stunned.

Then she went out to the balcony and sank into one of the warm sun chairs, too stunned even to feel the blazing heat of the sun, striped through the flapping blind.

She looked out at the volcano, at the perfect blue of the bay, and knew it was all over. She had failed, and the future would happen.

She had failed them all. Her parents, Max, Cara, all her friends at ZEUS, all those Janus had killed or imprisoned, all those children he had changed, all those lost in the mirror.

The black hole would devour the world and there was nothing she could do about it.

Then she jumped.

Something buzzed, wasp-like.

In her pocket the mobile phone was ringing.

CHAPTER TWENTY-THREE

Beauty and ugliness. Two eyes. A jagged mouth.
Does this god of Time have one face or two?

He looks forward and he looks back. He sees all
we do.

Illegal ZEUS transmission: Biography of Janus

The road was high above the sea and the view of the blue
bay was stunning.

David drove carefully; Rebecca fidgeted, wanting him
to speed up, but it wasn't safe, she could see that. The
narrow carriageway twisted and clung to the edge; in
places the road had no parapet and even glancing down
the sheer side to the rocks below made her dizzy. No
wonder Venn's car had crashed over the cliff. The amazing
thing was that he had survived.

She was thinking about that, wondering about how

much Shee there was in the mortal, when David muttered, 'How far now?'

She glanced at the map. 'The lay-by is a mile ahead. On the right.'

He nodded.

Silent, tense, his fingers clutched the dark leather of the wheel. A rosary of white beads swung above the driving mirror. The car smelled faintly of perfume and hot leather.

Then she said, 'That's it.'

It was a place to stop and gaze at the view, a sliver of hard shoulder, barely wide enough for a few vehicles to park.

David pulled over and edged the car as far in as he could. Then he turned the engine off, and there was a startling silence.

After a moment Rebecca slid her window down.

Heat shimmered; she smelled the salt of the sea, the acrid harshness of some herb, rosemary maybe, or sage. 'Now what?'

David flexed stiff fingers, rotated his shoulders. He looked at his watch. 'We wait.'

After a few seconds of silence she said, 'Did you know Leah?'

'Of course I did.' David smiled. 'I was their best man!

She was a fantastic woman. A great friend.'

'But you're used to it – her being dead. That's how you think of her now.'

He nodded, slowly, considering. 'Yes. I suppose so. It's hard to say when that starts to happen – not straight away. But yes. I think of her in the past.'

'So what about seeing her again? Talking to her? Isn't that going to be . . .' She wanted to say *wrong*, but the word disturbed her. 'A bit weird?'

He stared out at the shimmering tarmac. The car rocked slightly as a bus roared by.

Then he said, quietly, 'It is. And I won't pretend it doesn't scare me, Rebecca. It scares me stiff.'

Jake saw Gideon slip the half-coin into his pocket.

Well, at least he didn't have both of them any more. He was too tired to feel relief.

Summer said, 'Gideon, sweetkin. I wouldn't want you hurt. Please stand aside. And let me deal with this mortal who was so foolish as to steal from me.'

She slipped down from the horse. Her riding habit shimmered; it became the dark glossy feathers of a starling, shimmering with metallic greens. Her eyes were dark and bird-black.

Gideon didn't move.

'Go,' Jake muttered.

Gideon shook his head. He said, 'Summer. Please.'

She smiled.

Jake looked at Janus. 'You know you can't trust them,' he gasped, his throat so dry he could barely make the words.

Janus shrugged. 'Oh I'm a mere observer here, Jake.'

'You want your mirror destroyed? That's what she'll do. Are you going to sit there and watch that?'

Janus sat unmoved on the Shee horse. His straggly hair was windblown, his uniform torn and frayed. He went to speak; then his gaze flicked quickly over Jake's shoulder towards the house.

Jake turned.

Wharton was running full pelt over the grass; he had the shotgun and now he levelled it at Janus. 'Jake! Move! Back towards the house.'

Summer was so amused she giggled aloud. 'George, you are so stupid! Do you really think such a thing as a weapon scares me?'

'Not this one.' He jerked his head sideways. 'That one might though.'

Summer's head turned.

There was a shape on the lawn, a small darkness within the shadow of the house. As the moon came out and flickered over them all, glimmering on the hair of the Shee, Jake saw Summer's eyes go green as a cat's.

'You!'

Piers came out of the shadows. His coat was silver; his face calm.

Summer folded her arms, amused. 'How *did* you get back?'

'Perhaps you underestimated me, Highness. Perhaps you always have.'

She shrugged, scornful. 'You're nothing. Venn's slave. Do you think you can stop me?'

'I have my orders.'

'From Oberon? What does he care for you? Do you really think he'll ever even release you?'

'He's promised to.'

Her laugh was cruel; behind her all the Shee tittered in imitation. She shook her head. 'You've changed, Piers. You used to be scared of your own shadow. But there's nothing about you that could ever trouble me.'

Piers nodded, almost regretfully. 'Ordinarily, madam, I would agree with you. However at the moment, I have this.'

He brought his hands out from behind his back.

The Shee hissed. The horses whickered, wide-eyed. They stamped and stared.

Jake saw a small wand of what looked like bone. It was carved, and scraps and feathers were tied to it by leather thongs. 'What's that?' he muttered.

Wharton said, 'Take a bit long to explain. Belonged to a friend of mine. Pretty powerful piece of kit.'

Jake had guessed that from the look on Summer's face. She seemed half disgusted, half fascinated.

She said, 'The shaman. That painted boy! It smells of him.'

Piers stepped towards her. He held the thing out, and to Jake's amazement Summer stepped back, wrinkling up her nose. 'It's foul. Pieces of dead mortal. Take it away.'

It had power; Jake saw how it disturbed the Shee; how the host edged and fidgeted away from it.

'I'm afraid I'm not going to do that,' Piers said.

With a swiftness that none of them expected he swept the wand in a great curve in front of them and from it, like smoke from a burning brand, came a ripple of grey fog.

Gideon grabbed Jake's arm. 'Move!'

The fog was a thin line, a rising wave, a curtain so thick Jake felt it muffle him like a blanket; he stepped back into Wharton, who hissed, 'Run. *Now!*'

Somewhere Piers was laughing. The Shee horses were rearing and circling in confusion. Jake pulled clear of

Gideon and ran for the house; the door was open, and a glimmer of the moon showed him Maskelyne waiting on the steps.

They got there just in time. With a word of anger Summer shrivelled the fog; she galloped forward, extended one finger and sent a bolt of lightning straight at them.

Jake leaped up the steps, stumbled, but Wharton had him. They were inside the tiled hall, and Maskelyne was standing between them and the Shee.

'Look out!' Wharton roared.

The scarred man held up his hand, palm outward. The bolt struck him, and went through him, and scorched into the earth. For a moment there was only darkness where he had been.

Then he stepped in behind them and slammed the door.

'Bloody hell!' Wharton said, into the astonished silence. 'Why aren't you dead?'

Piers snapped, 'Get the iron bars in place. All of you, up the stairs. Jake!'

He stopped.

Jake had the mobile phone out; he was stabbing numbers into it.

'What are you——?'

'I have to speak to Venn.' He looked up. 'Janus is out there and all he's done is our fault. I have to tell Venn. Before it's too late!'

'Jake? Is that you?' Sarah had the phone jammed to her ear. 'Jake! I can't hear you! Are you still in the city?'

'No.' His voice was throaty, hoarse. 'Listen, Sarah, listen and don't talk. I'm back at Wintercombe, my time. We're all here, except Dad and Rebecca because they've *journeyed*. Operation Leah has started, but you're right, you were right all the time. We have to stop it.'

Her heart thudded; she jumped up.

'Keep talking.' She pulled open the heavy hotel door; beyond was a corridor of others, all identical.

'I know something about Janus. Sarah, *Janus was the boy*. The small boy whose life I saved on the beach, in our last test. That was him. He should have died and he didn't. *We did that, Sarah!* We kept him alive but he should have died.'

In mid-step, she stopped.

The phone crackled, his breath was fast, as if he had been running. Behind him she heard Wharton say, 'Oh my God.'

'Did you hear me?'

'Yes. Yes of course. What's happening there?'

323

'The Shee are on us. But we're in the house, we should be safe. Sarah, there's something else.' A rustle. Then, '*I've got both halves of the coin.*'

She almost cried out. She felt as if the black depths of the mirror had flashed wide and enfolded her; as if it was in her body, her brain, relief and joy and terror all at once.

There was a lift door; she slammed the buttons but couldn't wait for it; even as the slow whine of its ascent began she was fleeing down the stairs, yelling for him, not caring who heard. 'Venn! Venn! You have to listen to this!'

The phone crackled as if Jake said something else but she didn't hear it. At the foot of the stairs was a glossy lobby of marble; she ran past the reception desk and burst through glass doors into the sweltering heat of an Italian afternoon.

'Venn!'

He was a tall figure on the shady cobbles. She ran after him and grabbed his arm and made him turn.

'Venn! Wait!'

'I've said all I want to say.'

'Jake's just called! Here.' She thrust the phone into his hand. 'Listen to him! Just listen!'

She stood back.

Eyes blue as ice, he put the phone to his ear; still looking at her he said, 'Jake? Where the hell are you?'

She watched him.

The phone crackled; she could imagine Jake's voice; the words pouring out of him, the urgency, the horror. People strolled past her; a small car edged by and tooted, but all she had eyes for was Venn. She saw the moment when the impact of the knowledge came to him, saw in the drawn lines of his mouth when the pain arrived, the bitterest of understanding. He said nothing, but he looked at her, and she gazed back.

Finally, he took a breath. Then he said, 'Are you sure? Absolutely, totally sure?'

Jake must have been vehement. Venn turned and looked down the street. Then he said, 'OK. I get it. Guard the mirror. Leave this to me.'

He clicked the phone off and put it in his pocket.

They stood in silence in the hot shimmer from the cobbles.

Sarah was the first to speak; she had to know. 'He told you?'

'Yes.'

'That Janus was the little boy?'

'Yes.' He raised his head and laughed, a harsh bark that chilled her. 'Imagine it, Sarah. Such a small act. Such kindness to produce such consequences.'

She nodded, came closer. She wanted to touch him, hug him even, but he would hate that so she put her hands in her pockets. 'What will you do?'

'What can I do?' Abruptly, he turned and was walking. She hurried after him, alarmed. 'You're not going to find . . . yourself. You can't, Venn. Listen!' She did grab him now and swung him round. 'You have to let her go. You heard him. They have the coin – complete. We can't play around with time any more. It's too much of a risk – yes you might save Leah, but what else might we unleash? It's over, Venn. Over.'

He pulled away, his face unreadable, and walked away.

'Where are you going?' she screamed.

Venn stopped without looking back. His voice was a whisper. 'To say goodbye.'

It terrified her.

'No. Please.'

'I have to, Sarah.' He folded his arms, hugging himself tight. 'I have to speak to her, just once. For the last time. I won't warn her. I won't give anything away. But I have to.'

'It will hurt you,' she whispered.

Venn nodded. 'Some pain is worth bearing. Wait for me.'

She stood and watched as he walked down the narrow street, striped with sunlight, tall among the passers-by. Then she stepped behind a parked car and put both hands to her face, breathing hard.

This was so dangerous! How would he feel when he saw Leah, spoke to her? How could he stop himself warning her?

Sarah gripped her hands to fists. She moved the secret itchy switch in her head; saw her body flicker out, her shadow on the wall vanish.

Keeping close to the houses, she ran after him.

The road led to a small piazza filled with café tables, their striped umbrellas yellow and white against the glare of the sun. Venn ducked under one, and she lost sight of him; then stepping to one side, she saw him again. He was standing very still, and as she followed the direction of his gaze she saw a tall dark-haired woman, dressed in jeans and a white linen shirt, lounging in one of the chairs, her longs legs crossed at the ankle. She had a drink in front of her and she was writing a postcard; others, small rectangles of blue sky and terracotta buildings, lay on the table, bright in the sun.

The woman looked up. Sarah felt a prickle of astonishment down her spine.

She had seen the portrait at Wintercombe often

enough. That laughing, strong face, so like her own. That tangle of dark glossy hair.

Leah.

Her great-grandmother.

Leah wore sunglasses on her forehead; she tipped them down over her eyes and smiled.

Venn stood there. He seemed stricken, frozen, gazing at her until she laughed and said, 'For heaven's sake, what's the matter with you?'

Venn forced a smile.

Then, walking very slowly, as if into some terrible danger, he crossed the piazza and slipped into the chair next to her.

CHAPTER TWENTY-FOUR

I release spirits.
I am the sun.
The wave of the sea.
The white bird.

Be open.
Be unleashed.
Be free of all you fear.
Be free of all you love.

Shamanic spell of the Katka tribe

'Contact Dad!' Jake raced up the attic stairs, Gideon beside him.

'That's not possible.' Maskelyne, a fleet shadow, ran after them. 'What you told Venn – about the little boy. Are you really sure?'

'Janus told me so himself.' He burst into the attic.

The mirror leaned. In it he saw a hot road, a blue sky. Horatio gave a shriek of joy and scrambled from the cradle, leaping on to Jake's neck and hugging him, chattering non-stop. Jake tossed him in the air. Even in his panic he felt overwhelming relief at just being here.

At being home.

Piers hurried in and went straight to the window.

'Are they still there?' Wharton said.

'Are you kidding? They're going nowhere.'

Jake turned, into the thin grip of Maskelyne's fingers. The scarred man's voice was urgent.

'Janus – don't you think he might have been lying? He's a master of time – he'll have known what happened on that beach, the way we selected that child for the test. What proof do you have that the child was him?'

Jake stared at him, shocked to stillness. 'None. But—'

Wharton came up behind. 'That doesn't matter now. We can't help them or hinder them. The Shee are our problem.'

He turned to the door. Gideon moved up beside him; with a glance at Jake he tapped his pocket and nodded.

The room flickered with moonlight.

The handle turned and Summer strolled in.

Her feet were bare and she no longer wore the hunting

habit. Instead she was dressed as when he had first seen her, a short black dress, simple and unadorned, and she looked no older than him.

'It's so stuffy in here,' she snapped.

All the windows banged open.

Moths came in, leaves flew through. Starlings and jackdaws, a whole flock, fluttered and flapped to the sills, lining up on the rafters overhead. Sharp beaks squawked, bright, attentive eyes watched everything.

Jake turned and saw Janus standing in the doorway of the room like an uninvited guest at a party. He stared at the mirror in delight, at its shimmering landscape of heat.

'That's the place where Venn's wife died? We can see what will happen?'

Maskelyne said, 'If the Mirror wants us to see.'

'Ah, but it will to please you, won't it? Like when you and I worked on it, all those centuries ago.'

Maskelyne's face was dark. He turned away.

Summer pouted and threw herself into a chair. She stabbed a finger at Jake; he felt fear thrill through him. 'He has both the coins. Get them.'

Two of the Shee birds fluttered down and shimmered into people. Male, tall and beautiful, one grabbed him and the other rummaged through his pockets.

'Now look here,' Wharton said but Summer just

snapped, 'Oh shut up, George. I'm in charge here.'

One of the Shee held up a half-coin and it glimmered in the moonlit room. She clapped her hands, reached out and took it. 'The other?'

The Shee searched.

Then said, 'He doesn't have it, Highness.'

Summer's fine eyes narrowed. She stood and came over to Jake and faced him, toe to toe.

'What have you done with it?' she hissed.

He shook his head. 'I'll never tell you.'

Summer laughed. 'Oh they always say that. I assure you, when George is screaming in pain, or dear Piers is a pool of water that I am pouring on the fire, you will tell me. I—'

'Queen! HELLO!'

The voice was small and anxious.

Startled, Summer looked up.

The wooden bird sat on the curtain rail, hopping up and down with anxiety. 'Hi. It's me. Remember me? Well, it's just – I know where the other half is – I mean, which of them's got it. But before I tell you, you'll have me back in the host, won't you? Please?'

For a moment Summer didn't move.

Then, with her perfect lips, she smiled.

At the same time a white van raced into the road in

the mirror and squealed to a stop. The doors were flung open and two figures in uniform dived out.

Jake stared.

'Dad!' he breathed.

'Three twenty. Will we make it?'

David had the barricades and signs out of the back door and was dragging them to the junction. 'Have to. Come on, Rebecca. Quick!'

She ran back for the red striped tape, unrolling it hastily so that it fluttered in the warm breeze from the bay. They attached it, then dragged the signs up and the coast road was cordoned off, diversion arrows pointing back along the main highway.

David stepped back and looked at it, breathless. A car came behind him; he turned, in a sweat of fear, but the driver was a woman who slowed, stared at the diversion signs, muttered something in Italian and backed the car up.

Then it roared away.

Rebecca wiped sweat from her face. Her hair was sticking to her scalp with the sultry heat; the uniform was far too tight. She undid a button on the collar.

'That's it then.'

David bit his lip. 'Back to the van. And wait.'

* * *

In the hot piazza Sarah edged close to the café table. She held her breath, her invisible hand resting on the white frame of a chair.

Leah said carelessly, 'Anyway, you've been such a time, Venn.'

'Have I?' he said, quiet.

'And what on earth is that rubbish you're wearing? You didn't have that on an hour ago.'

He looked down at the grey clothes of the End World. 'No. I didn't.'

Words had dried up in him. He wanted just to stare at her, to say nothing, to drink in her presence and her laughter. Her scent.

Leah clicked the pen and put it away, then gathered the postcards up quickly. 'Where's the car?'

'Outside the hotel.'

She went to stand, then stared at him. 'Come on then.'

'Leah . . .'

'What's wrong?'

'Nothing. At least . . .'

Leah sat back down. She took off her sunglasses and Sarah saw her eyes were dark and intelligent and full of life.

'Don't tell me you've changed your mind. You know I

want to get down to Paestum before tonight. I thought you did too! Those temples look fantastic and—'

'*Leah*,' His voice was a whisper of pain.

He reached out a hand on the white table; after a moment Leah took it and played with his fingers, rubbing the frost-bitten scars. She looked at him, curious. 'If I didn't know better I'd say you were scared, Venn.'

'I'm never scared.'

'I know. That's what . . .' She tapped his fingers. 'Is there some bad news? Is it David?'

He shook his head. For a moment his ice-blue gaze passed over Sarah's face, as if he was searching for her, for some sort of help. She moved closer.

'Then what?'

'Leah.' He leaned closer. 'Why did you marry me?'

She laughed, surprised. 'I often ask myself that question. Because you're you. Impossible. Surly. Reckless. Hell to live with. Just what I was looking for, in fact.'

'You never give me a sensible answer.'

'You ask such stupid questions.'

He said softly, 'What do you love most in all the world, Leah?'

She shrugged, leaning back and looking down the street. Then she said, 'Freedom, Venn. Just like you.'

He nodded. His eyes were glints of blue. He said, 'So,

if you could . . . change things. Make the world work out the way that suited you, no matter what the cost, no matter what happened to everybody else. If it cost everything that might ever happen. Would you do it?'

She tipped her dark head sideways. 'I can't make you out today. You haven't been drinking?'

He shook his head.

'Then . . . well. I don't know! It's a complicated thing, isn't it? Life. It's not all about us.'

'I don't care about anyone else.'

'Then you should. Anyway, I don't believe that. You may have some crazy dream that you're only half mortal, Venn, but I know better.'

He made a small sound like a gasp. 'Leah, listen. *I have to . . .*'

Standing close behind, Sarah laid her hand lightly on his shoulder. He didn't jump, or give any sign that he felt her, but his stillness told her that he knew she was there. She squeezed her fingers, feeling the warmth of him.

Leah looked expectant. 'What?'

Venn shook his head. When he looked up again his eyes were bright and his face drawn, as if he had aged a little in that moment. 'What a strange world we live in,' he whispered.

Leah touched his chin. 'A strange, terrible, beautiful world. But we wouldn't have it any other way. Would we?'

'No,' he said, so softly Sarah barely heard him. 'No. We wouldn't.'

Leah stood up, pushing her chair back noisily. 'Coming?'

Venn stood too. He said, 'I just have to go back and get some cash. Wait here a few more minutes.' He glanced down the street. 'I shouldn't be long now.'

Then he leaned over and, very softly, kissed her cheek.

Surprised she said, 'Well hurry, won't you? And please change those awful clothes.'

'When I come back,' he said, 'I won't be wearing them.'

He turned.

'Venn,' she said.

He looked back.

'We might slow the speed of darkness but it still comes anyway.'

Venn nodded.

Sarah stood as he pushed past her. He walked away fast, not once looking behind.

For a moment she waited there, watching Leah watching him. Then she reached out, light as a Shee moth, and touched the woman's hand, the woman who would have been her great-grandmother, and now never would be.

Leah moved her fingers aside absently, and stood up.

Sarah turned. She ran after Venn, her breath caught like a sob in her throat.

David looked at his watch again. His foot tapped, impatient. 'Come on,' he breathed. '*Come on.*'

The road was quiet, the sea impossibly blue.

Rebecca said, 'Three twenty-five. Five minutes to go.'

'They're waiting for Venn?' Summer said, fascinated. She jumped up. 'Is this where he saves her? I'm not sitting here while that happens. I won't have it.'

Janus stared at the mirror, the blue lenses of his glasses pale in the moonlight. 'He really will do it,' he breathed. 'He must.'

Summer glared at him in fury. 'I thought you were on my side.'

Janus smiled, a twisted, mirthless spasm. 'Well, you thought wrong.'

Jake couldn't move. His father's face, furrowed with worry, stared at him through the mirror as if the brown eyes could see him.

'Summer?' The bird soared down and landed with a clatter on the table. 'Highness? Will you set me free?'

'Oh get out of my way.' Summer flung it aside; at her slap it became a small female Shee lying on its back in a scatter of blue feathers, one eye still a black bead.

It leaped up, with a whoop. 'At last!'

'So who has the other half?' Summer demanded.

The Shee pouted. 'What about my eye?'

'*The coin*, idiot!'

'All right. OK.' The Shee extended a tiny finger towards Gideon. 'It's him. He's got it.'

Summer turned but Janus moved first. He grabbed Gideon's wrist and Gideon cried out, as if a great pain had stabbed through him.

'It's mine,' Janus snarled. 'You can't destroy my work. I won't let you.'

'Leave him alone,' Summer spat.

Janus ignored her; he forced Gideon's hand open; for a moment the half-coin was there, glimmering, then Janus had wrenched it free. 'You will never destroy my mirror,' he said. And turned for the door.

Summer gave no shriek, made no sound. She struck the tyrant down from the back with a bolt of power that scorched the room; he fell crashing, his legs giving way, one arm flung out.

The half-coin rattled from his fingers; Gideon pounced on it like a cat on a mouse.

'No one,' she hissed, 'steals from me.'

Janus lay still, and broken. The lenses of the blue spectacles were a mass of cracks; they had fallen off and Jake saw his eyes, and they were the pale eyes of the little boy, the eyes that had stared at him over the mother's shoulder. Wide now, seeing nothing.

Wharton knelt and felt for the man's pulse.

He looked up, appalled.

As, with a vivid flash inside the mirror, a car came round the bend in the road.

Rebecca jumped. *'They're here!'*

She could see Venn's blond hair, the smaller shape of the woman next to him in the passenger seat. But surely . . .

David said, 'Wait a minute. That's the wrong car. That's not Leah. What the hell . . . ?'

He opened the van door.

Venn's car screeched to a halt, skidding so wildly that gravel flew up in a great wave. Even before it was still he was out, and Sarah with him; they ran full-pelt to the barricades.

David gasped. *'Wait!* What's going on? O?'

Venn didn't answer. Instead he took hold of the signs and barricade and tore them away, tape flailing out in the wind. He dragged the whole thing to the edge of the road and flung it over the cliff in a furious, savage effort; the crash of wood and plastic shattered down the long fall. Sarah helped him; she tossed sign after sign over, tears blinding her, stung by the salt wind.

David grabbed Venn's arm. 'Venn! Stop! What's happening?'

Venn stepped back. His face was white, his eyes bleak with a wild, bitter intensity. He said, 'Operation Leah is off. The road stays open.'

Then he turned, and stalked to the shade of an olive tree.

David looked at Rebecca, who shook her head in amazement. They stared at Sarah. 'For God's sake, why?' he asked, quietly.

She had no desire to tell him. 'Ask Jake.'

'Jake? But—'

'Jake knows. It had to be like this.' Suddenly she remembered where they were, that it hadn't even happened yet. She pushed him away. 'Get out of the road. They'll be here any minute!'

David blinked. For a moment she thought he wouldn't, that he'd make some crazy effort to stop this. But he stepped back, behind the white van. 'Becky. Do as she says.'

The car was coming. They could hear it accelerating round the bend, too fast, too carefree. And suddenly Sarah knew she had to be with Venn for this, that the Venns had to be together, so ignoring David's shout she ran and ducked under the gnarled branches.

Venn was standing very still. 'I'm not sure if I can watch this, Sarah,' he whispered, his voice brittle.

Turn away, she wanted to say. *Time is merciful; it hides the past.*

It was too late; in that instant, while Jake stared and Wharton swore and Summer put her hands together, the car flashed past, and Sarah had a brief glimpse of them both inside, of Leah, and Venn, a different, younger Venn, laughing, Leah's blue scarf flapping in the wind.

The squeal of the brakes came. The red bulk of the lorry. Far ahead and round the twist in the road a scream, a scorching crash, the terrible long, crumpling fall of metal into the sea.

Venn sat rigid, hands clenched white.

No one spoke.

Slow and serene, unaltered in their beauty, the luxury yachts cruised over the blue bay.

CHAPTER TWENTY-FIVE

There is no country you can find
Where I will never be.
There is no future you can make
That I will never see.

Ice to sun, day to night,
Death to life are we.
Matching halves and enemies
To all eternity.

Ballad of Lord Winter and Lady Summer

There had been an appalled silence, and then Summer had laughed.

She had put long fingers to her red lips and laughed a soft, gleeful, terrible sound. Wharton couldn't bear it. 'My God, you really have no heart,' he breathed.

She smiled at him, then stood lightly. 'Gideon, come with me. I have a whole palace to prepare. A wedding feast.'

'No,' he said. 'Summer, listen . . .'

But already she was gone, and Gideon with her.

Piers looked round. 'Wow. Look at that!'

Where the body of Janus had lain was nothing. Not a stir of dust, not a shard of blue glass, as if it had never been there at all, as if he had never even existed. Jake came and stared down at the spot. For a moment, faint and yet real, he felt the grip of the little boy's hot hand in his own.

They waited for hours.

Jake paced, Wharton stared out at the night, Piers made sandwiches which no one but Horatio ate, and Maskelyne sat in brooding silence. The room was dark; no one bothered to put the lights on or find a lamp. None of them really wanted to talk. But at five thirty in the morning, just as the very faintest glimmer of dawn was coming, the mirror rippled.

Jake turned on his heel. 'At last!'

David came through first, holding Rebecca's hand. They both looked utterly drained; Jake grabbed his father and hugged him tight, relief flooding him.

'Are you all right?'

David shrugged. 'Tired.' Then he said, 'I need to know why, Jake. Why Venn changed his mind. Sarah said to ask you.'

Jake nodded. He took David aside, talking quietly.

Wharton was looking at Rebecca. 'All right?' he said softly.

She seemed on the verge of tears. 'It was all so horrible, George.'

'Can't have been easy.'

'Venn's devastated.' She tugged the cap from her hair and threw it down. 'I just never want to have to see the past again. Reading about it is enough for me.'

She looked past him.

Maskelyne was sitting like a shadow, watching her. Wharton said, 'It's all been kicking off here too,' but she wasn't listening. Maskelyne stood up. 'Becky . . .'

Before he could say any more the mirror gave another spark and a shiver; the surface imploded into vacuum, and all the papers in the room fluttered in a great cloud.

Venn walked through them, and Sarah was with him.

Jake breathed in in huge relief. For a moment the crazy thought had come to him that they would never see her again; that Leah's death meant she had never been born, and so – but here she was, weary and grey as the shabby dress she wore, and she crumpled on to the first chair she came to as if she had been utterly defeated. And yet of all of them, she had what she wanted.

Venn looked stricken. His face was white, his eyes cold and forbidding as of ice. For a moment none of them dared even speak to him, Piers fidgeting and Jake silent, until David went over and gripped his arms silently and they stood together, face to face.

'Jake's told me. You did the right thing. Janus will never—'

'Not now.' Venn pushed past him. They heard his footsteps racing down the stairs.

A door slammed, with echoes that rang through the house.

In the silence, Piers sighed and opened the attic window. Far and faint over the Wood, a watery light was faint in the eastern sky.

'He's not . . .' Wharton hesitated. 'He hasn't gone to her, has he?'

It was Piers who answered. 'No. At least. Not yet.'

Jake went to his room. He meant just to get changed, but he was so tired he put his head back on the pillow, and in a sleepy second all the things he had seen were running through his mind in jagged motion. The stretched city of the future flickered and jerked like a film-strip, and there were foggy Victorian streets too, and the crash of a guillotine that fell on him, and Moll laughing, and bombs that screeched and exploded at his feet and turned into horses and hounds of grey steel that hunted him down the long aisles of the greenwood.

What woke him was a small, delicate tap at the window.

His eyes snapped wide.

Gideon was looking through the glass.

Jake slid his feet out, padded over, and unclicked the casement. Gideon hauled himself in, a scatter of ivy and tawny leaves gusting with him. He brushed himself down.

'How did you get away?' Jake looked out; the pre-dawn glimmer was pale through the dark gnarled branches of the Wood.

Gideon lounged on a chair, his coat russet as autumn. Instead of answering he said, 'So it's all over.'

'Summer must be so smug.'

Gideon laughed his mirthless laugh. 'You would not believe how she is.'

'At least the mirror is safe.'

'Until she asks me for the coin.'

'It doesn't matter any more. She won't care about the

347

mirror now.'

'I do, though.' Gideon scrambled up and walked to the door. 'Will they let me go through it, Jake? Will they take me with them?'

Alarmed, Jake said, 'Who?' but Gideon was already gone, so he scrabbled for some shoes, pulled them on and hurried out into the corridor. The house was silent and dim, the Long Gallery lit by slanting rectangles of wan light. The storm had blown itself out; all that was left was the soft stillness of an autumn dawn.

But where was everyone?

Suddenly Sarah stepped down from the servants' stairway, looking pale. She had changed out of the grey dress into jeans and shirt – her face was scrubbed, her hair still damp. He wanted to talk to her, to know more about what happened, but she said, 'You'd better get down here. Quickly.'

In the kitchen an enormous fire was roaring in the hearth, and Venn was throwing papers on to it. Calculations, notes, journals – all the work of months. Jake saw the red cover of Symmes's diary flung on; with a yell he dived for it, picking it out before the pages blackened.

'What are you doing? Are you mad!'

'It's over,' Venn snapped. 'All of it.' He dumped a box

of papers in a great shower of sparks, and turned as it flamed up behind him. 'Leah is dead. That future world we saw, that city, that black hole devouring everyone and everything, will never happen. That child who became a man with dreams that he could rule some sort of empire of time will never have the mirror. None of it will ever happen now.'

Jake saw Piers, chewing his nails, small and unhappy at the kitchen table.

Venn stepped back. 'I've finished with it all, the books, the wild journeying, the rough magic.'

'What about the mirror?' Sarah asked.

He glared at her.

'The mirror above all. Because if it stays here, Sarah, I'm afraid I might not have the strength to withstand it.' He managed a bitter smile. 'After all, there's all the time in the world to try again.'

He turned to Jake. 'Give me the coin.'

Jake hesitated. Then he took the half-stater out and dropped it in Venn's frostbitten fingers.

'The other?'

Jake looked at Gideon. Gideon frowned. His thin fingers dipped in the pocket of his russet coat, and paused.

'*Now*.'

'If I give it to you, what do I have to offer Summer?'

'Nothing. Which is as much as her promises are worth.'

Gideon took out the other half. 'What about your promises?'

Venn came and took it from him. 'I don't break my word.'

He held up the two halves, one in each hand, two divided fragments of a single face. They were so close! Jake could barely breathe, couldn't take his eyes from the empty air between them.

Sarah was staring too, in fascination and terror. 'Please. Be careful.'

Venn laughed. 'You've changed your tune.' He closed a fist over each fragment and turned to Piers. 'Get Maskelyne. And anyone who wants to go with him.'

Rebecca was curled, knees up, on the bench in the cloisters when she heard the footsteps behind her.

She knew it was him. He always moved so quietly; there was nothing loud about him. He was a true ghost.

He said, 'Becky?'

When she didn't answer he sat beside her. The bench barely creaked.

In the silence she said, 'I never really knew who you were. All those years when I was small, you were barely there, so shadowy and frail and see-through. Even later, when I could talk to you, there was always so much of you that was secret.' She smiled. 'Sometimes I even wondered if I was making you up.'

Gently he said, 'Becky, you may as well know this now. I'm not letting you come with me.'

She looked up.

Maskelyne kept his scarred face from her.

'Not *letting* me!'

'I have to deal with the mirror. Venn promised me that when Operation Leah was over it was mine, and that's only right, it's part of me, I made it. And it's too dangerous a thing to stay in this world.'

'Where will you go?'

He shook his head. 'I'm not telling you that.'

'So am I *part of you* too?' She twisted round to look at him. 'You have no right to make decisions for me.'

He began, 'Your life here . . .' but she stood up and he was silent. Then he stood too. Facing him she said, 'I decide. No one else.'

'But . . .'

'Listen.' She looked aside into the cobwebbed archways of the cloister. 'I've made up my mind. I thought it would be different, but, since what happened to Leah, I realize I want my life. This one. Here and now.'

He nodded.

'Not that I don't want to come with you,' she said hastily. 'Travel time, to see all those fantastic places and I'll be a wreck without you around. But – I'm staying.'

He took her by the arms and kissed her forehead. 'That's how it should be.'

'Will I see you again?'

Maskelyne smiled the ghost of a smile. 'Becky, eternity is endless. If you ever need me. If you're ever in trouble, use this.'

He took something from his pocket and gave it to her. It was the small bone wand, the one that had released her from being a girl of cobweb. She shivered. 'That thing! It was the shaman's.'

'Now it's yours. It will call me. And I promise you, I will come.'

She nodded.

There was discreet clearing of a throat. Piers said, 'Um, sorry to break this up, folks. But His Excellency's waiting.'

When they came into the attic it looked bare, because everything had been torn away. Papers, wiring, computer screens were all gone.

Venn, staring into the blackness of the mirror, swung round. Facing Maskelyne he said, 'It's yours. Take it.

Take it away. I never want to see it again.'

David frowned. 'O, listen. Maybe we should take more—'

'Time? That's what scares me.' He looked at David. 'There has to be no temptation. Do you understand?'

Reluctant, David nodded.

Wharton, on the window seat, said, 'I think it's the right thing to do. Bloody end it here.'

'Sarah? Do I even have to ask?'

She said, 'You know what I think. It should be destroyed. But this is the next best thing.'

Venn turned to Piers. 'What do you say?'

'You're asking my opinion?' Piers was startled.

'This once.'

'Then, Excellency, I say the teacher is right. The mirror is a danger to us all. Even the Shee, maybe, in the end.'

Venn nodded. Then, as if the thought had just come into his head he said, 'You're free, Piers. I dismiss you. Go where you want, do what you want. Without the mirror, I don't need you.'

Piers chortled in glee. He pumped the air with a fist, hissed, 'Yes!' and then, seeing Wharton's grin, shrugged with a studied carelessness. 'Thanks. But I think I'll stick around. After all, you can only lie in cowslip flowers sipping honey for so long. Believe me, the boredom is epic.'

353

Maskelyne stepped up to the Mirror. 'Gideon?'

Gideon pushed past Wharton quickly. 'I'm with you.'

'No guarantees. You may never get back to a normal mortal life.'

'Anything is better than the Summerland.' Gideon rubbed the lichen swirls from his face. 'I have to try. There must be somewhere she can't find me.'

Maskelyne nodded. 'The two of us, then. Unless . . .'

They all looked at Sarah.

With a pang of something like pain Jake knew what she would say, and it happened, because she walked over and stood by the obsidian glass. She smiled at him sadly. 'Goodbye, Jake. You too, George. David. Becky. It's been great.'

Venn said, 'Sarah . . . are you sure?'

'I'm nothing here now. A sort of Replicant. I'll never have been born at all.' She shrugged, lightly, tucking the blonde hair behind one ear. 'This way, at least I get some sort of life.'

Jake said, 'I'll miss you.'

'Me too,' Wharton growled. He stood. 'Take care of yourself, Sarah Venn, wherever you end up.'

'I will,' she said. 'And I'll miss you. All of you.'

Maskelyne nodded. He touched the mirror frame and the silver letters lit, as if a shiver of fire passed through

354

them. The coiled ammonite glimmered.

Venn stepped forward. 'I could never have had a better great-granddaughter.' He slipped off the silver bracelet from his arm, looked at the amber stone of the snake's eye a moment, and then gave it to her. She clipped it on her wrist. Then he reached into his right-hand pocket and brought out the half-coin that she had brought from the future, and held it out.

Eyes wide, she took it. 'Just in case,' he said. 'We Venns, we're the guardians of eternity.'

She slipped the chain over her neck.

Maskelyne looked round at her and Gideon. 'Don't be scared, whatever happens. Just follow me.'

He spread his arms wide and began to speak. It was a language none of them knew; Wharton thought it must be ancient, older than Latin, old as the shaman tongue, and maybe the silver letters around the frame were written in it.

Because the mirror answered.

Its voice was sly and eerie, as if the spaces between the stars had whispered. Maskelyne replied, then he stepped forward, his hands on the silver frame.

Through into darkness.

To Jake's amazement there was none of the usual implosion, no roar of vacuum. The Mirror was simply an empty space, and Maskelyne turned, beckoning to Gideon and Sarah. One on each side, they stepped in after him, and were instantly gone in the darkness, but Maskelyne remained like a man standing in a doorway.

He smiled at Rebecca. 'Remember,' he said. Then he reached out and took hold of the frame from the inside. He folded both sides inward, towards himself, until the glass was a narrow slit. Then he folded top and bottom together, and the mirror collapsed to a tiny aperture of darkness, and then that too was folded, once and again in on itself, and disappeared.

Where it had been just a scatter of dust lay on the bare boards.

The attic was silent.

Wharton breathed out. 'How in God's name did he do that?' he muttered.

No one answered.

Venn went to the window and opened it, as if he needed the fresh air, and leaning with his hands on the sill, looked out.

Then he turned and looked at the cats and the cradle and the space where the mirror had been.

'One last thing, Jake, to do,' he said.

On the cliff top the wind was cold. The sea tossed, dark

and wild. Although the tempest had blown itself out, the eastern sky was scarlet, and great ranks of cloud travelled in stately ranks to the horizon.

Venn, his coat flapping, said, 'This is not a world that has been kind to me. But I'd hate to see it lost.'

Jake thought of the contorted future they had avoided. 'Me too.'

'So.' Venn took something from his pocket.

Instantly, a huge commotion rose from Wintercombe. Turning, Jake saw that out of the Wood, above every branch and every tree, in a vast cloud of wings, starlings were rising. Thousands and thousands of them took off and gathered, a great murmuration of glossy purples and metallic green, swooping and regrouping over the lichened roofs of the Abbey.

Venn laughed, bitter. He pulled his arm back, and threw.

The half-coin spun, high, and then it fell like a golden star, the shining, jagged face of the Greek god turning over and over in the rays of the rising sun, and with a great screech the starling host swooped for it, but already it had plummeted between them, hit the water and was gone in the sheen of a wave, barely making a ripple.

Jake imagined it sinking and sinking, fathoms deep, deeper than sound, coming to rest in a puff of yellow sand, only the single eye of Zeus gazing up towards the sunlight.

Slowly, he turned his head.

Summer was standing beside them.

'Do what you like,' Venn said, still staring out to sea. 'The coin is deep and lost and you can't touch it. It will lie there for ever.' He turned to her. 'You could kill me now. Suddenly, mercilessly. Like you did Janus. That's what death is, Summer. There's no way back. And whatever the prophesies say, whatever you try, I will never be the Venn you entice into the Wood for all eternity.'

She smiled, and turned away. She walked past him over the cropped grass, and a few of the court landed and stared and whispered around her, in a sudden flutter of glossy green and purple clothes.

'I don't need to destroy anything, Venn,' she said, walking lightly. 'And I certainly don't want to kill you. Because you're mine now. For ever and ever. And you know it.'

He stared after her. 'I've released your changeling.'

'So you think. I'll find another. Mortals are cheap.' She clapped her hands. 'Away! All of you.'

The starlings burst into the air. They split and fountained and rustled in a vast cloud that bloomed into bizarre joyful shapes high in the sky, and suddenly there were so many of them Jake thought for a moment the black hole had come from the future and was devouring the world. He and Venn stared up, as the darkness over their heads dissolved into millions of rustling, shimmering birds that streamed like arrows down into the depths of the Wood.

Summer turned away. At the Wood's edge she paused and waved sweetly. 'Soon, Venn. I'll be waiting.'

He frowned. Then all that stood there was a tree, and its shadow.

Jake said, 'Is she right?'

Venn was still. 'Without the mirror, all that's left is my own strength. I'll have to hope that's enough.'

Jake nodded. Then he said, 'Hear that?'

A whisper of music far off, so delicate, so enticingly sweet it made him shiver.

'Don't listen,' Venn snapped. He turned, and Jake followed him through the leafless Wood, but just at the edge, where the lawns of Wintercombe began, he paused, and looked back.

The green aisles of the trees were heavy with birds.

Each of their million eyes was a glitter of darkness.